MW01267575

LAST of
HER
LEGACY

A GUARDIAN SERIES

DANIELLE M. PEPE

Copyright © 2013 Danielle M. Pepe
All rights reserved.

ISBN: 148261958X
ISBN-13: 9781482619584

Prologue

Fire fell from the sky, and for nine days the heavens cried. He stood at the edge of paradise looking down at his fallen brother, tears soaking his cheeks. He never wanted to do it: he never wanted to cast his brother down to the unknown, but his brother didn't give him much of a choice. He tried to take what was not his to take; he wanted to rule what could never be ruled. He wanted to overpower Michael.

"I will fight you to the death if you give me a reason to," Michael yelled.

"I have my army, loyal to me and me alone, big brother," he yelled back, wrath dripping from his fangs. His sword glistened in the moonlight. Black as night he struck Michael, but Michael was too fast and drew his sword at the last minute—it was then that the war began.

Just before Michael defeated his brother, he swore to take paradise and earth, being the ruler of all time. He swore upon his creator.

As Lucifer lay beaten and bruised in the depths of the unknown, in the world of the dead, the only power he had left was his power of creation. And upon his creations demons were born, abominations of pure souls turned by sin.

Chapter 1

"This is bull and you know it," I said as I stuck my head out the window, letting the wind catch my dark curls. A big wooden blue sign to my right read "Welcome to Picture City" with a sun and a beach carved into it. I held down a laugh as we drove, watching as the light caught my silver eyes in the side mirror.

"I know, honey, but it will be great. Just give it a chance," Sarah said, placing a gentle hand on my knee.

Sarah was all I had now; she was the closest thing I had to a mother. She and her husband, Jack, who reminded me so much of my father, had taken me in when I was three years old after my parents were brutally murdered by a demonic creature. I grew up with them and their two beautiful sons who were older than me but not by much.

"Whatever, I'll give this a chance but I won't like it," I argued as we pulled up to the small one-story, two-bedroom house overlooking the glassy blue ocean. This was my home, my new beginning, my new life in a small town sitting at the edge of an endless sea, where the cloudless blue sky shines bright and seasons never come.

Sarah laughed her silvery laugh and nudged my arm.

I had to admit, the house wasn't too bad. It was owned by the council and loaned to us for eight months. Queen palm silhouettes

1

cast shadows on the cherry wood porch, where an old wicker table and four chairs sat. Around back a blanket of cream-colored sand covered the ground where it lay flush with the ocean. Inside the house huge windows covered the back wall, and white silk curtains twirled around, illuminating the living room. A sectional took up most of the area with a flat-screen television on a stand. On the far side of the living room was a small hallway, where my bedroom was located across from the bathroom. Sarah's room was beyond the kitchen on the other side of the house.

My room was painted an eggshell white, and blue torn curtains hung from the only window that overlooked the front yard. A dresser, bed, and nightstand were all I had to start my new life. With no possessions to my name, besides one lonely picture of my parents and me on the day I was born, my room stayed empty.

My name is Alikye Macayan.

For as long as I can remember, I have lived amongst humans— but I am not one of them. I am part of a unique race that was created by the archangels. My family and I are called guardians; we protect mankind from hell's creatures, the monsters you only hear about in stories. The stories are all true, and it's my job to keep them hidden. We keep the innocents away from the evil that surrounds the world. Humans don't know who we are, for we stay in the shadows and keep to ourselves.

In my creation I was given gifts to help win my battles. Enochian magic covered my slender body; the markings, which resemble multiple tattoos, were made to protect me against human death, giving me extensive healing powers. They were also used to bind my soul to my body. Unless I was in danger or using too much of my powers, I could hide them to the world.

I am human-like: I breathe, eat, and sleep to survive. I feel emotions. (Well, a little more than humans do, which is not always good when I'm angry.) The only difference is that my senses are unparalleled, and my body can withstand more. My speed matches that of a cheetah. I have the agility of a cat, and my strength is that of a dozen full-grown men. My vision is phenomenal during the day and even better at night. If I concentrate I can distinguish a person's footsteps from half a mile away. I can sense what type of being is coming toward me before I see it.

I was a warrior of paradise, a machine built to fight, and now I stood in the driveway, living a life I never thought I would live—a life of normalcy and high school and, worst of all, a life where I was the same as humans. The thought of this new life brought me to my knees in pure agony when Sarah and Jack had made the decision for me a few weeks back.

Like most humans would say, *I never thought it would happen to me. I never thought this was how my life would turn out.* But for me it was a true shock. My family could sense something was wrong with me—they saw it in my behavior. They saw it in the way I fought, not only against hell but also against myself. Fire burned in my eyes every time I made a kill, but I never did it for the people. I never liked humans; they were a foul breed, a mistake filled with many flaws. Some thought I was on the verge of turning, going against my kind for the dark ones. Others thought I was suicidal. Suicidal, maybe, but turning, I would never. Demons were worse than humans, and I loved the fight too much. I loved the earth the way it used to be, so beautiful and full of life. I was fighting to one day get it all back. I was fighting for the adrenaline, never caring if I died. I never feared death, which would make sense as to why I was here for the next eight months—to learn who I was supposed to be and the importance of what my destiny entitled me to do.

****

I stood in front of the house, in the gap between the open door and the jamb, with a smug look on my face and my arms crossed over my chest. Most of the time I acted like an adult, but today I took pride in acting like a child, acting my true age, which was sixteen. Jack carried my bags in the house, one full of clothes, the other full of weapons. He kissed Sarah good-bye and came to my side, pulling me into the house.

"What? No last remark before I leave?" Jack joked as he wrapped me in his arms and kissed the top of my head.

3

"If you wanted to punish me that badly, it would have been nicer to send me to hell with a knife and a bottle of water," I retorted as I parted ways from him.

He just laughed and put out his hand. Something was in it.

"Y—You're kidding, right? You're just going to hand them over? I thought you said I would have to wait till I was mature enough for them?" I stuttered. Lying in the middle of his palm, a small metal object glistened. I sucked in a breath. At that moment my madness faded and my eyes lit up. It would soon pass, but for now I wanted to enjoy the warm feeling his gift had brought me.

"It was never mine to keep, Kye, and I think it's time you took it back." Jack said with a smile so heavenly you would think he was part angel (pun intended).

I took the key from him, holding it so tightly my knuckles turned white. It was finally mine, the key to a 1968 fire-engine-red Mustang GT convertible with a 335-horsepower Cobra Jet V8 engine. I had been in love with that car ever since I was a little girl. It had belonged to my father.

I jump hard into Jack's arms, causing him to stumble backward before catching his balance.

"So we good?" He laughed.

I nodded, too excited to speak.

"Ahem," someone interrupted. I turned my head.

I had nearly forgotten Derek and Lucas had arrived during my tantrum, and without a word they both stood to the side.

"See ya, Kye," Derek said as he pulled me into his arms. The hug was long. I snuggled my face into the opening of his chest and closed my eyes, taking in his scent. A mixture of earth and waterfalls filled my nose one last time.

Next was Lucas. His hug was quick and half-assed. He said not a word to me and only gave me a sad smile as he turned. Jack, Derek, and Lucas walked out the door and out of my life to continue protecting the human race, leaving Sarah to stay behind and care for me. It all felt surreal that I wasn't heading out with them, that at the end of the day, nothing would be the same. I walked to my room and fell to my bed, shoving my face in the pillow. I lay there, hours passing me by, trying to make sense of the insanity that tomorrow I would start my first day of real high school. The whole situation was unfair and all just to protect my name.

Chapter 2

I woke up early that morning, wishing all of it had been a dream. But when Sarah entered my room to get me up for school, I knew it was my real-life nightmare. I got out of bed and threw on some normal human clothes: dark skinny jeans, my very worn-out black combat boots, and a white James Dean tank top that fit snug on my tiny body.

I walked out into the kitchen where Sarah stood in front of the stove preparing a breakfast of fluffy egg whites, scrambled; turkey bacon sizzled in a hot oil-based pan; butter biscuits dripping in honey; and freshly squeezed orange juice. You would think by looking at her she belonged here as an all-American stay-at-home mom instead of a demon slaying warrior. But the six years she stayed home to raise her boys, before shipping them off to combat school, taught her everything she needed to know about taking care of others. Sarah turned toward me with a sympathetic look in her eyes. She knew I would have a hard time adjusting to normalcy, but she wanted me to get better like any mother would.

We sat in silence, devouring the tasty food until; finally, I got up for a second serving.

"It's going to be all right, sweetheart," Sarah said, moving her food from side to side before taking another bite. "Just pretend you're back at combat school, and you'll do great."

"I'm not worried about fitting in, Sarah," I snapped, emphasizing Sarah's name. "And this is nothing like combat school; at least there I could hit someone."

Sarah rolled her shoulder, her smile fading; she was trying her best to be in great spirits for me, but I didn't see it that way. She finished her breakfast and took all the dishes to the sink. The whole time I just watched her pretend this world was reality, when in reality this world was fantasy. I grew up in the *real* reality where darkness hunts the weak and nightmares come to life.

After breakfast Sarah tried her best to cover the scars on my face with makeup. During my last battle, I was up against a hellhound. Even with all my training, I still managed to dismiss the severity of the situation by going in without backup. My rash actions left me with four claw marks down the right side of my face, one going across my eyebrow. A month ago the jagged edges and thick red marks made me look more like Two Face, but after a while they healed enough to show thin pink lines, soft and new like baby skin. Light makeup and bangs cut short and sweeping to the side made the scars almost invisible.

******

The day was like any other day. We got notice of a mission not far from where we were staying. The information was vague. Nicholas Carter, an elder in charge of the East Coast of North America was the one who contacted us. Although he generally resided in England with the rest of the council, his jurisdiction was America. Also a Legacy, Carter was in his late eighties with dark-brown hair shaved clean like a soldier and pale-blue eyes almost like mine but not as silver. His refusal to resign from the council led his aging to stop like most Legacies, so he looked to be in his early forties.

A group of kids had gone missing after a weekend camping trip. Derek, Lucas, and I headed up to Vermont to assess the situation. On scene, blood covered the campsite and tents and sleeping bags were torn to shreds, but food lying around was untouched and well-preserved in its coolers. The story was, a bear had come during the night and attacked the five teenagers, but the evidence showed the bodies were dragged away and the drag marks were covered up by the forest. It was no bear; it was something else, something smart and demonic. Search parties were called off, and after a week had gone by, the kids were pronounced dead. The boys and I, accompanied by other Guardians Tanner and Haden, went in search for the creature. After three days the trail started to heat up when we found dried blood streaked along bushes and trees about a mile north of the campsite. A cluster of caves nearby smelled of rotting corpses—the stench was sickening. Derek ordered us all to stay back and camp for the night about a hundred yards away until we could confirm what was living in the caves. With all the innocents dead, I agreed with no arguments. That night Tanner and I stood guard while the others got some rest. I only had an hour left in my shift, before I had to wake the others, when I told Tanner to get some shut-eye, that I would be fine on my own.

Soon I was alone listening to the silence of the night. I remembered the smell of the air, light and crisp, the smell brought on by the beginning of spring. The trees rustled in the wind, and the sounds of animals sang under the full moon. I lay against a tree, eyes shut, taking in the serenity. That was, until the screaming startled me out of my daydream. A human scream can be the most deafening sound. The pain and suffering in a voice full of fear was like being stabbed in the chest over and over again, almost heartbreaking. Before anyone had the chance to stop me, I was gone, running in hyperspeed down the hill through thick brush. Branches broke under my feet as I made my way to the cave.

The screams got louder.

I entered the cave within seconds. The mixture of death and mildew was intoxicating, bringing me to my knees. Liquid erupted from my mouth as I vomited my last meal over a horde of rocks. After regaining my strength, I lifted myself to my feet and carried on. The others wouldn't make it for another couple of minutes, giving me enough time to grab the girl and get out. I walked farther into the cave, tripping over piles of human remains, some decomposing others still fresh and bloody with chunks of meat eaten from their bodies and limbs ripped off and thrown in every direction. I was still unsure of what I was dealing with, but I couldn't turn back and allow the fate of this girl to match that of those who lay beneath my feet. Eight feet high and twelve feet wide, the cave split into three directions. Drops of stale water fell from above me, cooling off my heated skin. I finally gave up using my nose as my personal GPS, and clinging it shut I started breathing from my mouth. Only the husky breathing, loud like an animal, directed me around the dark, twisted cavern.

Footsteps entered the caves. I heard whispers of my name being called, but the girl's scream led me away from my friends. I entered the creature's lair, widening my eyes in disbelief. The scene was far worse than anything I had ever observed: more bodies hung from hooks, organs scattered all over the floor, cages stacked high and covered in gore, bones stripped clean of any flesh and piled high in the corner. This was definitely no animal I had ever seen—at least not any normal one. No, this thing came straight from hell and found its perfect home where there was never a shortage of food. At least thirty humans were dead and were eaten or saved for later. But I could see no creature. There was only the sound of loud breathing off to one side and the screams of the girl somewhere else. I searched around, listening carefully to where the scream was coming from; it echoed off the wall making her seem everywhere.

Around the corner in a small nook, I finally located her. She was scared out of her mind with claw marks running down her back and across her chest. Her clothes were torn to shreds exposing most of her skeleton frame. As gently as possible, I took her hand, pulling her up to her feet, but instantly she fell back to the ground. I wrapped my jacket around her bloody body, pulling her into my arms. She stopped screaming long enough to repeat the same thing over and over, "Dog, dog, dog," and then fell into unconsciousness. Needless to say it only took thirty seconds to figure out what "dog" meant because right in front of me appeared a six-foot, three-hundred-pound dog. Blood-red eyes, a long snout filled with razor sharp teeth, and claws the size of kitchen knives came right at me. In the quickest move I have ever made, I was able to block the blow that would have surly killed the girl in my arms but not before I took a hit to my face.

The poison the hellhounds release in their claws is more like acid that burns through skin; to humans it's not deadly given the animal wouldn't want to eat tainted meat, but to a Guardian it's excruciating. With only the tips of its claws grazing my cheek in a split-second encounter, it was enough to tear open my face. Blood ran down my chin like a waterfall, and the taste of iron filled my mouth. My right eye was split in two, swelling shut. My body started healing right away, but like getting cut with a demon blade, the healing only did enough to clot the blood and set my eye back together. But my vision was gone for the moment, and the poison burned. The hound disappeared, giving me no chance of getting the upper hand. All I had now was my hearing to rely on.

From the time I entered the cave to the time I sustained my injuries, only two or three minutes passed, and by that time backup had finally arrived. Looking as if I had just walked off the battlefield after days of fighting, I slung the girl into Lucas's arms and ran for the mutt before any words were exchanged.

The fight lasted ten minutes, and in the end the head of the beast lay detached from its body. As for me besides my mangled face, my ribs were bruised, my shoulders were dislocated, and a few small puncture marks were indented in my leg. I couldn't take all the credit though. Lucas saved the girl, and the others helped me kill the thing. No one was pleased with me, and after a long, heated discussion over my stability, my family counted it as my third and final strike, which led to my sitting in the kitchen with Sarah, about to leave for high school.

*****

The drive to school brought me past miles of endless pastures and empty fields. The school was in the middle of nowhere, and the only entrance doubled as an exit. My Mustang roared up the half-mile driveway like a lion defending his territory. When I finally found the parking lot, all heads turned toward me and my ferociously loud car. I pulled up to the one-story school and parked in the back of the overflow lot. I threw my car into park and began marching up to my personal hell.

I was supposed to be meeting my guide at the front of the school, but before I even made it out of the parking lot, an energetic girl wove her way through the cars in my direction with a megawatt smile plastered on her face. She ran up to me as if we had known each other for ages.

"Oh my God, hi! You must be Alikye—I have been looking everywhere for you," she said all in one breath. "My name is Kady Scott, and I am your guide. You can sit with me at lunch, if you want. I mean, the worst thing for a new person is sitting alone, and I want to make sure that does not happen."

As Kady rambled on, I was preoccupied with studying the groups of people in their natural habitats. The jocks, preps, surfers, skaters, nerds, and outcasts each had their own designated area. It seemed like something out of a movie, so cliché. No one even noticed my presence as we walked through the crowds. Everyone just seemed to be more preoccupied with who was dating whom and some girl they knew who was seen hanging out with this guy who was, "So not cool." A few girls, who were dressed in expensive attire, turned once in my direction to tip their noses up at me while rolling their eyes. One boy, however, seemed mesmerized. His deep-blue eyes locked on mine, and a sudden shock ran through my body. His dark-brown hair, untamed and windblown, reached just above his eyes curling around his neck and ears. He had your typical swimmer's body and sun-kissed skin. It took me a second to realize I was gazing back at him. With an unpleasant grin, I turned my face and walked away. My attention then fell back to Kady, who had not stopped talking.

"Yeah, that's all cool; can we just go to class please?" I asked in an attempt to silence her.

"Oh. OK, this way," Kady said, beckoning to me over her shoulder. She was a tiny girl, shorter than me by an inch, with dark-brown hair, olive skin, and chocolate-brown eyes. She dressed like she belonged to a wealthy country club with her khaki miniskirt, pink polo with a popped collar, and wedged heals. However, her attitude toward me was accepting and completely nonjudgmental.

We walked through the center courtyard to the chipped red-painted lockers, exchanging smiles in silence.

"To the left is the huge auditorium, and to the right are the administration offices. Each hallway is marked with a letter and has six to seven classrooms. Past the courtyard and the lunchroom is the art department and the school gym. On the opposite side of the school is the band room," Kady explained, pointing in each location's direction.

"What hallway is my first class in?" I asked. Apparently the school didn't believe in alphabetical order; therefore, each letter hallway was scattered from one end of the school to the next without any pattern.

"If you go all the way down to the band room, your hallway is right across. I can walk you there if you want."

"No, thank you. I think I can handle it from here," I mumbled, trying to keep a smile on my face.

"OK, well, don't be nervous; you'll do great," she chirped with her megawatt smile. She gave me a small wave and walked down the hall into the crowds of people.

I watched her until she disappeared from my view. After observing the way simple humans interact with each other, my mind was set back to hunting. Nothing compared to being in the middle of a bloodbath battle, slicing the heads off hellhounds and thrusting my Silver Scripture Arrow into the throat of a level-three demon. Watching them explode into smoke and ash gave me a pleasant feeling. Those were the happy memories, when the boys and I smiled in victory together.

Chapter 3

Derek and Lucas had not slept in two days; they were still getting used to the fact that, for the first time in years, they would be on their own without Alikye by their sides. From when they started combat school together to when they were old enough to go on missions, the three of them had never been apart.

The boys were so opposite from one another, not just by looks but also by personality. Derek had dark-brown hair, short and clean-cut just above his ears. His eyes, like his mother's, were the color of liquid gold. And, like his father, he was tall and built. He was the know-it-all type and very stubborn. Lucas, on the other hand, was the smart and sensitive type. He had curly blond hair that fell just past his ears and eyes like emeralds. He stood a few inches below Derek at five feet eleven.

Lucas was in love with Alikye; his world began and ended with her, so he was taking the situation a bit harder. He first suggested that she get out of the game for a while because he could not bear to lose her. She took his actions as a betrayal, and the last words she had said to him were like a dagger being plunged into his heart: "After all this is done, we will never be the same." The look in Alikye's eyes was like fires exploding. The anger she possessed, so much hatred and rage, made Lucas realize what he was doing was the right thing.

Lucas knew she would never feel the same way about him. She couldn't; it was like Alikye could not feel the good in anything. She couldn't love him without hurting him more, so he walked out the door with a piece of himself missing. It was the only way to save her life—her soul.

Derek sat next to his brother in silence, knowing nothing he could say would help. To him, Alikye was like a little sister and his best friend; the feelings were strictly platonic. They had missions to fight, and with Lucas in that kind of mental state, they would only get killed.

"Hey, Bro," Derek said sympathetically as he stood up from the bed. He didn't know how to finish, how to make Lucas's pain go away. But he needed his brother, and more importantly he needed his brother to finally realize how to go on without her. Lucas turned his face toward the faded brownish carpet. "I know, dude- I know you miss her but she wouldn't want you to get yourself killed. And I need you to have my back." Derek finally finished.

Jack suggested the boys take a couple days to themselves to recuperate. So they settled in a run-down motel room in the suburbs of Richmond, Virginia. The room was small and plain with blood-red velvet curtains. Two beds lay flush with the white stained wall. Crumbled in the middle of each bed were plaid wool blankets that were too itchy for comfort, and across from them stood a chipped wood dresser, one leg held up by a few pallets of wood pieces.

They were on their way to Troy, New York, a small city located upstate. They were informed by other Guardians that a band of level-five demons were terrorizing the area. In studies of demonology, there were five levels, five being the weakest. Level fives were mostly used for finding souls to fill their boss's quota. The worst were the level ones; their main purpose was to kill, torture, and start wars.

Derek, Lucas, and Alikye had only once been face to face with a level-one demon. Orders were given to wait for backup from the more experienced Guardians like Jack. Alikye hadn't listened; she ran in, guns blazing. She did a number on the demon but almost got everyone killed in the process. If Jack and Henry (an old trusted family friend) hadn't shown up when they did, it would have been a bloodbath. *That was strike one,* Lucas had thought.

Their current mission was supposed to be easy; it should only take them a night or two. The hard part was to make up a cover story for the mischief, to inform the humans that what had happened was nothing more than a psychopath on the loose or a government conspiracy theory.

"I know," Lucas said, rubbing the sleep from his eyes. "I'm good, I promise. I just want to get the hell out of here and kill me something."

They had left the hotel feeling exhilarated, their blood pumping, heart racing. They both needed this case. They headed 420 miles north, traveling a good eight hours.

Lucas was the researcher. He had studies on many of the creatures and demons that walked the earth. He just needed the right information; each creature could be killed a different way and by different weapons, and each creature could have different abilities, so making a small mistake on what they were dealing with could be deadly.

Most myths and folklores had been told from personal experiences occurring many years back. After centuries the stories became nothing more than stories, but everything was still documented in old books and now on the web. Most of the stories were candy-coated, but with the knowledge from elders and what Guardian parents were to teach their children, the real stories came to light. Many people thought the only way to become a werewolf was through a bite. The way of the wolves could only be through bloodlines from the ancient people of dark witches. They used black magic to shape-shift. Mistakes were made, and the gods punished those and their firstborn sons with the transformation of one of the most feared animals. They change only on the nights of a full moon—when they lose all their humanity and kill at random, never remembering what they did during their change. Vampires had never actually been seen; they didn't exist. They were made from the imaginations of cannibalistic humans.

Freddy Krueger was made up from demons called dream walkers. They had the abilities to get in the minds of humans while the humans were asleep, making them do and see what the dream walkers wanted until the humans would take their own lives, giving hell a free pass to their souls.

The boogeyman, a very angry and vengeful spirit, would prey on a child's life force, or energy, taunting the child for nights on end, weakening them until they perished.

Killing demons was not possible with everyday human weapons and tools. Ancient beginning-of-time weapons were hard to come by. The legend went that when Lucifer was exiled from the heavens, he and his followers made it their mission to destroy the one thing that had destroyed him: humans. Lucifer wanted to be superior to his own race. When he disobeyed his father, he was cast down to hell, and his grace was taken from him. With rage and hate, Lucifer created the worst and scariest of nightmares to haunt and torture the human race. The angels created the Guardians to protect the humans and gave the Guardians weapons made out of the purest of the heavens. Knives, swords, and arrows were given to the Guardians, but over the centuries the weapons were stolen, destroyed, or forgotten. Only a few remained.

Lucas and Derek had only one dagger made of pure gold with the markings of their family name; some of the markings mirrored their bodies. They had asked Alikye for her *Arcus* and *Sagitta* (bow and arrow), knowing she would not need it. But she refused, holding on to her grudge. Alikye's father taught her how to use it, and when he died she was the heir to take it over. Without her consent it would be useless. That's how they all worked: the weapons knew their owners and would only comply with them unless they were ordered otherwise.

Chapter 4

I have always been loud, arrogant, and not afraid to get my hands dirty. (And trust me; the insides of some of the creatures I have killed would make a grown man gag and cry, and I was always the one with their intestines all over me.) I have always jumped into action without thinking twice, and I have never let anyone tell me what to do. I was stubborn, and I fought for it. I could break a nose with one hit, dislocate an arm in one twist, and break a neck in one pull.

But here it was different—I was different. I was quiet, shy, and weak. No matter how hard I tried, or how difficult it was for me, I was a sad excuse for a human being. But that was what I had to do to stay invisible. I didn't want to make friends; what kind of friend would I be if all I did was lie?

Derek and Lucas were my only friends, and for years I have tried to love Lucas as more. He was chosen to be my mate, my other half. As a friend I would always love him; he never thought so, but I did. I didn't mean the things I said to him. I was just so angry that he betrayed me. I wanted to forgive him, and a part of me already had, but I wasn't ready to tell him. He hurt me for all the right reasons. Plus I had to get through this huge obstacle before I dealt with anything else.

The bell rang, warning me that I was late for class.

I never liked school, not even my own school. I never fit in. At the age of five, I started combat school. It was mandatory that every Guardian attend to prepare us for the human world.

The first few years I endured school, but it took me away from the grief I felt for my murdered parents. You wouldn't think it, but anger is a dangerous emotion at such a young age. Releasing that anger by hitting a punching bag helped. By age eight classes were mostly about creature information. They taught us what the creatures were, how to track them, and how to kill them. Fight training got more intense—longer workouts, harder drills. At twelve I was taught to use my gifts while fighting. I became a machine. I was only focused on destroying every opponent I was given. My strength made me reckless and, therefore, overconfident. Killing the creatures took less time and effort for me than for any other student. Derek and Lucas were the only friends I ever had. The other Guardian children tried to approach me but would always back away. They were scared of me. However, as we grew up, they began to respect me. They wanted me to be the one watching their backs. I was only in the game for two years before being shipped here to Florida to start my first class at a normal human school.

This I was never trained for.

I ran, stopping just short of the door. This was the part where I walk in with everyone else already in their seats. The teacher would have already begun teaching, and I would be interrupting. All the attention would be on the new girl: me.

I took a deep breath, opened the door, and pasted a confused look on my face. My planned excuse was that I'd gotten lost on my way to this room, but the teacher never asked. He just smiled at me and asked me to stand in front of the class. He introduced himself as Riker James. He was a very attractive man in his late twenties. Light-brown hair fell in waves against his neck, and his face was unshaved and scruffy. His eyes were a pale green with dark lashes surrounding them.

"Everyone, I want you to say hello to our newest student, Alikye Macayan," he said. "Can you tell us a little bit about yourself?"

"Yeah…hi. I…um just moved here from…well, everywhere."

Sarah and Jack had come up with a cover story for me to tell people. They told me to be truthful about my parents and about how Sarah and Jack had taken me in. There was no record Guardians were ever born, and adoption did not exist for us. When a Guardian dies, the living children are given to the Guardian's closest friends. Sarah and Jack had known my parents since they were all in combat school together, since they were five years old.

"Jack is currently in Iraq, serving in the air force for the next eight months. Sarah and I decided to settle here until he returns home," I said in a bored tone.

"Are Jack and Sarah your parents?" asked Mr. Riker.

"Jack and Sarah took me in," I replied nonchalantly. "My real parents were murdered when I was three." A loud gasp came from the room. I guess I had not considered that losing both parents was uncommon among humans. It had been such a long time, I occasionally forget to miss them. Do not get me wrong; I loved them. However, I developed psychological damage in witnessing their gruesome deaths, so it was hard to show emotion.

*****

My mother was beautiful; I definitely got my looks from her. I remember one night, in the dead of winter, it was so cold outside that the water on the ground froze. My mother came into my room. I was three. She wrapped me up in a wool blanket and carried me to the car, my car. The heat was blasting, so by the time she set me in the front seat, it was nice and toasty inside. I had no clue where we were going.

Miles away was a building made of glass. Inside the glass were rows of color. My mother and I walked hand in hand down each aisle of flowers, gently grazing our fingertips upon each plant. The world outside seemed so asleep, but everything inside was awake and vibrant. Blossoming by the light of the moon was my mother's favorite flower, the night-blooming jasmine. The aroma from hundreds of small blossoms filled my nose and made me feel safe. "As long as you keep to the flowers, you will be safe. The scent will make the danger stay away," my mother said to me before I drifted off to sleep.

The following spring my mother and I spent weeks planting night-blooming jasmines in the front yard just beneath the porch. As each night fell, the jasmines would bloom into brilliant and stunning flowers, while the first sign of light would make them curl back into buds for the day.

The night of my parents' deaths I was asleep in my bed. I awoke from the sounds of hooves on the wooden floor. I knew it was a creature from hell from the smell of death and decay. My first thought was the flowers. I crawled out my window onto the porch. The colors of white and purple spread more magnificently across the grounds than they ever had before. I tucked myself among the plants, curled in the fetal position, with my mother's blanket wrapped around me.

From inside the house, my mother was sobbing. My father had been hurt badly, and blood was pouring out of his abdomen. He would soon be dead. My mother cried out as the creature struck her. She, too, would soon be dead. My parents' hands were tightly intertwined as their bodies lay motionless in pools of blood.

I felt my face and realized I had been crying. My body trembled as the creature slowly sauntered outside. He stood just above me, blood dripping from his fangs. His repulsive odor filled my nostrils, but he could not smell me. "The scent will make the danger stay away." I didn't understand until then what my mother had meant. The creature could not find me, and my life was spared.

Anytime I smelled night-blooming jasmine, I always thought of her.

*****

"Alikye, I am so sorry to hear about your parents," Mr. Riker said, bringing my attention back to reality.

"It was a long time ago. Jack and Sarah are great," I replied.

"OK. Anything else?"

I had a feeling my abrupt answer about my parents started to make him and everyone else a little uncomfortable and that he didn't really want me to say more. "Not really. Can I please just take my seat? I am very excited about my first class," I said sarcastically.

He laughed. "Of course; you may take a seat next to Andrew. Andrew, can you please raise your hand?"

Chapter 5

Lucas lay sleeping in the passenger seat of the car. He passed out the minute they left the hotel in Virginia. Now, eight hours later, he woke as Derek yanked the car into the driveway, slamming on the breaks. Not quite knowing where he was, he slid out of his seat and grabbed his bag from the back.

"How can we do this without her?" Lucas asked as they made their way to the house of a retired elder.

Without an answer from Derek, they walked to the door. Lucas knew he needed to drop the Alikye subject as complaining would get Derek and him nowhere and wouldn't bring her back any faster. An older, but not too old, looking man with salt-and-pepper hair and sad pale-blue eyes opened the door before they even had a chance to knock. It was the scent thing; everyone had a distinct scent. He welcomed them into his two-story Victorian home. The entrance gave way to a huge spiral staircase still with its original wood. The sitting area to the left was furnished with the finest of seventeenth-century furniture from Old England, and beautiful African china was set on the wooden table, steam coming from the small cups of tea. Derek and Lucas preferred the occasional beer, but out of respect for the old man, they sat down and enjoyed the tea with him. Small pastries were brought in by the man's house-keeper. Rolls dripped with honey, and small cakes offered melted chocolate and candy flowers. Bread slices complemented a variety of cheeses.

Lucas pulled out his laptop and started taking notes while taking small bites of each delicious dessert.

"Shame about the girl," the man said softly, shaking his head.

They both just smiled, neither saying a word. As an elder the man was strictly old school and didn't believe in the rehabilitation Alikye was getting, but he was sympathetic to them losing a loved one even if for only a little while.

"Well, if you ask me, she made the right choice," the man said, taking a quick sip of tea. "I would have never survived living under the same roof as the council, not even for a minute."

"So…what is going on here?" Derek began. "I was told that some chaos has been going on, and we were the closest to respond, but nothing out of the ordinary has been said on the local news coverage."

"Yes, well, it seems that the soul rating has spiraled out of control. People are selling souls for the smallest of reasons, and it just doesn't sit well with me. A car, a raise, good grades, and college acceptances are not worth all of eternity in the darkness," the man said with a nonchalant expression on his face.

He didn't seem like his heart was in this anymore. Time took a toll on Guardians over the years, but he seemed different, complacent. It was odd to sell a soul for so little. Both Derek and Lucas knew that, so they did what they did best: they got up and started to investigate.

They decided to start by interviewing the victims, hopefully not the way Alikye did it: by force. Their first guy, a twenty-two-year-old kid, seemed very willing to speak. He had sold his soul for a new Kia Optima, but when asked what happened, he couldn't remember anything, just that he felt empty. He was broken up about it. He said all of his life he had been a religious man, but his whole life changed one night after meeting a girl.

"When did all of this start?" Lucas asked, still taking notes while sipping his cola.

"Two weeks ago. And now I don't know what to do. My soul feels empty," the kid whimpered, tears pouring out of his eyes.

This wasn't any normal demon. They don't have the power to force people into selling their souls. They trick humans all the time, but force and memory loss wasn't their work. The boy had also said he felt empty, that his soul was missing. After two more interviews of willing victims, the stories seemed to be the same: lives changing, religious folks, small rewards, and the feeling of missing souls. This was no demon—this was something else. But Derek had no idea what it could be that was doing this. Lucas started in on the phone calls. He searched pages on the Internet made by other Guardians. When the Internet became popular, Guardians came up with a way to jot down information on what they had seen or heard of the old legends and myths on one blog. It was a page that could only be accessed by other Guardians. The mass amounts of codes and passwords would take even the best hacker a few years to gain access, but that would never happen. Lucas was scrolling through the pages, trying to find something that made sense, but he came up with nothing.

Chapter 6

His hand went up. In the far back of the room, the boy I had seen earlier, the beautiful boy with sapphire eyes. His perfectly sculpted chest steadily moved in and out from under his fitted pale-blue T-shirt. He twisted his head, moving his copper hair from over his left eye. His eyes followed every movement my body made as I strolled toward him.

When I arrived at my table, I set my belongings on the floor next to me, still feeling his eyes on me. He tilted his head my way, cocking one eyebrow and smiling as if he was waiting for me to speak first. He finally surrendered his white flag—"Hi, I'm Andy." He leaned toward me, handing me a book, his fingertips grazing my hand. I froze.

His touch sent chills down my spine. I could feel my blood pulsing through my veins. His aroma wrapped around me, sending electric waves through me until my entire body was paralyzed. I was trapped in his gaze, seeing flashes of colors appear in my head; my mind was frozen in time, frozen with images of Andy. I saw an immaculate fire burning around us as we stood only inches apart, never taking our eyes off each other. The image disappeared, being replaced by another one of him sitting in a field of early morning flowers that stretched their petals up toward the first light of day. The sun shone through the cotton-ball clouds, barely touching his flawless skin as he held a rose in his hands, placing it gently in my lap. The next image was of a raging tornado ripping through the land, destroying everything it touched except for him. He stood in the middle of it with not one drop of rain on his skin, and again there I was with him, looking up to the sky, smiling. All of a sudden, I felt my skin heating up, a burning sensation that should have had me screaming, but instead I welcomed the pain. It consumed my every thought until—

"Alikye," boomed the voice of Mr. Riker, shocking me back to reality as he called out my name for the answer to a question on the blackboard. I answered the question without hesitation, blinking in the soft lights of my surrounding.

My heart beat through my chest, my palms turned sweaty, and my head still spun with bliss. Dumbfounded I asked myself the same question over and over: *What just happened? Did he see the same thing?*

I had to calm myself down and center my energy. My stomach cramped up, and with every heavy breath I took, the muscles deep in my belly tightened. Again Andy locked his steely blue eyes on mine, his smile widened. I could feel my energy pulling me toward him. I wanted to speak to him, but my words were lost. I raised my hand to answer the next question, trying to distract myself from wanting him, ignoring his every attempt to make conversation. He tried again. I managed to look at him with slight hostility so that he might think I hadn't seen what I just saw; all the while my heart screamed his name.

The bell rang and, with a quick glance from Andy, I ran out the door. I didn't need him to find an excuse to talk to me. There was just something about him that didn't sit well with me. Good or bad, I was not about to find out. I stood at my locker for a moment, clearing my head, bringing my heart rate back to normal.

I heard Kady's footsteps coming up behind me. She had a light step to her walk, even and steady with a lot of confidence. She walked with pride and her head held high. Humans would never be able to read a person by the way they walked, never be able to detect a certain individual by a step, or a smell, like I can. Every person is different, but it's something that can't be seen. It's kind of like a personality trait. Everyone has his or her own walk, and like a snowflake, no two are the same. It can also describe a lot about a person: who they are, what they want, how they feel at that moment. And just like a person's face, scent and movements also imprint in my mind.

Kady reached me, placing a welcoming arm around my shoulder. I was actually relieved to have her next to me. My attention fell upon her and the new guy she was with. She introduced him as her boyfriend, Greg. He was tall, lean, and exotic looking, your average soccer player, so to speak. His dark-brown hair was uneven and a long mess of curls, lying just above his shoulders, matching his evenly toned brown skin and brown eyes. He appeared to be of Spanish descent.

We talked for a little bit before the last bell rang. Greg was quite the character; everything was a joke to him. He kept me laughing, which was never an easy thing to do. And I was surprised at my reaction.

"So we have this block together, and you'll have third block with Greg," Kady said.

"You know what—it sounds great to have someone in class to talk to," I replied, honestly hoping Andy wouldn't be in another one of my classes.

Kady and I sat together in American history. It was not hard for me to recognize the stories the humans were made to believe in and the thoughts that were planted in their heads by Guardians. The truth about wars, economic breakdowns, and even life came from my race. I enjoyed being taught as a human. It was fascinating to me to learn what they believed. Younger Guardians never had the privilege of hearing what the elders told the humans. We were always just told, "It's done." To finally hear the stories my people made up was funny, smart, and entertaining.

Our teacher went over the criteria for the semester. We would be starting with the Civil War. Guardians were never involved in that particular war and neither were the demons. It all fell on the American humans. History was useless to us because we were taught to never look behind for answers. We were taught to never learn from our own mistakes but from others who have had more experience. The same mistakes were never repeated by learning that way.

Mrs. Cofflen, a thin, older woman with light hair and dark eyes, began her lecture, and all I could do was listen. Every word she spoke was like showing me a new meaning to this life, human behavior at its worst, and the different needs from one country alone. They were at war with each other, killing their own people for standing up for what they believed in. The election of President Abraham Lincoln outlawing the slaving of men and women in America made a huge impact that caused a four-year war. I wouldn't choose to pick a side, but it showed a different side of the United States that I never knew existed. I did not want the class to end. I wanted to absorb all the information I could. I wanted to learn how the war ended and why. I could not fathom why humans never learn from their mistakes. Every ten or twenty years humans seem to need another war to occupy them. They must have given the demons everything they needed for control and domination, which only seemed to prove my point about mankind in the first place.

On the other hand, in the mites of war there were the humans who sat on the sidelines in the middle of something that was devastating, they looked to something else. In the tragedy of loss, the destruction of homes, the sadness that those people felt, they always had the courage to pick themselves up and start over from nothing. They knew what they lost was forever but did not dwell on the darkness that could have come of it. With all the ignorance, there was more passion; with the bad, there was more good; and with all the self-indulged politics, there were always those people who would never back down for what they believed in and would fight for a better world.

The bell rang, sending each student out the door for a free period of lunch. Kady saw how intrigued I was with the class, like I was a child in a candy store and couldn't decide what to eat first. She never brought it up, but I knew she was curious about how a subject that was taught every year since the fourth grade had grabbed my interest while all the other students drooled on their desks, bored by the facts of the past.

The lunch area was already starting to fill up. Spread throughout the grassy courtyard were twenty concrete benches attached to round tables. The inside cafeteria was a small room that could only fit about thirty students at a time. There were ten carts with food and drinks for sale that offered students a variety of greasy, processed foods. As a nonhuman being, I had a massive appetite, and my body naturally ran ten degrees hotter, burning a lot of energy. That meant I never had to worry about what I ate, or how much. I grabbed a few of the things I commonly ate: a double veggie cheeseburger, two sides of fries with barbecue sauce, a chocolate cupcake, and a Code Red Mountain Dew. After I purchased my lunch, Kady and I walked to her table where Greg was already sitting, waiting for our arrival. Kady brought her lunch from home in a brown paper bag. It consisted of a ham and cheese sandwich on multigrain bread, a bag of carrot sticks and ranch dip, one homemade cookie, and a diet Pepsi.

I was dreading being introduced to some of Kady's girlfriends. I had decided last class I would be OK with hanging out with Kady and Greg only during school, but when no one else arrived at the table, I let out a sigh of relief. As soon as that thought crossed my mind, I felt him getting closer. His scent was overwhelming. His footsteps were powerful and controlled. My body turned stiff, paralyzed, so I couldn't turn to see his incredibly beautiful eyes as he came from behind. It was just my luck that the only person I hung out with in a school pushing a couple thousand students would be friends with the boy that made my skin crawl. He sat down next to me and smiled his superstar half-smile, tilting his head a little to show me his lack of intimidation. For a moment I tensed up, not wanting him to accidently touch me.

"Alikye didn't expect you to be here," Andy said without moving his eyes away from mine.

"Good! You two have already met, so we can skip the boring introduction," Kady interrupted with a megawatt smile.

"We have first block together. Mr. Riker paired us up. He's a pretty cool teacher," I said, avoiding any conversation with Andy.

"He's the soccer coach, the one I was telling you about. You should try out for the team. It's a lot of fun," Kady finished.

"You should tell me more about it," I replied, turning all my questions to Kady and Greg.

The rest of the lunch hour, we just talked about random teen subjects. They caught me up on the gossip around town, the best places to go, and everything on the to-do list for a new girl. They asked me questions about myself, but they didn't pry too much. If only my family could see me now.

"Oh, isn't this cute. Andrew finally getting into charity work, I see," a voice I didn't recognize said from behind me. I could smell her though, and her scent, strawberries and cream, was unrecognizable. She wasn't in any of my classes. But when I turned around, my photographic memory recognized her as being the girl on the front lawn before school. She and two others, who dressed a lot alike with short, strapless, floral-printed dresses and stiletto pumps, were the girls who were standing with Andy and the rest of the jocks. She had bleach-blond hair that fell down her back, bright hazel eyes, and tan skin that looked like she had just walked out of the tanning bed.

"Amanda, how pleasant it is to see you once again," Andy said and began to turn toward me. "Have you met—"

"Yeah, don't care." Amanda blew him off and turned her attention toward me. "Word travels fast. I know all about you, girl, and to tell you the truth, I'm not impressed either." The two clones behind her, who also had the same blond hair and fake tan but not as pretty as Amanda, started to giggle. "Just a small warning to you—Andrew is mine. Just because we are not together now doesn't mean we won't be soon enough. You are just a new toy for him to play with, but he will be fed up in a matter of days." Amanda said matter-of-factly as she strutted off with her two clones at her heels.

Chapter 7

The rest of the day went on as anticipated. The classes were premature, and the humans were cliché. I didn't see how Sarah was so optimistic about this whole situation, how she thought this would be good for me. I was programmed to fight, to live under the radar. I was trained to protect humans not *be* a human.

After lunch Andy kept apologizing for Amanda's behavior and reassured me he was not some dumb jock who played with girls' emotions. I told him I would be fine and that it didn't bother me, which it didn't. Andy was nothing to me and never would be, so Amanda's comment was more like telling me the sky was blue. It was information that was irrelevant to why I was here. Kady, on the other hand, felt the need to explain the situation.

Apparently Andy, Amanda, and Kady had been friends since Andy and Amanda were in second grade and Kady was in first grade. As they grew up, their friendships with Kady started to perish, but Amanda and Andy started to grow closer. Kady met Greg when she was a freshman, and the three of them became estranged. Amanda wanted nothing to do with Kady anymore, and she fell into the popular crowd. It wasn't until early summer that Kady and Andy started to mend their friendship after Amanda broke up with Andy for an older guy she met when she spent the summer in the Hamptons.

Third block, I had Math. Greg sat next to me to catch me up on all I had missed. Forth block, science, which would have been boring if not for Amanda, who kept coughing rude remarks at me. I shrugged it off as petty and listened to the teacher. With my academic scores so high, another gift I was given as a Guardian and for my photographic memory—my first, third, and fourth blocks were all senior classes, and I was the only junior in there.

School finally ended, and I rushed out to my car undetected, hoping to get out without small chitchat and other unnecessary conversations. But Kady saw me as I was reaching for my door handle.

"Alikye, hey, wait up," she screamed from across the parking lot, grabbing the attention of the whole student body.

Damn, she saw me, and so did Andy who was now making his way toward me. I figured it would be rude of me to jump in my car and speed out of there, so now there was only one thing left for me to do. I jumped on the door of my car, leaning up against the windshield. I didn't care how many people told me it would be smart to keep the top up, that the school wasn't liable for stolen property if I wouldn't take the time to lock up my vehicle. I didn't care since it would take me a whole ten minutes to find the thief and knock out his or her teeth.

I sat there, my foot propped up, my arm resting on my knee. The sun was hot on my face, the smell of salt and coconut danced around my nose. The wind blew through my tangled curls tickling my neck.

"Hey, what are your plans today?" Kady asked.

"Homework I guess." I didn't know where this was going, but I could only guess that she wanted me to accompany her in some kind of after-school gathering. I agreed to be friends with her in school, but after the school day ended, I was hoping to be left alone in my own place of solitude to sulk in self-pity.

"Well, we are going to dinner at six thirty if you would like to join us. It's a hot spot for teens and they have really good food."

"I'm not sure. I will have to check with Sarah, but I will let you know."

"You should come. It will be a lot of fun," Andy said before he gave me his award-winning smile, sending goose bumps down my body and ending at my toes. A shiver ran through me as he took a step closer, his warm breath on my neck. "Seriously." Then turning on his heels, he walked away with Kady, leaving me to myself.

I walked through the back door as Sarah was coming into the living area with a small tray of cookies. I never realized how blissful she was acting as a real mother, but her smile showed me everything. I was hungry. At lunchtime I managed to eat a little over fifteen hundred calories, but that did not appease my four-thousand-or-more-calorie appetite, and that smell was seductive. Sarah knew my weakness: freshly baked sugar cookies with a load of sprinkles cooked into them.

I finished the whole tray as I told her about my day. She seemed impressed by my attempt to change. Her face lit up when I told her about the friends I made and about trying out for soccer. I think she started to envy me, my new life. In the back of all Guardians' thoughts, they always imagine life as a human, always feel a small part of themselves missing, never having the chance to really be free. Because we were created to have traits of humans, our souls long for the real chance to be human. It's the angel part that overrides the human instincts, that keeps us rational, but it's the human part that lets us feel. I personally never wanted any of this, and I was pretty sure I was the only one who didn't. I envied all of them, the Guardians.

"I don't see how any of this is a good idea," I said.

How could I? By my being here, in the same world as humans, living their lives, something was bound to happen. What if they notice something different about me? What if I mess up and use my gifts in front of them. What if I am being hunted, and I have no other choice but to fight, and they see me fight—they see me kill, something that they might see as human? What do I do then?

"Kye, honey, this is your last option. You need to make this work. You know if the…" Tears began to form in her eyes.

"I know, that's why I'm here. I'm the last of the Macayan legacy.…I got it."

Sarah walked me out to the porch. She understood my despondency; it was a lot to go through for such a young girl. I was barely sixteen, and already my life was becoming confounding. What the hell was I going to do?

I dug my toes into the soft white sand. The water was still for miles and miles across the ocean. The sun sat in the sky of clouds. I loved the tranquility of resting underneath the large Queen Palm that sat in the backyard among the five smaller palm trees.

Sarah had left me to myself. She told me if I needed her she would come back out, but I didn't need her, and I didn't need for her to see me like this. I would rather just lie on my chair and feel the salty breeze brush up on my heated face. I would rather listen to the silence of the ocean. I would rather the tree fell on my body, crushing me to death. No, I didn't need her, I didn't need anyone.

A few hours passed. I was so into my own mind I had not realized Sarah had company over. I could hear a woman and a man or maybe two men. I heard them all laugh. What was so funny? I could hear my name—they were saying Alikye. They were not her friends. They were my future friends, and I didn't think they would come over to my home. How the hell did they know where I lived? I never told them. I wasn't giving them the gratification of getting up and welcoming them to my home that I had no intention of ever inviting them to.

"Kye, honey, I told your friends it would be OK for you to go out to dinner with them," Sarah yelled from the doorway.

Freaking fabulous.

I ignored her, keeping my eyes closed. I was concentrating on my surroundings, exercising my senses. I was listening to the sounds of the trees rustling in the wind and the faint sound of a sailboat a few miles away catching what little wind we had. I could hear a school of fish swimming through kelp on the bottom of the ocean. And then I heard *them.*

Three sets of footsteps walked down the porch and into the sand, entering my private sanctuary.

"Hey, Alikye, are you ready to go? We figured we would pick you up," Kady said.

"Sure, just give me a minute," I annoyingly said, still lying in my chair. This was not how I wanted to spend my night, but now I had no choice since they went around me to ask Sarah, and I needed to stay on track with my plan to get out of here.

I walked inside, eyeing Sarah. What was she thinking? I ran to my room and put on black tights and a tight-fitting grey sweater. I kept on my combat boots, not caring if they went with the outfit. I left my room and ran into Andy who was standing in the hallway. He was becoming very persistent.

"Hey, Alikye," Andy said.

"Hi, Andy. What's up," I replied nonchalantly.

"I'm glad you're coming."

I gave him a small smile. "Sure," I mumbled. I didn't want him to read too much into why I was going. It wasn't a date.

I walked with him down the hallway, and his hand gently brushed mine, sending an electric tremor down my body. Heat rolled up my arm in tendrils, pressing hard against my heart. I jumped in surprise. He acted like he didn't notice, but the small jolt made him turn his head and smile—I knew he felt it, too. I knew he felt all of it.

Chapter 8

"May I please start with an order of cheese sticks with a side of ranch and a basket of onion rings? For my dinner I'll take a veggie cheeseburger with fries and extra barbecue sauce," I said to the server after she had taken everyone else's order. For a human I ate a lot. For a Guardian I never ate enough. I had what every girl wanted: to be able to eat when I wanted and what I wanted without gaining any weight. I loved food.

We went to Scooters Bar and Grill located on the corner of Bridge Road and Southeast Lares Avenue. It was a small, low-key place known as the locals' hangout. In the center of the restaurant was a large horseshoe shaped bar with five flat-screen televisions displaying various sporting events. Three pool tables were located in the far back corner adjacent to a stage used for Wednesday night karaoke. The wood paneled walls were decorated with pieces of history from the small beach town. Pieces of the Reformation, a British ship that wrecked off the coast in 1691, hung on the wall beside the Spanish currency found in the ship. A lobster trap, a buoy, and pictures featuring the old Flagler railroad station also hung on the walls. An antique Donkey Kong video game plaque was nailed on one of the corner booths. A young woman in a short jean skirt, cowboy boots, and a black laced top stood in front of a digital jukebox, her hand on her hip, scowling through album after album probably trying to decide on a cheery tune to dance to.

The place was upbeat and full of laughter, a great place to just kick back and relax. But I had never been the type to just kick back and relax. I was always wide-eyed and on full alert. I guess when you go through life with demons trying to kill you, that's the type of person you must become to survive.

Andy sat to my left, eyeing me as I ate my food. He would turn to watch me dip my fries in my sauce and delicately place them on my tongue to absorb the sweet and salty goodness. I felt the heat from his body. I tasted the pungent smell of his Giorgio Armani cologne. I curled my lip at him to silently inform him he was disturbing me.

What was with this kid? All day he had been throwing me signals, and all day I had been rejecting him. Don't get me wrong, Andy was very attractive, his dark-blue eyes could melt a girl's heart, and his messy dark hair that fell in front of his eyes every time he shifted stances could drive a girl crazy. He was absolutely beautiful. And the way he made me feel—nervous, unsure of myself. Andy had a magnetic hold on me, and I couldn't explain what it meant or why it was happening. But I despised it, I despised him. I couldn't like him—he was human. It would be forbidden. I closed my eyes to get him out of my head, to stop thinking about what it would be like to give in to his temptation.

"So, Alikye, how do you like this place so far?" Andy asked, cocking his eyebrows up and curling the side of his mouth just a smidge. Could he be more obvious? Is this really how the male brain worked? Was chivalry really dead? My race would never behave like that. The age of thirteen, which for humans was usually around the time puberty happened, was when our parents would tell us who we were mated to. We all knew the day would come. There was no need for flirting or using egos to win a girl's attention. It was easy: you knew your soul mate, and you spent the next few years learning to like your mate and then eventually falling in love. No games, no stupid pickup lines and creepy eye twitches, no random dating and heartbreaking break ups. It was simple—this was who you were going to spend the rest of your life with whether you liked it or not. Only if life was that simple, the complication of love would never turn something good into evil.

I turned a cold shoulder to him, not wanting to answer his question. To be honest I hated being here, spending precious time wasting away in a podunk town where gossip spread like wildfire. Attending a human school where I had to bite my tongue and allow a shallow plastic Barbie doll to push me around. I missed my old life hunting demons and taking out my anger with a blade to their ice-cold hearts. I missed being me, being around people I never had to lie to.

"Fine. The food's really good," I replied nonchalantly.

"Would you like for me to take your plate?" The server asked politely when she noticed my clean plate with nothing but a used napkin crumbled on top of it.

I nodded.

"You sure do eat a lot for a girl," Andy said after the server cleared our table.

"Yeah, I know. I like food."

"Well, I like a girl who can eat. It tells you a lot about her."

"I bet."

I was just about to ask Kady more about soccer when my body froze. The faint scent of strawberry and cream fluttered across my nose then smacked me in the face. *She* was here or at least somewhere in the vicinity. I locked my eyes on the wall in front of me. I took a deep breath, slowly releasing it. The world around me froze. A shimmering veil of pink glided gracefully through the air. My eyes watched patiently as the veil danced around the room to the far back. Past the bar, down a short hallway where a neon restroom sign hung from the ceiling, Amanda, accompanied by her two clones, walked through the door. I didn't want the confrontation, so instead of staying and letting Amanda rip me a new one, I put a twenty and a ten on the table and slipped out of the booth. Without a word I walked to the front door. I didn't look back to see the others staring at me with disbelief. Their eyes on my back told me everything. I grasped the cold bronze handle. Before exiting the building, I looked back to the hallway where the pink veil was now far gone and watched the three girls giggling as they strutted into the main dining room.

I left before they saw me.

Guardians only have three rules, besides being in cohorts with demons.

1. Never kill or even harm a human.
2. Never save a human from natural causes.
3. NEVER fall in love with a human.

I stood outside on the sidewalk where the night took to the starry sky. A light drizzle fell.

One day. I'd only had one day, and already I was being stalked by a creepy, but gorgeous, guy. I made an enemy with a vengeance to ruin my life. And now I was being chased out into the rain so I didn't do something stupid and blow my cover. I couldn't go home; Sarah would ask questions I didn't want to answer. I couldn't go back inside, too risky. I looked to my left and felt the salty breeze push me toward the beach. It was a three-mile run, two minutes in hyperspeed. I always loved the beach at night—the silky sand between my toes, the cool water on my skin, the salty air against my face. I loved the silence of the night, the sound of the waves crashing on shore. I took off running, the scenery blurring around me as I ran, the string of lights coming off of each passing car, the dust swirling beneath my feet, and the wind brushing through my hair. It was the complete freedom of being invisible. I never wanted to stop. I wanted to run forever. To escape from the hell I was living. To escape from what I was and who I was. It was all colliding together, resulting in the end of me—my real life and my forged life.

I got to the beach in no time. The small parking lot was empty. Beyond that a brittle wooden pavilion stood between two wooden walkways that led down to the beach. Six wooden benches sat snug next to one another with the right amount of coverage under the pavilion. I sat on the center bench closest to the sea. Two feet in front of me, down over the concrete ledge, was a garden of flowers and plants that stood safely guarded by orange netting.

I looked out into the night where the moon shined bright, sprinkling the ocean in specks of diamonds. I thought about Derek and Lucas and what they might be doing at that minute. I wondered if they were thinking about me. I thought about Lucas and what he must think about me, what I must be doing to him. It was never my intention to hurt him. I loved him, just not how he wanted me to love him. I had enough issues to work out on my own without having to bring him into the picture. I knew that much. What I didn't know was how being here would help me work them out. If my parents were still alive, would I still be in this situation?

Back when I was first told about Lucas being mated to me, my reaction should have been different. I remember smiling at Jack and Sarah when they told us. Lucas was sixteen. The female was always the first to know, when she turned thirteen. The male's age didn't matter, and he had to wait until his name was called to a female. Every girl my age, and some older and even younger, wanted their mate to be Lucas. They all cried when he was finally spoken for. I cried later because I didn't want him. I didn't want anyone. All the movies show that when a girl falls for a boy, she gets goose bumps all over her body. She gets butterflies in her stomach. The first kiss ends with a leg that pops up or knees that go weak. Did I want that? Probably not, but it was nice to think about finding my own guy, my way. A guy who would cross the ocean for a chance to see me if only for one moment. A guy who would go to the ends of the earth just to find me. A guy who would burn with so much passion his fire would never dissipate. A guy whose fire would burn only for me. Would I ever feel *that* in Lucas?

I was lost in my own mind when behind me a set of headlights pulled into the parking lot. I shook my head in annoyance. How did they find me, and what have they been doing for the last thirty minutes? Kady parked her white Ford Explorer in the spot closest to me. All three doors opened at once, and one by one they piled out of the SUV, staring straight at me.

"Alikye," Kady yelled. "What the hell happened? We have been looking everywhere for you. Sarah said you might have come here. I guess she was right."

They went to see Sarah. Great. I was trying to avoid that, or I would have gone home and hidden in my room. I guess I couldn't blame them. I did disappear on them.

"Sorry. I saw Amanda, so I left before she could start shit with me," I said, reassuring them it was nothing they did. I still didn't like them much.

"That's what we figured after she came over to our table and started talking our ears off," Kady said sweetly, making a face as she said it.

"Yeah, but don't worry pretty girl. I got your back," Andy said as he took the seat next to me. His hot breath tickled my neck.

My heartbeat ran wild with how close Andy was to me. If only he knew how he affected me. Damn it; then he would never leave me alone.

"You walked all the way here? You must have just gotten here a few minutes ago," Greg said.

"Do you have to be so close? Heard of personal space?" I said, backing away from Andy.

He laughed at me and scooted closer, touching my leg with his. "I would love to be in your personal space anytime." He threw his head back, laughing even harder, but then he smiled and moved away. "OK," Andy said, placing his hands in the air, palms out. "I get the point."

Chapter 9

Two weeks had gone by, and Sarah was still buying my act of compassion for me and for the humans. However, I was starting to buy my own act, like I was supposed to be here. I'd grown accustomed to waking up and only having to think about school and friends. Kady's kindness had been rubbing off on me, and Andy was still persistent on a date, even though we spent every day together.

One morning at the breakfast table, Sarah surprised me with brand new cleats and shin guards for team tryouts.

"Can you please act human, Little Miss Speedy Gonzalez?" She asked, teasing me about using my abilities as an advantage in making the team. "It is only fair."

"I wouldn't dream of it." I grinned sarcastically.

"Kye—"

"I was thinking of it, just a little," I said with a higher pitch.

With a huge smile on her face, Sarah shook her head at me.

***

Kady and I walked to our usual lunch table where Greg and Andy were hysterically laughing at something their friend Holden had said. Holden was a sophomore who was also trying out for the soccer team. His dreadlocked blonde hair fell midway down his back. He had green eyes and was slightly smaller than Andy in height and build. As soon as we sat down, Andy started making jokes about Holden and I not making the team. Little did he know.

When I walked from the locker room out to the field, I noticed the black and red cement bleachers were packed with students. The football team was in one section, awaiting its turn for the field. The rest of the student body crowded the bleachers, overflowing onto the track where the band was trying to practice marching. The cheerleaders sat cross-legged on the grass with their pom-poms in their laps. Amanda stood close to Mr. Riker with a clip-board in her hands.

I passed by her, making my way toward Kady, but when I looked at Amanda, she groaned at me, scrunching her perfectly done-up face.

I walked on the field, ready for tryouts to begin, knowing that I would kick ass. Andy, Kady, Greg, and the rest of the team were playing against me and the other newbies. I was trying out for a midfield position, one that demanded constant sprinting from offense to defense. When Andy heard my position, he loudly called me out as the person he was guarding. I furrowed my eyebrows and maliciously giggled at him.

Mr. Riker blew the whistle to begin the scrimmage. From center position Holden quickly passed me the ball, landing me one-on-one with Andy. I simply glided around him with the ball at my feet. He never stood a chance in taking the ball from me. I ran down the field, kicking the ball ahead of me, continuing to slip gracefully around my opponents. I slightly used my hyperspeed to maneuver around but not enough to raise suspicion. It would have been easy enough for me to make it past midfield, through the defense, and to the goal with no help from my teammates. But I wanted to give the other rookies a deserved chance to prove their skills, so I passed the ball back to Holden in a give-and-go play with Andy at my heels. As Holden kicked the ball back to me, I scissor kicked it right past Greg's untimely hands. Seasoned players and rookies alike were awestruck by my abilities. Andy huffed and puffed and demanded a rematch. I accepted.

For the second scrimmage, I was playing the center position. I looked over at Holden, giving him a knowing nod. This time around I was being blocked by Andy and two other defenders, and Greg was readied at the goal. Mr. Riker blew the whistle for us to begin. I swiftly pulled the ball back to me and kicked it through Andy's open legs. Then, spinning to his backside, I regained possession of the ball. I heard Andy trip over his own feet as he tried to keep up with me. The two other defenders flanked me as I passed the ball to Holden who was open and in position to score. He forcefully kicked it toward the net. Greg dove on top of the ball and saved the would-be goal. He then cleared it down the right sideline to Andy at midfield. I ran to his side as fast as humanly possible. I proceeded to let him dribble the ball a few steps toward my goal before I stole it. Andy had no idea what had just happened. I didn't realize how easy this sport would be for me and how my abilities could contribute. In no time at all, I was back at the opposing goal and ready to score. I faked out Greg by acting like I was going to kick the ball to the left side of the goal. This forced him to abandon the right side. I shifted my body position and kicked the ball into the top right corner of the net for yet another surprising feat. Greg fell to his knees, dumbfounded at his rookie-like mistake. After my second goal, Mr. Riker blew the whistle to end the day's tryout. He announced that the new team roster would be posted on his classroom door the following school day.

I looked around to find Andy with a look of defeat upon his face. As he walked past me, he took off his sweaty jersey, exposing his dripping wet chest and chiseled abs. He was about six feet tall with a rock hard stomach and large biceps. He wore his gym shorts low exposing a V between his hipbones. All I could do was stand rooted to the ground, staring in a hypnotic trance at his incredible body. My grin fell from my face as I felt a spark light inside me and my knees go weak. Flashes of light crossed my vision, and then I knew without doubt, he knew what he was doing to me.

***

During my drive to school the next morning, I realized just how excited I was about my tryout the previous day. The feeling of success without a consequence of harm was better than I could have ever imagined it would be. Since my arrival in Picture City, I had been cooped up and unable to use my natural abilities. I found soccer to be a satisfying alternate activity. The quick maneuvers and on-the-spot decisions reminded me of fighting beside Derek and Lucas.

As I scanned the white sheet of paper with my finger, I found my name in the third slot. Even though I knew I would make the team, seeing my name on the list solidified my place in high school and put a genuine smile on my face. Holden came up behind me, wrapping his arms around my waist and lifting me off the ground.

"Can you believe it?" Holden asked. "I mean, yeah, I knew you were going to make the team, but me? I'm the only sophomore they're allowing on the varsity team. And it's all thanks to you."

"I didn't do anything—it was all you," I replied, locking my arm around his.

"If it wasn't for you teaming up with me, I'd be on the junior varsity team instead of varsity, which makes me a shoe-in for the next two years," Holden said, beaming as we walked down the hallway.

"Well, we make a great team," I said, leaving him and walking into class.

Mr. Riker was the first to greet me at the door with a huge smile and an even bigger applause. I smiled back shyly when the entire class turned their attention on me and Stacy, another girl who had also made the team. Like the first day of school, I tried not to say much. I just took my seat next to Andy who was grinning like a hyena.

"What?" I snapped at him.

Andy raised his eyebrows. We had come such a long way in our friendship.

"Nothing," Andy said evenly. "Just thinking about all the time we'll get to spend with each other. All the late…night…sweaty…practices together."

"Or you could get your head out of the gutter and think about all the times I'll be stealing the ball right out from under your feet like I did at tryouts, or have you forgotten already?"

"Beginners luck, but if you are that good we'll make a hell of a team, don't you think?"

"Creepy much." I grunted because something in his eyes was giving me goose bumps. A seductive look mixed with his usual cockiness, like I was a game to him, an animal on the loose that couldn't be tamed. He wanted me more and more each day because he couldn't have me. But there was more to it—it was like he *had* to have me. I was the piece he needed in order to finish his puzzle. I was the final mark on the board. And the worst part was, I was enjoying it.

Chapter 10

Lucas had just come back from Westfield, Massachusetts. He decided to go alone so Derek could finish the Troy interviews. Two days ago another soul was stolen with the same signature as the others. The thirty-two-year-old man was of Western European descent and belonged to a local Lutheran church located across the street from Stanley Park. The happily married father of two came upon the creature in the form of the woman he most desired. The man described her to Lucas as having jet-black hair that fell past her waist and a caramel complexion like an ancient warrior from the Amazon rainforest. She was tall and muscular and spoke with a Portuguese accent. Under her spell, the man asked for a Harley Davidson motorcycle in exchange for his soul. The next day she was gone. *Nothing is making sense anymore,* Lucas thought when he was done.

It had taken days for Lucas to finish with the interviews. All the signs pointed to a Barter demon, one who negotiates with humans for the selling of their souls. This case shouldn't be this difficult, Lucas thought to himself as he paced back and forth on the screened porch. The sun was setting for the fifteenth night since he and Derek had arrived at the old man's house, and he was no closer now than he was on the first day.

After extensive amounts of research, luck was finally on Lucas's side. The answer was staring him right in the face the whole time, but because he had been thinking about Alikye, he didn't see what was there. His intelligence was the quality he was most proud of, but he felt stupid for allowing thoughts of her distract him.

"From this day on, I'm back!" Lucas exclaimed, giving himself a pep talk as he punched the air. "No more obsessing over Kye. No more thinking about what-ifs. I'll deal with it when the time comes."

Lucas felt like a one-hundred-pound weight named Alikye was lifted from his shoulders. He used a finger to scroll up through his contacts on his Android until he found Derek's name. Derek answered in two rings, sounding disappointed.

"Sorry, dude. Nothing," Derek sulked. "It's all the same, but I just don't know."

"That's because you're not me." Lucas beamed cheerfully as if he had just solved world hunger.

"You didn't," Derek said with a smirk, in disbelief.

"Oh…but I did. It's a Nimphica!"

"That's impossible, Bro."

Lucas knew it was a long shot, but all the facts pointed directly in the Nimphica's direction. He didn't know much about the creature, but he remembered hearing the stories as a young boy.

Nimphica's were very rare creatures. Like Haley's comet they only came out every seventy-five years. Once out they only remained for a period of five weeks. They fed off the essence of human souls. The female creature originated in the mythology of ancient Israel, the religious capital of the world. She could shape-shift into any man's desired woman, and she only preyed on religious men. She seduced them into handing over their souls for next to nothing in return. Unless a Nimphica was killed within her five weeks of feeding, the souls were lost forever.

"How do we kill it?" Derek asked.

"We have to find her first…"

Lucas finished up on the phone, saying good-bye to Derek. He was very proud of himself for finally figuring out what creature they were up against. In the past three cycles that Nimphica's had walked the earth, no Guardian had been able to find one, let alone kill one. Lucas was determined to be the first. He wanted to be the one to find the creature and slay it with only Derek's help. He needed to prove to himself that he was capable of doing so without Alikye by his side.

Chapter 11

Saturday morning I was awakened by the sweet sound of Sarah asking me to run a few errands. I accepted the tasks, baffled by the everyday human nature of the activities. She asked me to travel to the next town, ten miles due south, to get fresh fruits and vegetables from the local farmers' market.

"Why can't I just get the groceries from the supermarket that is five minutes away?" I whined, as I rolled out of bed.

In a tone that dripped with sugar, Sarah replied, "Please, Kye." She placed her hands lightly upon mine. "You know how I love to cook with the freshest vegetables."

"Fine," I mumbled while throwing on a pair of jeans and a tank top. "Anything for you."

Sarah walked out of my room with a smile on her face that let me know she was thankful.

I decided to take the scenic route along Beach Road. Palm trees lined the street for the five mile stretch paralleling the intercostal. I drove with the convertible top down and the wind in my hair. The salty air rested on my skin. The modern homes on the right side of the street astounded me with their colossal size. I didn't understand why humans felt the need to spend massive amounts of money on material possessions.

"When the time comes that I have to raise my future children, I will be satisfied with having a small home like the one I barely knew," I said out loud.

For the first time in weeks, I was finally alone with my thoughts. I didn't want to believe that I actually had feelings for Andy, that the feelings had been good all along. Every minute I was away from him, I was thinking about him, and every time I saw him, I got those butterflies that reminded me of how love was supposed to be. When he texted or called me, a huge smile appeared on my face. When he would show up on my doorstep without warning, I pretended to be mad, but really I was a giddy little girl on the inside. I couldn't show him how I felt, and I had to try to ignore those feelings if I wanted them to disappear. If I ignored my feelings, then they wouldn't exist. If I couldn't be with him romantically, at least I could be friends with him.

How did I even make friends? The four of us formed a bond so quickly. At first I was nice to them just for Sarah, but now, after hanging out with them, it was hard not to be a sincere friend. Kady instantly included me in her life without any judgment. I enjoyed being around her because she took me away from the life that I would go back to, one of hate and death. She brought me to a place where, for the first time, I could be a normal teenager. Yes, I got along with the other girls in combat school, but those girls only talked about fighting demons and learning new techniques on how to defeat them, even though that's all I ever did want to talk about. But with Kady it was different. I loved our friendship; we could gossip and have it not mean anything the next day.

I pulled into a parking spot in front of the farmers' market and grabbed the shopping list off the passenger seat. It was busy, and with all the voices crowding me, my thoughts couldn't be heard. I walked from stand to stand, aimlessly grabbing the items on my list, absorbing all the colors and smells of my surroundings. Now I knew why Sarah sent me here. The variety and quality of the produce was nothing I would have been able to find in a grocery store.

***

I arrived home to find Kady's and Andy's car in my driveway. As usual, they never thought to call before showing up at my house. Sarah seemed to find their presence comforting. As I cautiously tiptoed through the too quiet house, my bare feet stuck to the cool white tiles. As I made my way to the backyard where my friends usually waited for me, I could sense the energy of a warm group of friends.

Walking through the French doors, I was taken aback by the company of my soccer team and coaches. They had decorated the backyard in full Bulldog colors. Balloon centerpieces dotted the buffet table that was covered in delicious homemade food from Mr. and Mrs. Scott. White Christmas lights wrapped the many palm trees, and tiki torches lined the perimeter of my backyard. Sarah rushed up to me, embracing me in a mom-like hug out of pride for my making the soccer team. As I took in the sight of my peers, I noticed the happy faces of Holden and Greg and the unwanted glare from Amanda. I felt a little bit overwhelmed by my sudden appreciation of my human life. I could never fathom how many people could care about me in the short time I had been in Picture City. I had started to view my new human-like life as more of a pleasure than a pain.

When Sarah let go of me, I caught Andy intensely staring at me, sending chills down my spine. I quickly shook off the feelings of lust toward Andy as Kady, overly excited, leapt to hug me. Andy strutted toward me, bare-chested, the wind blowing his crisp scent past me, bringing me back to a trance. He then wrapped his strong arms around my petite body, subjecting me to a stone-like state; unwittingly I locked my arms around his neck, my head resting at his collarbone. Sarah loudly cleared her throat, calling everyone to the buffet table underneath the pristine bundle of Queen Palms. I pulled away from Andy, eyes wide. Turning too quickly I stumbled but was caught by arms encircling my waist.

"Whoa there. I'm finally getting to you huh?" Andy said.

If only he really knew. "No, I'm just hungry," I lied.

"If that's your story, but soon, Kye, you'll cave. Very soon," Andy said, releasing me from his hold.

If he kept this up I was afraid I would soon cave. But for now I was happy just being around him.

Stars mottled the sky in brilliant splendor as the party continued into the night. The coaches built an immaculate bonfire about twenty yards from the breaking point of the tranquil waves. With only half the team remaining and the adults inside for coffee, we all sat comfortably around the fire, taking in its warmth.

"So our first game is in two weeks—you ready for it?" Greg turned from Kady to me.

"Of course she's ready; she dominates on the field," Kady said before I had the chance to answer.

To be honest I was a little nervous. The team meant a lot to the school. Although football was the pride in most towns, soccer took the reins in this one, and we were one of the only schools to allow a coed team, so we had a lot more to prove. I knew I was going to be fine on the field. It felt as natural to me as if I were fighting a demon. But the pressure to win was more intense; therefore, I was uneasy.

"She's right. I'll be fine," I lied.

Chapter 12

Seven men in less than three weeks—that's how many victims the Nimphica had taken by the time Lucas figured out its pattern. Five different states, never the same town or city, and never once was a shred of evidence left behind. But she wasn't invisible and she was predictable. Papers covered the wood floor in the study, and maps with yarn running this way and that covered the wall. Black and red Sharpie markings were written on each page, displaying a clue to where the creature was going next. *Seven different men and all different beliefs: Catholic, Christian, Lutheran, Baptist, Jewish… So who's next, and what religion has she not gotten to?* Lucas thought as he ruffled through the stacks of papers. There were too many religions to guess which church she would be hitting next, and if she changed her MO then he would be back to square one. Time was running out with only two weeks to go.

"What's our next step?" Derek asked, walking into the room. Lucas turned around with a tired look on his face and black bags under his eyes. He was working nonstop to find the creature, trying to prove something to everyone. Derek didn't have to be told by anyone about how great Lucas was. Derek already knew he was a great partner and a great brother. Together they dominated. Derek was the muscles while Lucas was the brains; Alikye was just an overzealous teen out for revenge of some sort. She could have been the greatest Guardian ever if not for her rage. But without her it was time to show the others what the two of them could do. Derek was just worried Lucas was pushing himself too hard.

"Honestly, I'm not sure, dude. The only thing I have noticed is she moves fifty miles from one place to the next every three days. The first day I'm guessing she hunts, the second day she seduces, and the third she takes the soul and leaves in the night. Her pattern, though, seems to follow the same pattern it did the last time she was here. I received an old notebook written by the Guardian who was on her last case. His son found it among his things and sent it to me last night. I've been going through it all night, and it all seems the same." Lucas grabbed the brown leather-bound notebook from the piles on his desk and threw it over to Derek. In one swift movement he caught it with no effort and began shuffling through the pages.

The book was old but beautifully preserved. Although the web gave them enough information, back in the day before technology went viral, Guardians kept all their memories written in their own books and passed them down from generation to generation. Now, with the younger generations, it was memorized and jotted down in personal blogs with secret codes and passwords. But creatures that haven't been seen in decades were forgotten about, and the information was gone unless they found an old notebook.

The man's name was Thomas Everson. He and his two partners Gorge Tamer and Joseph Summers were all only fifteen when they got their orders, but back then the world didn't take to the supernatural so lightly, so the victims weren't willing to speak to them. Only two told them the devil took their souls and later were found dead by their own hands over the guilt and grief of what they had done. They hit a dead end, and the case was lost. Twelve victims lost their souls; five were dead within a few years. Thomas wrote every detail he could find. He wrote down every town, every church, every name…

"That's it!" Derek said, jumping to his feet, throwing the book on the desk, and scattering papers everywhere.

Lucas looked up, furious at the mess Derek had just made. It took him days to organize everything, and now he would have to start from scratch.

"What the hell? Do you know how—"

"Yeah, who cares. Look," Derek said, jabbing a finger at the names on the list.

1. Josh Hastings
2. Fred Marshalls
3. Terence Jacobs
4. Brock Yule
5. Cho Lang
6. Isaiah Amish
7. Jonathon Kale
8. Owen Miller
9. Hail Yuima
10. Karl Undergo
11. Matthew Fabreeze
12. Liam Collins

"OK, I see the names. They were the victims. What's your point?" Lucas said between his gritted teeth. He'd read those names only once, passing them over to read the story. He found the names irrelevant to the case. His theory was that names caused an attachment; therefore, he never memorized the names of the victims. Unlike Derek and Alikye who always needed a name. It was their way to find vengeance for that person.

"Right, you don't do names. Well, Brother, if you had you would have seen how important a name can be."

Lucas read over the names twice, really seeing them this time, and like a lightbulb being turned on in the darkness, his eyes flashed brightly at Derek who just watched and smiled because now they knew how to catch the beast. They knew where she would be next, and this time they would be right there waiting to put her down for good.

The information led them to a small town outside of Boston, Massachusetts. She wouldn't be there for another six hours, and they still needed to find a way to kill her. They settled for a small motel room five minutes from the Mormon Church.

Her next stop.

After comparing the names from the notebook and the names of the men Derek and Lucas had interviewed, they found their final clue. The Nimphica went after the same blood, the same soul. To make sure their theory was correct, they called Carter in England and had him e-mail them a list of the victims from the last attacks, which only confirmed their suspicions. Those lost so many years ago, Carter realized it too, had never been put into the database and registered to the Nimphica's case. It was actually Carter's father who had been the hunter. Lucas found out that information days ago, and it wasn't until now that Carter had finally found his father's notebook in a vault under his name. Now with all the case files together, they had all the evidence needed to be one step in front of her.

Owen Miller was one of the victims who had taken his own life days after the attack, leaving behind a son, who had a daughter, who now had a grown son. Three out of the seven had the same last names. The rest were hard enough to track down giving the women changed their names, but it was enough to realize the pattern. Kevin James Miller-Grant was her next mark, a twenty-three-year-old father of an infant son. Martha Miller, his mother, was the granddaughter of Owen, and she only had one son.

After settling their things in the room, Lucas and Derek set out to Kevin's home. The Nimphica would have to meet Kevin tonight; it was up to them to watch Kevin's every move. The day was still bright, so to keep any suspicion off them, they parked down the road, still in view of his house. There were two pairs of footsteps inside and a baby crying. He was home, but it was just a matter of time before he left and the creature subdued him in her fantasy.

After a few hours passed and the sun started to dissipate in the distances, Kevin finally left his house, kissing his wife and child. He got into his old beat-up Chevy and turned down the street. By the looks of where they lived, they were getting by with little to no money, and the birth of a child only made things harder. His house was small and brittle with bars over the two front windows.

The yard hadn't been maintained in years, leaving brown dead patches of grass and dirt. One lonely dying tree sat next to the broken driveway.

Kevin made a right onto the highway heading south. After two more turns, they ended up on a back road moving toward the motel the boys were staying at. Derek made sure to keep a few vehicles in between them so they weren't seen. They stopped only once at the gas station and watched Kevin buy a lotto ticket, then went off to the church. They sat behind Kevin and listened to a man make his speech from the podium. Every so often they would catch Kevin glancing over at a plain woman with blond hair and brown eyes. She was pin thin with no attractive marks.

"Maybe just a friend, there is no way that could be the man's dream girl," Derek whispered.

"Not everyone is attracted to beautiful women. Just so happens he's not shallow. Plus he's looking at her in shock like he didn't expect to see his ugly dream girl." Lucas finished gesturing over to the two of them, making split-second eye contact.

The speech lasted longer than an hour. The man talked about things that were of no interest to either boy, and by the looks of Kevin and his mystery girl, they, too, were uninterested. They waited for Kevin to stand up and leave before following the rest of the people out to the courtyard for small chitchat and refreshments that were promised. The two boys stood by a tree in earshot of Kevin who was being approached by a few other men and the woman who had her eye on him.

"Sorry to hear about your child being sick. I hope the test results come back with good news. My wife and I have been praying for a full recovery," a man said to Kevin. After shaking his hand, the man joined a woman who was with another group.

"I truly am sorry. I heard and had to see you. I've been driving all night," the woman said, walking up to Kevin, taking his hand in hers.

"H—how is this possible? You can't be real," Kevin stuttered, obviously flabbergasted.

"I am, and I'm here to help you. I'm here to save your child," the woman replied, moving in closer to him. "Are you willing to do *anything* to save your son's life?"

Kevin nodded, still in shock.

Derek and Lucas listened to her deception. She was taking something so precious and using it as a bargaining chip. Of course he would do it; any parent would sacrifice his or her own life for his or her child's. Alikye's parents did. They could have tried to escape, but the chance that their child would pay the price was too high, so they died saving their daughter. Now this woman was doing the same thing by promising Kevin a healthy life for his maybe sick son. Derek wanted to run to her and rip out her throat, but that would only piss her off and expose Derek and Lucas. So the boys stayed back and watched in the shadows, waiting for the weapon that would kill her.

Carter had found the name of the weapon in his father's notebook. If only they'd had the information before, she could have been stopped seventy-five years ago, but it was pointless to ponder about what-ifs. So instead they worked on a way to stop her once and for all. The weapon was an old ancient dagger made from the wood of a tree that grew in Israel centuries ago and was burned down by a man who was being influenced by demons. The tree was believed to hold the magic that could kill anything evil. One of the first, a Legacy, was able to obtain a single branch from the ashes and with that turned it into a dagger. The only problem was, that Legacy's name died out long ago leaving only one survivor who held the key to the safe where the dagger lay. But that one survivor was off the grid, and her whereabouts were never found. Carter, with the help of the council, worked for hours trying to open the door to the safe. And although it required the blood of the Guardian, in case of an emergency, there was another way.

After they talked for nearly two hours, she bid her good-byes to Kevin, giving him a place and time to meet her tomorrow. Derek and Lucas went back to their room, waiting for Carter to call, knowing that tonight Kevin would be safe from the Nimphica. The phone rang, startling the boys. Derek hit the answer button and put it on speaker.

"Were you able to get it?" Derek asked

"I'm sorry, not yet. It's going to take longer than I thought, but there's one other thing you're going to need," Carter said, pausing for a moment. "You're going to have to find fresh sheep's blood. There's an address I'm sending you—you can find it there. The man will be expecting you, but it's going to take a few hours to get there. Unless you can find your own sheep. It won't take much blood, just enough to soak the tip of the dagger."

"I'll leave right away. Lucas can stay behind to keep watch on Kevin. She won't strike until tomorrow night. We will have plenty of time," Derek said, shutting the phone. He grabbed a few supplies, gave Lucas some instructions, and left the room.

Derek arrived back at the motel late in the afternoon. Lucas had gone off several of times to check on Kevin, but so far no Nimphica.

"Any word from Carter yet?" Lucas asked when Derek walked in to the room with a jar full of blood inside a bigger jar full of melting ice.

Derek shook his head, placing the jars in the mini fridge and falling over on his bed. Within minutes his eyes were closed, and he drifted off to sleep. Derek woke up a few hours later to his phone ringing on the side table. He got out of bed, refreshed from his small nap, and answered it.

"Did you get it yet?" he asked into the speaker.

Lucas walked in, eyeing his brother. Derek put the phone on speaker and placed it on the bed. "Repeat what you just told me. Lucas just walked in."

"We almost got the safe opened, maybe another hour. I'm looking right now at your time though. Problem is how do we get it to you?"

Silence fell in the room as the three men considered their options. To fly the dagger over on a private jet would take too long, and express mail was now impossible. There was only one way, but Carter was not going to like the solution.

"I have an idea," Derek said. "Just call back when you have the thing. I need to make a phone call." Derek walked over to his phone, sitting down at the small table by the window. He scrolled down to a name, hitting call. After a few rings, a man answered the phone. "Hey, it's Derek. I need your help."

"Is my girl OK?" the man asked in a strong European accent.

"Yeah she's fine; it has nothing to do with her. Can you help me?" Derek grunted.

"Of course. Just tell me what you need."

The sun was setting by the time the man showed up with the dagger. Carter had argued he didn't want him helping, but the man was an asset to the Guardians, so Carter had no say.

"Shasta, it's good to see you," Derek said, shaking his hand.

"Nice to see you, too, mate. So how is my girl doing? Has she gone insane yet living with all those humans?" Shasta asked referring to Alikye.

"She's fine, but you know her—not the happiest chip on the old block," Derek joked.

After more words were exchanged and a quick good-bye, Shasta disappeared in an instant, teleporting back to Paris for whatever reasons he had for living there.

Chapter 13

The instructions were easy: find the creature, dip the dagger in sheep's blood, and plunge it into her heart. It was sudden death, and all the souls would be returned. At least it sounded easy, but nothing was ever that easy. Lucas took the dagger and strapped it to his hip. He placed his black body armor over his chest, forearms, and lower legs. He wore dark blue jeans and a tight black shirt that showed off his muscular body. Derek wore the exact same except he had a sword strapped to his back and a gun to his leg. The look of the two brothers standing next each other was a masterpiece not even Michelangelo could capture.

The night was cold with a light drizzle that soon turned into a downpour. Derek and Lucas arrived at the old church outside of the town's limits. By the looks of it, the church had not been used in years. Black ash covered the outside walls, and the stained glass windows had been blown out from what looked like a massive explosion. Overgrown vegetation blanketed the ground with vines wrapping around the brittle building. Apparently the church was first built in the late eighteen hundreds by a man who brought the town out of heavy depression, preaching the word of God. He became so crazed that later that decade he trapped half of the town inside the church and lit it on fire. He then told the authorities God asked him to punish the sinners to bring paradise to their small town. Almost a hundred years later, it sat hidden in the woods, forgotten about.

The boys waited for Kevin and his mysterious woman to show up. It was this spot that Derek overheard the creature tell Kevin to meet her at ten o'clock. The boys got to the church thirty minutes early to set up for what would be known as one of the most epic battles of their time. The storm started to get worse forcing the boys to head inside the church and wait for their arrival. Kevin was the first to pull up, jumping from his car with a jacket hanging over his head. He headed inside, and wiped his feet off on a small patch of burnt carpet. He placed his belongings on the ground and took a seat in one of the remaining wooden pews, eyeing his surroundings. Derek and Lucas hid behind two oversized pillars in the front of the church next to the podium.

Derek passed Lucas the jar of sheep's blood he purchased at a butcher shop that catered to these kinds of things. Lucas grasped it in his hands, twisting off the top. He took the dagger from his hip and placed the end of the blade in the blood. Lucas then held it to the side, allowing it to dry, and then placed the jar on the ground away from the fight zone. After what felt like hours, the burnt splintery door creaked open as the woman, the Nimphica, gracefully strutted in and ran her thumb down Kevin's jawline.

"Do you know what you want, baby?" she asked softly.

"Yes. My son—I want him better," Kevin whined, placing his head in his hands.

"OK then, let's make the deal." She smiled.

Derek nodded to his brother, signaling for their next move. With no words spoken, Lucas went left and Derek went right. Slowly and carefully they crept behind all the burned and demolished wreckage. The only light in the church was the few candles burning, casting shadowy figures dancing along the walls and floors. Using hand signals like baseball players, Derek told his brother to stay while he made his way closer to the monster, crawling from pew to pew. He rose up again, nodding to Lucas who mirrored Derek's moves. Kevin and the woman were deep in discussion, her hands sliding up and down his pale, thin arms. Kevin wrapped his arms around the woman's waist, suddenly stilling before their lips met.

"It's OK, baby. Go ahead," she whispered in his ears.

"But you're dead—you died fifteen years ago—I know, I was there," He whimpered.

"Oh, baby, no. I only look like the woman who died. I'm alive. I'm real." Again she ran her long, pale, skinny finger down his cheek, smiling.

"I don't know if I can—not like this."

"I'm only this." She moved her hand up and down, pointing to her body. "To make it easier, do it for your son." She smiled, moving her lips to his.

Derek looked over to his brother mouthing "GO" now that the Nimphica was distracted. Lucas jumped out from behind a statue of the Virgin Mary encased in ash and mold. With the dagger positioned in his right hand, he aimed for the woman's heart only to be thrown back by her surprise kick to his hand releasing the blade. Kevin, completely shocked, stepped back a few paces. Now the woman, as graceful as a ballerina, blocked each punch and kick Lucas was throwing. Every time he made contact with her, she was always a step ahead, hitting him two more times. The fight went on and on, and all Derek could do was protect the human at hand. Derek reached over, grabbing Kevin, pulling him to safety. He reached around his back, grasping his sword, releasing it from his back holster. From behind he struck the monster bringing her to her knees. The blow wouldn't kill her, but he knew that it would hinder her for the moment, allowing Lucas the chance to have the upper hand. He sat astride her, pinning her arms to her thighs, raising the dagger in the air to make the final blow. He was about to plunge it in her heart when he suddenly stilled without moving the knife from above her chest.

"Umm…What the hell are you doing. Lucas?" She panted.

"Kye?" His eyes lit up like the Fourth of July. All seriousness vanished from his face.

"Yes, it's me, ass. Now can you please explain to me why you're sitting on top of me with a knife to my heart." She raised her hands palms up, surrendering. "I know I said I was mad, but I'm over it." She looked just like Alikye. Beautiful auburn hair fell around her body in soft curls, and intense smoky-silver eyes gazed in wonder. She wore a dark-blue strapless, satin dress that clung to her curvy, slender figure, showing off her flawless sun-kissed skin.

Lucas backed away crawling on his hands. He sat stunned, running both hands through his long blond curls. She jumped to her feet, dusting off her dress, and moved toward him.

"Well, baby, that was not what I was expecting, but I guess we are even now." Her voice was the same, soft yet strong but sweet like a child's. It was Alikye's voice, no doubt about it.

"Kye,...I'm so...I mean, I didn't...I'm sorry, Kye."

"Lucas, baby, it's fine. Can I please see that dagger before you hurt yourself." She smiled, showing off a mouthful of perfect teeth.

"What?"

"Lucas, that's not Alikye. The Nimphica just wants you to think that," Derek shouted, running toward his brother.

"Lucas, please, don't listen to him. It's me, baby. I'm here," fake-Kye begged.

Alikye never begged. In all the years he had known her, she never once begged. It was new to him, hearing her sound so small and helpless. The way he always wished she would be around him. He always wanted to protect her, but she never needed protection, and now, for the first time, she needed him, wanted him. Lucas jumped to his feet, putting his body between the woman he loved and his big brother. "Dude, what the hell do you think you're doing?" Lucas yelled.

"What do you think I'm doing? That's not Alikye, dumbass." Derek grabbed for the knife, but Lucas expected it and pulled it out of Derek's grasp.

Fake-Kye huddled behind Lucas's back like a small child hiding from an enemy. "Why is he trying to hurt me, baby?" she cried.

"Dude, what is your problem?" Lucas snapped.

******

She was playing to Lucas's only weakness, playing the innocent lover. Derek knew then the only way to do this was to be the one who killed her. But how? If he pushed too hard, Lucas would do everything in his power to protect her. But if she obtained the dagger, this whole battle would be over, and she would be gone. "You're right, man." Derek turned to fake-Kye. "How are you, sweetheart?" She smiled at Derek then turned back to Lucas.

"Lucas, baby, can I see that dagger?" She asked sweetly.

"Here, I'll take it, dude. It's pretty gross. I'll clean it first." Derek needed to hurry. He knew that in the end his brother would always choose Alikye over him, but this wasn't her, and he didn't understand why Lucas couldn't see that. Fake-Kye was playing on his emotions; if she kept up the whining, pathetic little girl act, he would cave. Derek moved his hand back, and before Lucas or the Nimphica knew what was happening, Derek threw his fist hard into Lucas's temple, knocking his head backward, making contact with the monster's face. Like a domino effect, they both fell to the floor, Lucas knocked out cold. *Two birds, one stone,* Derek thought. He rushed his brother, grabbing the knife before it ever hit the floor.

"NO!" Fake-Kye screamed, but her spell didn't work on him, and in one swift movement, he slid to the floor, plunging the knife into her heart. She screamed in horror as her body started to convulse, flashing in and out of each woman she had ever become. Her body then erupted into a ball of fire as she finally burned to ash on the wooden floor. Derek fell to his knees in front of his brother, rubbing his forehead. He sat for what felt like days before he finally heard Lucas start to stir.

"What the hell happened?" Lucas asked, blinking in the faded candlelight.

"You don't remember...*baby*." Derek smirked.

"Oh shit. I thought I was dreaming...and stop laughing at me. How was I supposed to know better? It was an easy mistake, but please tell me you were able to kill that bitch."

"Yes, I killed her but not before I had to punch you in the head to get the dagger." Derek laughed, fisting both hands in front in his face.

"Yeah, yeah, I'll give that hit, but next time I won't be so forgiving. And, dude, can we keep this part to ourselves please?"

Both boys laughed as they got off the floor and headed for the door, pride staining their faces. They killed the creature no other could kill, and as they got into the car and headed to nowhere, the weight of the last few weeks finally lifted from their shoulders.

Chapter 14

"Have you ever been to anything like this before?" asked Kady. "I know you have traveled a lot."

"Yeah…sure," I lied.

Everything I knew about high school was from a full day of viewing movies based in high school settings before I enrolled. Bonfires, dances, football games, people cheering: unrealistic scenarios to make money at the box office.

I didn't understand why girls felt the need to spend the day together just to get ready for some superficial school tradition. But Kady just would not let it go. This was the first time I had ever been in Kady's house. She lived in a two-story, Spanish style home in a gated community on Gomez Drive. From Kady's bedroom bay window seat, the lush backyard stretched for what seemed like the fairway of a golf course. A large oak tree paralleled the house, its branches reaching toward her window close enough for her to touch. A tree house sat perfectly erect between the branches. Kady and her father had built it themselves, board by board. In her room a four-poster canopy bed stood flush with a lavender wall. Synthetic white calla lilies and purple beads coiled around each post of the queen-size bed. A large white carpet lay immaculately in the middle of the room upon the parquet wooden floors. An early-nineteenth century vanity sat in the corner. On either side of the mirror were three draws that held all of Kady's female essentials: makeup products, hair accessories, flat iron and blow dryer, and her assortment of nail polishes. A full length mirror hung on the back of her door, covered with pictures of her with family and friends laughing and having fun. Compared to my chaotic and unpredictable life, her room embodied the stability of her youth thus far.

When I sat crossed legged on Kady's memory-foam mattress, I took in her perfect room. As I gazed around the room, she emptied the plastic bag of T-shirts and decorating supplies onto the bed. The routine of making T-shirts for school functions seemed so devout to her. I would have settled on just wearing a plain black T-shirt with "Bulldogs" written across the front. But as I watched Kady cut, alter, and perfectly design her shirt, I was intrigued and wanted to do the same. While the painted shirts were drying, Kady French braided my hair, incorporating black and red ribbons throughout. After getting dressed we checked ourselves out in the mirror. I was pleasantly satisfied with the way the shirt delicately fell off my shoulder. The bottom was trimmed just a little bit, showing a small strip of my torso. I completed the outfit with my combat boots and a pair of cutoff jean shorts. Kady's shirt was identical to mine, but with her sense of style, she paired it with perfectly hemmed khaki shorts and Sperry Topsider shoes.

Kady glanced up at the clock and realized that we were already late for the annual homecoming football game and bonfire at our school. We said good-bye to her parents, who were on their way out of town for the weekend, and hopped in her white Ford Explorer. As we headed west on Bridge Road, we cranked up the music when "Hurricane" by 30 Seconds to Mars came on the radio. With a twenty-five minute drive to school, we knew Greg and Andy would beat us there. As the previous song ended, we were thrown into a fit of giggles when "Cooler Than Me" by Mike Posner started playing.

"Hey, who does this song remind you of?" Kady asked through suppressed laughter.

She didn't even have to finish her question. I knew exactly whom she was thinking of: Amanda.

Trying to change the subject, I asked, "Do you think we hurt the boys' feelings when we uninvited them to drive with us?"

"Maybe. But they need guy time just as much as we need girl time," Kady responded. "Speaking of girl time, so Andy..." She wiggled her eyebrows up and down.

"Come again," I tried playing dumb.

"Oh, please don't give me that. I see the way you two look at each other, so spill."

"Kady, I swear there is nothing between us." Oh but how I wished sometimes there could be something more between us, but I wasn't about to say that out loud.

"But you like him?" Kady asked with a huge smile on her face. I think it was more of a statement than a question.

"Even if I did, it doesn't matter. I could never go there for reasons you wouldn't understand."

"But you like him," she repeated.

"Whatever," I replied nonchalantly as Kady turned the volume of the radio back up.

As we drove the familiar roads to the school, the night cast a shadow of darkness upon the streets. Not a headlight from an oncoming car or a streetlight helped light our way through the barren landscape. The usually friendly trees appeared menacing amongst the shadows, bringing me back to the days when nothing in my life had any beauty. An eerie silence overcame the vast fields of cattle with the bringing of each nightfall.

Using a tube of lipstick as a microphone, I wailed the lyrics in Kady's direction. We were jamming when Kady realized that she could barely see the road through the dense fog. As we drove over the state turnpike overpass, she refused to let up on the gas. Since we had already neglected to attend the first half of the football game, Kady did not want to waste another minute. Up until this point, I really did not think that I would need to use my Guardian abilities living in this human world. The hairpin turn would have never been noticed under such harsh conditions. When we got closer to the turn, the fog began to thin, but it was too late. Kady gripped the steering wheel so tightly her knuckles turned white. The look on her face was one of pure terror. Her expression jolted me back to the reality that was staring me in the face: there was nothing I can do.

Kady jerked the vehicle to the right, overcompensating in her attempt to make up for the delayed reaction. With her rash movements, I was slammed into the passenger door like a rubber chicken. As I righted myself, I quickly realized that we were in the grass and only on two wheels. If she had just let the vehicle balance itself out, she could have braked to a stop. Kady's human instincts caused her to act irrationally instead of methodically. Therefore, she was unable to consider coherent thoughts in that split second. Kady roughly pulled the wheel to the left, making the tires screech like banshees.

I knew what was to come; I could feel the imbalance in the vehicle. I sensed how each infraction Kady made affected the vehicle's tire placements upon the pavement. There was no time for me to tell her that her actions were wrong, that they were too forceful.

The SUV had spun 180 degrees, now facing the opposite direction. The next thing I knew, the vehicle was flipping. The first impact was between the passenger side and the ground. My right side smashed against the door, dislocating my shoulder. The pain was present, but not overpowering. The window shattered inward, and shards of glass embedded in my skin. As the vehicle continued rolling, the distortion of the metal drowned out Kady's horrified cries. I gripped the center armrest, waiting for the motions to be over. I attempted to look at Kady, but the pressure pinned my head back. The vehicle came to a sudden stop as the roof wrapped around a mature bay oak tree. What felt like an eternity was really just a few seconds. Despite my years of training to be alert at all times, I was not paying any attention to the surroundings that might have now taken the life of my best friend.

Chapter 15

I woke up less than a minute after the crash, slightly disoriented, and quickly assessed the situation. I had to get myself adjusted before attempting to help Kady. I gripped the armrest on my door and used my left hand to push my shoulder back into place. The sound of my bones sliding past each other rang in my ears as they realigned. I picked all the glass shards out of my face and arms; each cut healed without scarring. The magic in my blood kept me safe from any man-made objects. My Enochian tattoos protected my body from the accident.

I looked over to find Kady unconscious, the steering wheel pinning her legs. Her left arm was caught in the locked seat belt, keeping her from falling on top of me. Blood dripped from her limp head, leaving shiny wet trails down her hair. Kady's swollen right hand dangled in midair in front of my face.

I looked for a way out of the car. The two passenger doors were flush with the ground, making their exit impossible. I pulled myself upright by grabbing hold of the steering wheel. Feet first I inched my way to the backseat, avoiding Kady's wilted body. The rear driver-side window was blown out during the crash. It was my only exit. Reaching up I gripped the sharp edges of the frame. Glass pierced my skin as I heaved myself through the opening. Blood streamed down my arms, dyeing them red. I jumped from the mangled vehicle onto the grass matted from the accident. As I walked onto the road, glass crunched beneath my boots, scraping against the pavement. Wisps of smoke and the smell of gasoline came from underneath the crushed hood. Small flames burst out from under the windshield, painting it black with soot.

Time was running out. I needed to think fast. The clock was ticking on Kady's life. Within minutes the car would be engulfed in flames ten feet high and there'd be no way to escape. She would lay there trapped and helpless in her own hell as the fire melted the skin off her bones. She would suffer through minutes of torture before finally burning into the darkness. She would beg for her life as she turned into a pile of ashes. I would watch my best friend die.

I knew what I could do. I had the ability to save her, but it could put my identity in jeopardy. Guardians were never supposed to save humans from natural causes. We were only allowed to intervene when a supernatural being was threatening a human's life. But I was a Legacy, and I trusted Kady enough that if she knew what I was, she would be accepting of me. The time had come, and even with the car about to explode, I needed to get Kady to a hospital in case of any internal damage.

Kady woke screaming and writhing in agony. I jumped up on the car's side, glancing down through the broken window. Her pale face and glassy eyes told me she was in shock. I gripped the door in both hands and pulled it from its hinges like yanking a feather from water. I ripped the steering wheel off her legs, listening to the blood flow back into her numb limbs. For a minute Kady stopped screaming, allowing for a slight whimper. Now that I was close to her heart, I could hear all the blood pumping evenly, suggesting no internal bleeding. The flames started to rise, heating the night in poisonous gases. The windshield splintered and cracked. It could shatter at any moment.

I pulled Kady close to me as I put one foot in between the steering wheel and locked the other in place on the top of the car.

"Wrap your arms around my neck," I repeated over and over, trying to get Kady to comply.

"H—how," Kady stuttered.

"Kady, please," I pleaded, tears filling my eyes.

I wasn't sure if it was the crackling of the heated metal or the pain in my eyes, but Kady gripped onto me for dear life and nodded. I pulled on the seat belt, dislodging it from its seams, and pulled Kady to the top of the car. I jumped from the burning vehicle with Kady curled in my arms, watching as my surroundings and the sudden explosion blurred into the distance.

I placed Kady gently on the grass a quarter of a mile from the scene. Besides a little blood loss and a concussion, she seemed like she was coming back to life.Like a deer in headlights, her expression was more fear than gratitude. I was losing my friend, and there was nothing I could do to fix it.

"Alikye, your stomach."

I looked down to the area her eyes were locked on. With all that was happening and my body not processing my own damage, I saw a shiny thick piece of metal lodged into my side, its jagged edges sticking out. In any other case, the pain would have registered, but with adrenaline pumping through my veins, my body felt numb. I grasped the shrapnel in my palm, causing a fresh wound to appear in my hand, and pulled it out of my flesh. It slid through my organs flawlessly, causing little pain. I sat for a minute in silence, waiting for the wound to heal, taking deep breaths in and out so I wouldn't get lightheaded from my own blood loss. Kady stared in awe as my body lit up in Persian indigo-blue Enochian markings. Covering both my arms and most of my torso were the magic tattoos given to me by Michael himself.

Headlights appeared from a few miles up, giving me no time to explain. The vehicle was still burning high into the sky, lighting up the way for any passing car.

"I promise I will tell you everything, Kady, but I need you to keep quiet. They can't know. No one can know." I pleaded for her silence. I knew she understood everything she saw, and if asked she would tell them everything. My life depended on her now because the council could never find out.

It was actually quite easy to make a human believe what we wanted them to believe, but this was different circumstances. I had

79

saved her when I should have let her die. I had shown her what I was capable of instead of pulling her aside, hiding her from the truth.

"Please." Blood poured from a deep gash on her upper arm. I took off my shirt exposing my flawless abs and untouched skin. My Enochian marks faded as the seconds ticked by.

"You promise?" she said in a low raspy voice.

I nodded.

Chapter 16

It never occurred to me how baffling life could be sometimes. One minute you're alone down a dark road waiting for help, and then the next you see the one person you don't want help from because that would mean you owe them a favor. Or someone who can be the true definition of evil would actually surprise you with true compassion. I was sent here to really feel the good in people, but it wasn't until that moment that I saw it, that I knew what I was supposed to learn. Amanda had been running late for the bonfire as well—at least that's what she had told us later. She jumped from her car and ran over to us, phone in hand, screaming at the emergency operator to hurry the hell up. I had never seen her so pale and scared before. I always expected her not to care for anyone but herself, but at that moment she threw her arms around Kady, tears running down her face. I could see she truly cared for her old best friend. And at that moment everything changed for me.

Down the dark abandoned road, a storm of sirens sped to where Kady and I were sitting in the grass with Amanda. Two police vehicles headed the line along with two ambulances followed by a fire truck and another police car at the rear. A swarm of uniformed personnel surrounded Kady and me, asking an abundance of questions. I wanted to sit with Kady, but they kept us apart with our own bands of medics. Between questions I looked over to her. I was worried that Kady would talk about what had really just happened. She said she wouldn't, but under the circumstances she might have felt threatened. She smiled, reassuring me she was OK, that we were OK.

The firefighters dealt with the dying fire while the paramedics stayed busy checking our vitals and sticking us with needles. Following protocol they began rendering emergency care with my airway being priority, followed by oxygen and hemorrhage control. They hooked me up to a non-rebreather oxygen mask. A nice man attached a cardiac monitor to my chest and a pulse oximeter onto my index finger. He performed a rapid, full body assessment in order to rule out any major injuries. I kept implying I was fine, but he insisted and said, "Sorry, miss, it's protocol."

I looked over at Kady and saw they were doing the same to her. Because her injuries were more extensive, they started an IV of lactated Ringer's solution, which was a sterile non pyrogenic solution of electrolytes in water.

After checking our blood pressures and noting both were at a normal 120/80, they finished up with Kady by splinting her arm and bandaging her head and a few other cuts.

I listened in as the paramedics and officers discussed the situation and compared notes from our statements. They kept saying how lucky we were to still be alive, after looking over the vehicle. They also couldn't understand how my body was matted in dried blood with not even a scratch to indicate where the blood came from.

"She must have gotten it on her when she carried me out of the car. It's my blood I assure you," Kady had told the officers when they first arrived.

"Ma'am, what happened to your shirt?" The officer asked me.

"Her arm was bleeding pretty critically," I slightly lifted my shirt off Kady's arm to show the officer the gash on her upper right arm just below her shoulder. She groaned a little, pulling back her shoulder when my hand gently grazed her wound. "It's the only thing I had to cover up the wound."

"Yes, ma'am. Smart choice." He looked over the gash, signaling toward the medics. "I'm not a doctor, but she may need stitches."

That was when they separated us into different ambulances.

They didn't believe the story we gave them. There was just too much blood that I wasn't able to wipe off me in time, but they didn't have reason to believe anything different.

I wasn't too worried about *why*; I was more worried about whether Kady would really keep quiet. I could only imagine what would happen to me if my people found out. It would definitely mean the England office for me for sure. I'd have to work side by side with the elders, going over important information—something I never wanted to do. I promised Kady I would tell her everything about me, the entire truth that no human had ever known to my knowledge. My judgment assured me that I could trust her. I was 100 percent sure; she was my best friend after all. The nice medic that was handling my case came back to me with a jacket to cover up with, given I was only in a sports bra and a pair of shorts. He wrapped me up and allowed me to get in the same ambulances as Kady. I held tight to her good hand as we left for the hospital.

*****

I sent Amanda to the bonfire to tell Andy and Greg what had happened. For reasons I didn't want to understand, I was hoping Andy would drop what he was doing and rush to my side. I wanted to be near him—I needed to be near him. To feel the heat from his body rush through mine. To have the sweet sensation of his scent wrap around me.

I shook my head to get the thoughts to escape from it. I needed to be there for Kady. I needed to comfort her in this crucial time. I had to explain what had just happened. That thought scared me to death. It would be her choice if she wanted to believe me, to trust me, to be my friend after this. I didn't think I could stand losing her. My stomach filled with nausea. That pain was something that couldn't be healed by my gifts. I needed to get to her and feel that she still loved me, for me. To know I was no different than I was yesterday.

The fluorescent lighting wisped by me as the medic rolled me through the emergency room. Kady was taken first and was being examined by a few doctors. I was taken to another room.

The area was small, only a few beds separated by white sheets. The smell was atrocious. To any normal human, it was just a faint smell of chemicals and sterile products with a hint of urine. To me, it was the smell of death and decay, blood spilling from numerous victims, infections and bacteria spreading through dying skin and organs. I held my breath for a moment and started to breathe through my mouth. I again concentrated on the scent of Andy to retract my thoughts—the smell of his cologne and the natural scent. It was calming and pleasurable. I lay back in my bed, and memories of him had me reminiscing about the first day we met and how he made me feel.

Doctors came in and out, baffled over my healthy appearance. Besides the small amount of exhaustion I felt for all the healing power, my body was fine. I told them that time and again, but every time I asked to leave, they just shook their heads and said they had a few more tests to perform.

I protested, trying to get up. I had to see her. Hands grabbed my shoulders and pushed me down. I let them and then tried again to get up.

They gave me something to ease the nonexistent pain, and after a few moments, I started to feel the effects. It wouldn't last long but for the minutes I did feel it, it made me happy and light-headed. Made me forget about what I was doing—someone I had to see.

"This will help you calm down and make you sleep a bit," The nurse said.

Another nurse came in and said I had a visitor. I jumped up too quickly, thinking it was Sarah, but the dizziness almost knocked me to my butt. I tripped over my feet trying to catch my balance when I felt the warmth rush threw me, numbing the drugs. The nurse looked like she was about to scold me for getting out of bed, but Andy laid me back down and assured her I wouldn't do that again.

"You scared me half to death, pretty girl." Andy sat on the bed next to me, his voice a little shaken as he spoke. Without his touch, the effect from the drugs came back hard, knocking me into a hazy state. I didn't sense him coming. I then realized I couldn't even smell all the scents from the hospital that was becoming unbearable. My gifts were gone. I felt normal, human even. The drugs must have counteracted my senses.

"I'm…f—fine. I wasn't going to fall….," I mumbled, stumbling over every word.

"The accident, Kye. When Amanda told me what had happened…I don't know. I freaked."

I started to laugh, wanting him to touch me again so I could think straight, so I could remember what I had to do and why I was here.

I could see he was getting frustrated with me, but I didn't know what I did wrong. Then he grabbed my hand and I remembered.

The accident. Oh shit, Kady. I rubbed my eyes trying to remember what had happened. Whatever the nurse gave me did more than numb my senses. It was making me disoriented.

"Kady. Did you see her? Is she OK? The doctors won't let me see her. They keep saying I need to rest. But I need to know…" I rambled on, my words scrambling. Did Andy even understand what I was saying, or was it only in my head?

"Hey, she's fine," Andy said, taking my hand. Again the effects of the drugs dissipated. Everything came back to focus. "Greg's with her, and she keeps asking about you, too. How are you?"

"I'm good now. I'm glad you're here." I tightened my grip on his hands. "I was hoping you'd come."

I saw the look in his eyes soften. "You scared me, Kye, I didn't know…" He trailed off, looking up at the ceiling. He squeezed his eyes shut, shaking his head back and forth.

"I…," he started to say but stopped when I pulled him toward me, crushing my mouth to his. After the shock wore off, he deepened the kiss. Something occurred to me earlier, and I couldn't keep denying him. Like a wave crashing to shore during a hurricane, the magnetic pulse between us intensified. The passion from that one little kiss shot electricity from me to him and back to me. He wrapped his arms around my waist, sliding his hands under my hospital robe they gave to me to wear. The touch of his hands was like fire burning a hole through my skin. My blood rushed to my heart pumping so loud I think the person in the next room could hear it. The monitors I was hooked to picked up on it, and the beeping quickened. I then slid my hands through his beautiful hair, gripping tight, pulling him closer. The kiss hardened for a minute before Andy pulled away, locking his eyes on mine. He cupped my face, and one last time grazed his lips against mine. Without a word we just stared at each other in a lustful pleasure of our first kiss.

"I hope that was you and not the drugs," he joked.

"It was all me. I wanted to tell you for a while." I shrugged my shoulders, smiling. For a while now, I had wanted to tell him how I felt. Denying the truth was becoming pointless, hard even. "Just the timing never seemed right."

"And you pick a hospital after an accident to, well,…show me." Andy moved his hands back around my waist. I laid my head on his chest, listening to his heart speed up. I felt the soft thumping on my cheek.

"Well, better now than never," I said sarcastically, biting my lip.

"So I finally get a chance with you? You're not going to wake up tomorrow and blame it on the drugs right?"

I hesitated watching his expression falter.

"No, I want to be with you." I lay back down and intertwined my fingers with his.

Nothing more was said. Being with him was all I needed just then.

Chapter 17

I sat cross-legged on my bed, my arms folded against my body. Kady sat in front of me, her eyebrows furrowed, waiting for me to explain like I promised. She looked so beat up; dark bruises covered her right eye and cheekbone. Kady's hand was in a cast, and nine stitches were placed in her upper arm. Her back and ribs were showing early signs of bruising. With Kady's parents out of town and not being able to come home till the morning, Mr. and Mrs. Scott asked the hospital to release her into Sarah's care. We made it home a little after two in the morning, and all I wanted was for Kady to get some much needed sleep, but she wasn't having it. Instead she turned her chocolate-brown eyes my way and insisted she was fine for now.

I knew I had to tell her something, but just how much would be enough. I hated lying to her, and the last thing I wanted to do was give her some stupid excuses like adrenaline helped me lift you out of the car, and the trick of the light made you see something that was not really there. I could tell her nothing and threaten her not to say a word. Plus who would believe her anyway. But I couldn't. I couldn't keep lying to her, and I wanted someone I cared about to know my secret. I rubbed the cold from my arms, locked in her wondering gaze. I took in a deep breath to begin.

"The war first started between a son and his father. Lucifer was the most beautiful and loved angel in paradise, even more so than his older brother Michael—"

"Wait, I'm so confused—Lucifer as in the devil? What's that have to do with anything. Kye, what does this have to do with what I saw? And please do give me a trick of the light crap because whatever you are, it's not human." Kady threw her hands in the air.

I threw my head back, laughing at her serious yet amused look on her face. "OK, if I'm going to tell you the whole truth, you have to know the whole story, and by the way Lucifer is real, and before you ask I have never met him nor would I ever want to," I said with a chuckle. "So when humans were created, all the angels were asked—told—that they would be equal to the humans, that not one angel or archangel would see themselves as better than them. Out of greed and envy, wanting power and so on, Lucifer started a war by disobeying his father. Michael defeated his brother, casting him and a third of his followers down to hell.

"Sickened by all that had happened, Lucifer created an army of demons and monsters and unleashed them on earth to take out the human race because archangels including Lucifer are forbidden to step foot on earth's plain. Michael, the big and powerful older brother, created his own race using parts of his own soul in the form of humans, and so Guardians were born. Michael created eighteen stronger and more powerful than any demon to protect the human race from extinction. They were the first of many Guardians; they were the Legacies, more angel-like than human. A bloodline that if ever broken the Guardians would cease to exist, and their souls would be lost forever. With the deaths of all Guardians, Lucifer would be able to find a way to walk the earth, and if you know the history, the apocalypse would begin. Until Lucifer created more demons by using human mothers, the other five archangels had no other choice but to create Guardians more human-like than angel"

She took a minute absorbing all that I said, shaking her leg up and down in a nervous twitch. "What's the difference between the two?" Kady asked. She smiled, making me feel better about how much I was telling her.

I didn't have to share the origin of my creation; all I had to tell her was the main pinpoints to what I was. But for some reason, the

88

tingle in my stomach, the way my body felt relaxed, the way it felt easy to breathe with her, I wanted to tell her everything. I wanted her to know the truth behind it all—no secrets, no lies.

"Legacies were created by Michael. It's like we hold the string to our kind. If we die off, the string is cut in half and it falls. We all fall. Guardians were created by the other archangels with the same gifts except Legacies are stronger, faster, and harder to kill. Five Legacies were ended over the times; four disappeared and joined hell, believing humans were not worth the fight. Nine Legacies remain, including me. With my parent's demise and no other siblings, I'm the last of my Legacy."

"Also the first eighteen were given weapons made by Michael himself. They were forged by the metals of heaven, made in the fires of purity. They are powerful against hell and can kill any demon created by Lucifer. The others were given weapons as well, but most were destroyed; only the true weapons made by Michael could never be destroyed."

"So what's yours then?" Kady asked nonchalantly.

"Solid gold bow chiseled with Enochian verses and the names of my family and edged with blades. Four arrows, tips made of steal and feathers, each from the archangels' wings. All the weapons are indestructible and each is chiseled with Michael's seal."

Kady's eyes widened. Although I had a human physique, I wasn't human. I was an actual angel hybrid. She didn't jump, didn't tell me I was crazy or say I needed help, that what I was saying could never be true. Kady sat beside me with her soft hand on my knee, motioning me to continue.

"The true elders, the ones who have decided to keep on living long after their expiration date, make up the council of Guardians. Six out of the nine are Legacies, and once they pass on, the name will then go to their children. They make the rules and decide everything, from marriage to death. When I hit the right age, I will then be able to take my place as a council member. Including me, two of the last Legacies are also inexperienced orphaned children. We fight—we protect mankind—it's what we do, and it's what we were made for. It's our destiny."

Kady laid her head on my pillow, looking up at the ceiling. The time was now three in the morning. We were tired, and my eyes started to feel heavy, but my soul felt relieved. I knew telling her was the right thing to do.

"So you're not human?"

I hesitated, raising my eyebrows in thought. "Um…Yes and no."

"So monsters are real?" Kady asked as her eyes started to close.

"Yeah, but you have nothing to worry about. I'm not going anywhere."

"I know. That's why I'm not scared." Kady's breaths evened out as we both fell asleep.

Chapter 18

Andy and I set sail on a whirlwind of romance like two young lovers who only had the summer together. Passionate time was spent wrapped in each other's arms, promising one another a future neither could guarantee. One night while lying in the bed of Andy's truck, watching as the stars fell from the sky to an unknown abyss, I heard a song on the radio that reminded me of our new relationship. A story of a couple who only had a few months together, but in those few months had fallen deeply in love. They made promises of letters and phone calls, promises that they would never lose touch with each other and that they would wait until the day they could meet again. By the end of the summer, good-byes were made. Tears fell to the ground, and the longing for their next kiss lingered in the air. But it was always the end to a tragic love story. The dream was theirs, but we both felt as if it belonged to us. Little did Andy realize, our story would end the same, but I didn't have the heart to tell him the real summer would never be ours.

We spent most our days on the beach basking in the sun followed by picnics in the park with all my favorite foods: strawberries dipped in heavy creams, fresh rolls of cinnamon bread with an assortments of cheeses and delectable varieties of homemade spreads. Andy always brought along sweet tea trying to wean me off the large amounts of Mountain Dew I was accustomed to.

By night he would take me sailing beneath the stars, and we would listen to the waves lap against the boat. We would curl up together in a blanket of cashmere, talking all night about everything.

I could never get enough of the way he made me feel. The magnetic pull between our energies like star-crossed lovers, our destiny written in the stars. Andy was the only person who could make me feel both hot and cold at the same time. He was the only being who could make me feel vulnerable.

Days turned into weeks and weeks into months. The days grew shorter while the nights longer. The air became thinner with every breath I took. The cool chill of the ocean breeze wisped across my face as I looked out to the sea. I listened to the music coming from a yacht a few miles out. Christmas lights were strung around the railing, illuminating the ocean in various colors. I never had a real Christmas before, had never experienced any holiday traditions, so when Kady and her family invited Sarah and me over for Thanksgiving, I jumped at the chance. After a big dinner, we all sat around the living area drinking eggnog and eating homemade pumpkin pie. I loved the way the pie melted on my palate as I savored every last morsel. Kady's father excused himself from the room, leaving a suspicious look on everyone's faces. After a moment she began to laugh as he came in carrying an enormous tree. A huge smile filled my face as we all danced around, setting the house up in beautiful holiday spirit. Greens and reds of all kinds filled the warm home with cheerful happiness. Music echoed throughout in jingling tunes and songs about Santa and reindeers. It all had a nice ring to it.

Two weeks before Christmas, Sarah waited at the front door one afternoon, grinning from ear to ear. I walked into the house after a long day of school expecting a snack and a "Don't forget to finish your homework," but not that day. No, that day I got a beautiful eight-foot Fraser Fir Christmas tree. The scent of pine brought me back to my first home where the tangy aroma spread through the house. Boxes of lights and glittery silver garland were laid out on the coffee table. Sarah even bought Christmas albums to play on the record player. I couldn't believe she would do this for me—give me the Christmas I never had. In past years we ignored every holiday. It never meant anything to us, and we were too busy defending the world to stop for the day and cherish human holidays. So that day meant the world to me. We spent the remainder of the day decorating the tree. We strung garland from the window sills, adding a dash of glitter for extravagant beauty. The tree was set up in the center of the window, lighting up the world from the outside porch. We draped lights around the palm trees in the backyard. The small lights copied the enormous star-lit sky above. The night was my favorite time, when the house would sparkle brilliantly throughout the street.

I heard a car pull up in my driveway and heard the steady sound of breathing.

It was Kady.

I stood up from the beach, wiping sand off my jeans, before Kady even made it out of the car. I ran to the front yard. To her I must have appeared out of nowhere because the minute she saw me she jumped.

"Does anything ever surprise you?" Kady asked, pausing for a moment to catch her breath. Her arms were full of wrapped packages.

It was still a week to go until Christmas, and I wasn't aware we were giving out presents. Sarah had told me about gift exchange, she told me to get something special for all my friends, but I wasn't planning on shopping until this weekend.

"Maybe…if I'm not expecting it," I said, exchanging looks toward her arms then back to her chocolate eyes. They sparkled in the dim light as she entered the living room and placed the boxes on the table.

"Oh, this. I know I'm early, but I couldn't wait." She handed me a rectangular box wrapped in gold with a big silver bow around it.

"Tell Sarah to come in. It's for both of you." Kady took the rest of the boxes and placed them snug under the tree. "Oh, and don't worry about the rest—you will have to wait till Christmas Eve."

Sarah didn't need me to call her name. From across the house, walking through the kitchen over to us, Sarah paused a minute to throw on her silk maroon robe she had laying over her arm. She smiled at Kady, and hugged her tightly.

"I saw it and had to get it," Kady said, practically falling out of her seat. I tore through the pristine wrapping, glimpsing over at her every few seconds. I couldn't help but giggle under my breath. Kady was so amazing about everything. It had only been a few months since she found out the truth about Sarah and me, but it didn't seem to change her outlook on life or opinion about who I was. She still treated me like her best friend. Still acted as if I was human and nothing had changed between us. Kady was more interested in knowing everything about me; she never once made it feel like she was afraid of what really went on in the world. She was always so angelic, which was ironic if you think about it. But she was, and I loved having her around.

The picture on the box was a beautiful white angel dressed in a white laced gown. She wore a gold halo wrapped around her head of golden locks. She cradled a small white light in her two hands.

"I know—corny—but I saw it and thought of you." Kady smiled taking the fragile angel from its case. "You put it at the top of your tree."

Kady's eyes widened in anticipation. She waited.

"Kady, we love it. You're very thoughtful honey," Sarah said, gesturing to me with her elbow in my rib cage.

I thought it was cute, and don't get me wrong, but wasn't that a bit stereotypical? Humans' thoughts on angels were sweet and cute: they fly around heaven with their big white wings, playing and strumming on their harps. But that was as far from the truth as anything. Yes, angels are beautiful and flawless, but they're also fighters, warriors of paradise. Archangels were the only ones with wings. The rest of us, not so much. And we couldn't even fly. Angels were nothing like the stories; they were strong, relentless, and great with a weapon. We also had nothing to do with the history of Christmas. Since the beginning all we did was fight a war between heaven and hell, good and evil. We protect no matter the cost. But Kady was doing her best to understand, so I did not want to be a know-it-all.

"It's perfect. Let's set it up, shall we?" I smiled.

Chapter 19

The final bell for school rang, releasing us for the next two weeks for break. Andy met me at my car, leaning up against the driver side door, legs crossed at the ankles. His hands rested in his pockets as he gave me one of his charming smiles. I walked up to him, pressing my body against his as he wrapped his arms around me, kissing my forehead.

"Well hello, pretty girl," he said as he moved from the car to open the door for me. I couldn't help but melt every time he was around. He held the only weakness I ever had. He was perfect, and he was mine. Andy slid into the passenger seat, placing one hand on my knee while hanging the other out the window. I drove from the school with the blur of students left in my wake.

Kady and Greg were sitting on the porch when Andy and I turned the corner to the backyard. A few nights back, Andy had decided on having our own little Christmas celebration at my house, just the four of us. Since Kady explained to me how hectic the holiday could be, visiting numerous family members, we would not get the chance to see each other that day. We rented *It's a Wonderful Life* through Netflix and baked brownies and sugar cookies with sprinkles. When the movie started to play, we all snuggled on the couch and turned out the light. I gazed around the room lit up by only candlelight and the tree. The vibe gave off a very relaxed feeling. Greg sat at the far end of the couch with Kady lying between his legs, her dark hair cascading down his chest. Andy sat next to me, his legs sprawled out toward the coffee table. I nestled against him, laying my head on his heart. I ran my fingers up and down his stomach, listening as his blood ran wild. I felt the heat from his body radiate off of him toward me, quickening his heart rate. He made no movements only a faint smile, but the inside of his body could not hide his true reactions.

*****

After a while throughout the movie, Kady and I busted out laughing when an angel part came on, and out of nowhere Kady said, "I wonder if that's true."

"If what's true. Kady?" I asked, holding back a chuckle.

"When a bell rings, Kye, do you think that means an angel gets his wings?"

Andy and Greg kept staring at us as if we had lost our minds, but Kady was having the time of her life, and I loved how she felt comfortable enough to make jokes about the supernatural, now that she knew the truth.

"Well, Kady," I said, trying to hold a straight face. It took me a few seconds to catch my breath before I could finish. "I don't believe so, and I don't believe they even have wings, but if they did that would be so cool."

"What are you two even talking about?" Andy interrupted.

It was so hard not to ask since the opportunity presented itself, even though my next question was mostly for my and Kady's amusement only.

"So, Andy, the question of the day: Do you believe in angels and if so would they have wings?" I asked, watching as Kady's face turned to shock. I just smiled, winking toward her.

She relaxed her face and turned toward Andy. "So what do you think?" She finished.

"Of course I believe in angels. And, yes, they would have wings. That's what makes them so majestic," Andy answered.

We all started to laugh.

After the movie was over, we all gathered around the tree to unwrap presents. I had asked Kady to help me find things for Andy and Greg and had Sarah help me for Kady. I realized I sucked at buying things for people, even if I knew and loved them. Kady had gone a little overboard on the gifts; she came from a wealthy family, having a credit card with no limit. Andy and Greg shared the same wealth. Greg's dad was some big time soccer player in Spain back in the day. After meeting an American woman, who would later become Greg's mom, when she studied abroad, his dad packed up his stuff and moved home with her. He said it was love at first sight.

I never had to worry about money. I didn't know where it came from or how much I had. All I knew was that I had a secret bank account that always stayed full and could never be traced by the governments or the elders.

The night ended in a mess of wrapping paper. The gifts I had gotten everyone were a big hit. Greg was speechless when he unwrapped an authentic signed soccer jersey from the 2010 World Cup of his favorite player, Cristiano Ronaldo. I gave Kady a silver bow-and-arrow necklace with an Enochian ruin for protection chiseled into it. Right away she got what it was, and later that night when we were alone, she started to cry, saying it was the greatest gift she could have ever gotten. She, in return, in the privacy of my room, gave me a leather box. When I opened it, I pulled out a dagger made of iron. By the looks of it, it must have cost a lot. The hilt of the dagger was a polished metal with a bare tree engraved into it. The blade was smooth and sharp. Iron was a deadly weapon to most creatures. I was never sure of the backstories, but in a lot of myths, iron had a compound that could bind a being to whatever dimension it was in. The bare tree represented the most natural element known to man, earth itself.

Andy was the hardest to shop for. I felt I knew everything about him, but nothing had any significance to it. I ended up not buying anything for him until a week earlier when the perfect gift finally occurred to me. The gift was priceless, set in a beautiful glass box.

Gold rimmed the edges with Latin ruins engraved around the entire surface. It was given to one of my great ancestors back in the fifteen hundreds by the love of her life, Shasta. Passed down over the generation, I had it shipped in from England. I had no use for it and was never a big reader, but a month ago in English class we were studying century-old literature and Andy's face lit up when Mr. Riker announced we were going to read a novel written by Sir Thomas More called *Utopia*. Andy went on and on about how he could read that book a million times and never get enough of it.

"Um…How?" Andy stuttered as he finished tearing through the paper, revealing the box. Snuggled in a blanket of gold velvet lay a first edition 1516 novel. The opened left-hand page showed a picture of a small island surrounded by water. The island was covered in fourteenth century castles, a large Viking ship lay anchored in the ocean accompanied by a smaller ship. In the background were hills and the largest of all the castles. In Latin the words read, "Vtopiae Instvlae Figvra," and on the right-hand page were Latin paragraphs and phrases.

"It's been in my family forever, sitting in a vault. I have no use for it, and I know how much you love that book." I knew there was no way Andy could read it. First of all it was written in Latin, and the English edition wasn't published until 1551. And second if he ever opened the glass box, the book would be ruined. But I guess it wasn't about reading it. To him it was about his love for old books.

"I can't, Kye. This book is priceless," Andy said, looking a little pale.

He ended up keeping the book since I refused to take it back. It was a perfect gift, and I couldn't help but love the way it made him happy—that I made him happy.

Chapter 20

I stood silently at the podium with the rest of my team. It was time for the award ceremony, to congratulate us for winning district and regional and for coming in second place at state. I stared out at the crowd of faces in the audience, the entire student body was sitting in the auditorium. Dean Franklin had announced this morning all classes would be canceled to join in the ceremonies. It had been years since the school had any major wins under its belt, so this was a big celebration for the Bulldogs' pride. The parents of the team started to show up, finding their seats reserved in the front three rows. I smiled at Kady's parents as they took their seats next to Sarah, having small talk before the administration asked for silence. Next Andy's parents and two older sisters walked in with Mr. and Mrs. Sardinia, Greg's parents. Although I had met Greg's family numerous times through dinners and parties, I had yet to meet Andy's because I was feeling uncomfortable about having to break their son's heart sooner or later. He would invite me over every week for family night, even telling me to bring along Sarah. But every time I would decline, making up some stupid reason about how it was a big deal and I wasn't ready for it.

When the seats were filled and the doors closed, Dean Franklin started to give his speech about the importance of school pride and how proud he was of all of us. Then, before he got into anything else, he decided to show everyone why he was so proud by putting together a video of the entire season that we would all get to watch immediately. Which was not good since I seemed to always be in the spotlight and since ninety-nine percent of the time, I used my hyperspeed and unnatural strength to win the game.

I held my breath, feeling my heart quicken in anticipation. My hands started to produce moister causing me to wipe them every few seconds. I looked over to see Sarah with the same fear in her eyes. She clenched her finely shaped jaw, scowling at me from across the room. Sarah noticed every time. She saw the lights stretch behind me, saw the blurs of the other teammates. If someone noticed what Sarah and I saw, I would have no choice but to leave tonight without any good-byes. I would leave my new life without finishing my journey. I would have to start over somewhere else where the chances of finding people that amazing again would be impossible. I didn't want to leave just yet, there was so much more I needed from this place, so much more soul searching I needed to do. It's funny when you think about it. Only five months ago, I would have given anything to leave. I would have left those people behind without ever turning back. But now I could never even imagine leaving them yet. I still wanted the time with them, still wanted the time to learn about friendship and love.

I looked over at Kady who was seated next to me and was smiling with pride. I nudged her arm.

"Hey, do you see anything odd about me, like supernatural," I whispered so low I'm surprised she even heard me.

She looked harder at the screen before she answered. "Right now?" she asked.

"Umm…Oh, now," I said quickly so she wouldn't miss it.

I was relieved when she shook her head. Then after a minute she realized what I was asking. Her head snapped back my way.

"Hey… You are such a cheater. No wonder you're so good," she joked in a hushed voice.

"Seriously, it took you that long to put two and two together"

"No, I didn't think you had super soccer powers," she grunted.

"It has nothing to do with soccer. It's all about balance and speed, which for me is just better I guess."

We went back to watching the screen. A few times I caught Kady really concentrating on the games to see if she could see something supernatural, but it turned out she saw nothing, which meant no one else did either. After twenty minutes of footage, showing everything from victories to defeats, the movie finally ended. The entire crowd got to their feet, screaming and cheering. They erupted in applause so loud I wouldn't be surprised if they could be heard them from the front of the school.

Dean Franklin walked back up to the podium, asking everyone to take their seats. After a few minutes of *excuse me's* and *settle downs*, the room finally fell silent once more. A man in a dark suit walked up behind the dean. He was younger than the other gentlemen he arrived with by ten or so years. He cleared his throat in the microphone, thanking everyone for their time. He introduced himself as Robert Wells, a sports scout for a school in Chapel Hill, North Carolina.

"I have been to many of your games, and I must say I have never seen so much talent in one school alone. Usually I would only offer one scholarship per school, but I am here today to offer three," Mr. Wells announced.

Mr. Wells turned his head to address us alone. "I have already talked with your teachers, coaches, and deans about my decision and was asked to wait until today to announce my three candidates."

I had absolutely no idea what this man was talking about, and to be honest it wasn't like any of this applied to me. I felt a small pang in my stomach when I thought about how nice it would be if I could care about this stuff. I liked playing soccer. I liked being able to run and be on a team again. But none of this applied to my future, so it was a little unsettling.

Until…

"Alikye Macayan, can you please come up here?" Mr. Wells said, signaling for me to join him.

I froze; I had no idea what he was asking me to do. I finally rose from my seat, walking over to him.

Everyone's focus was on me and me alone.

Chapter 21

The team and I were excused from afternoon classes. We were all told to meet back in Riker's classroom after we said our good-byes to our families. Sarah was standing in a group with Greg's, Andy's, and Kady's parents. Outside in the courtyard, they were congratulating her on behalf of me. They were telling her it was a great honor to receive something like that as a junior. I could see the hurt in her eyes as she lied about how proud she was.

Up at the podium, Mr. Wells offered me an early acceptance to his school along with a four-year scholarship as long as I played for the girls' soccer team. Since I still had to wait till the end of next year, the offer was good as long as I kept up my grades and played for my school next year. Mr. Riker assured him I would meet all requirements along with enough game time. Andy and Greg were offered the same except they would be starting after the summer.

I guess given the circumstances it was good I would be leaving. Andy was leaving anyway for school and now in a different state fourteen hours away. Even if I could stay, the chances of us working out as a couple were slim to none. I wasn't a naïve person who believed in high school love lasting forever. We would make it a month and then what?

Andy grabbed my hand, walking me toward his folks; I didn't really have a choice anymore about meeting them. Sarah embraced me in her arms, kissing my forehead. After saying hello to Mr. and Mrs. Scott and Mr. and Mrs. Sardinia, I braced myself for Andy's parents.

"Mom, Dad, this is Alikye," he said

"Congratulations. You must be so proud of your son. I know I am," I said as pleasant as I could. Andy's dad skipped the handshake, taking me into his arms instead. I was caught way off guard but accepted the gesture. Andy's mom, on the other hand, looked like she had seen a ghost. The quick reaction, though, didn't draw the attention of the others. For a moment looking into her face, she seemed familiar to me also, like I had met her long ago. Andy touched my hand, sending a shock through my body, releasing me from her trance. We both just glared into each other's eyes.

"And a big congratulation goes to you, too," Andy's dad said moving his eyes to his wife. "Don't you think so, honey?"

"Oh, yes, and I'm so glad to finally meet you. We have heard so much about you. You, my dear, are all Andy talks about"

"Dude, Mom, really?" Andy said, embarrassed, his cheeks starting to turn red.

*****

Riker was sitting atop his desk when I walked in to his class. He smiled at me and asked me to take my seat. Andy, Greg, Kady, and I took our seats in the far left corner. Holden, who had been waiting for us, pulled his chair closer, closing our circle. Amanda was the last to arrive. She came barging into the room, her heels clanking on the tile with her oversize purse dangling from her scrawny elbow. She plowed her way through the team, taking her seat next to Riker's desk, her clipboard still in hand.

"Let's begin. We only have an hour, and we have a lot to discuss," Mr. Riker said, bringing the room to his full attention. "First I am pleased to announce I have just received a phone call verifying our spot in the All State Championship Tournament, which will begin in early May. It's a weeklong tournament in Tallahassee."

"Seriously, we get to skip school for a week to play soccer?" Andy asked to confirm that what he was hearing was correct.

"Yes, Andy, only if your parents agree to it. Amanda's parents have generously offered to donate the money needed to pay for everyone's stay, including offering to rent us a bus."

Of course they did. Just so Riker would be obligated to let Amanda tag along. The only reason she was even on the team as an assistant was because her college applications required school activities, and the more the better. Amanda was the president of the student body and head editor of the yearbook and newspaper. She ran special events that would raise money for disadvantaged children. Even during the holidays she would volunteer her time in soup kitchens and hospitals. She was your teenage Mother Teresa except she didn't do it out of the goodness of her heart.

"That's amazing," I said sarcastically, plastering a fake smile on my face. "But I think I would prefer to drive. If we take three vehicles, we would be able to save at least half that money, and I don't know, if her parents don't mind, use the bus money toward new equipment."

"That's a great idea except there is a lot of paperwork to fill out to allow students to drive to school activities," Riker said.

I really wanted to bring my car with me, not just to get away from Amanda, but I felt safer with it, being that far away from home. I needed a way to convince him.

"Well, the administration has to fill out paperwork anyway. What are a few more sheets? Plus we'll have a school official in each car. It's brilliant." I could see Riker contemplating my idea, and in the end, after a unanimous decision, we all agreed to take three vehicles. Amanda wasn't happy with the idea since she didn't come up with it herself, but she had to play nice and agreed it would be OK with her parents to give the remaining of the money to the sports department.

"So we will need three volunteers to drive." Right away I raised my hand. Since it was my idea, I thought it only fair to drive. Kady, Greg, and Andy immediately established they were riding with me.

"I figured, and I guess that makes me your chaperon," Riker added.

Holden was about to ask if he could also ride with us when Amanda spoke up too soon. "Well, I would like to stay with you, Mr. Riker. I mean if that's OK with Alikye.

"Why, I figured you would volunteer to drive yourself," I said, looking from her to Riker.

"Please. Why would I do that when I could just ride with you, right?"

"Yeah, except I told Holden he could ride with me, so their won't be any room, sorry."

"Girls, please. Amanda will ride with you, Alikye. Holden will be fine in another car," Riker chimed in, getting annoyed with our bickering.

"Seriously?" I asked.

"Yes, now that's the end of it," Riker finished.

I could not believe Amanda weaseled her way into my car just to get back at me for stealing her glory, but what could I do? Riker made up his mind. I thought about meeting him after school to talk more about it, but that would never work, and I doubted he wanted to get on Amanda's bad side since she could decline her offer of paying for the trip. No, I had to be the mature one and keep my mouth shut. I mean, how bad could it really be?

Chapter 22

"So…Kady, come on just tell me," I begged as I laid my head back on Kady's bed. For weeks I had been trying to get Kady to tell me what Andy was planning for Valentine's Day. With only a week to go, I resorted to begging and pleading. "I hate surprises and you know that."

Kady got up from her desk and took a seat next to me on the lavish carpet in her bedroom. She laughed as I puffed out my lips, giving her the best puppy dog eyes I could. "Please just tell me. I promise I'll act surprised," I said, laying my head on her shoulder. She shook her head back and forth covering her mouth with two fingers, zipping them across her lips. All I was told was to pack an overnight bag with warm clothes and that we would be leaving after school on Friday. I think I was more nervous than excited about spending an entire night with him. I was always taught about sex, but unlike humans it was never a problem among my kind since we didn't do it until we were bonded to one another. If I were to lose my virginity to anyone besides Lucas, the repercussions were extreme. And if I were to lose it to a human boy…It's as forbidden as falling in love with one. It would mean the end of me as a Guardian. The risk would not be worth it. But worst of all my heart would forever belong to that person. For as long as I lived, I would never feel for another again.

I left Kady's house as the sun started to disappear in the distance. I wasn't getting anything out of her, so I finally threw up my white flag and decided I would wait until Friday. The week went by very sluggishly. Mr. Riker had set up intense workouts for the team to get ready for the competition. Between the weight room and playing against each other out on the field, by Thursday I was exhausted more than I thought I could ever be. The weekend could not come soon enough, and getting away for the night was all I needed to relax.

After practice I decided to go straight home. I pulled into my driveway, sweat dripping from my head and down my back. I threw my soccer bag over my shoulder, and my dirt crusted cleats hung from my fingers. I was filthy and covered in mud after some idiot left the sprinklers on, coating the field in water. All I wanted was a cold shower and a long nap, but lately the world had its funny way of making what I wanted complicated—when I walked through the front door and saw what I saw, all I could do was freeze.

*****

Derek woke to the sound of his cell phone ringing. With drowsy eyes he tried to focus on the front screen. He blinked a few times before realizing the caller was his father, Jack. He answered in a hurry. There was a few minutes of talking then a quick good-bye, and Derek went to Lucas's bed to wake him up.

"Dude, Luke, wake up. Dad just called," he said, shaking Lucas's shoulders.

Lucas rolled to the other side of the bed, yanking the covers over his head. They had just fought one of the biggest battles in history, and the last thing Lucas wanted was another mission right now. Lucas grunted, throwing his arms in the air to shoo away his brother. It was still dark outside, the sun barely touching the horizon.

"It's about Kye," Derek finished in a soft voice.

Lucas got out of bed and packed up his belongings while Derek did the same. They washed up, made their beds, and headed downstairs for morning tea and a hot breakfast. The old man sat at the breakfast nook, his eyes busy with the paper he had in front of him and a steaming cup in his hand. Placed around the table was a variety of fruit pastries, hot fluffy pancakes with homemade maple syrup, eggs, and bacon. Freshly made hash browns were mixed with onions, peppers, and mushrooms picked this morning from the garden. A pot of water sat on a hot plate surrounded by cups and an assortment of teas. The old man turned his face away from the paper and greeted the boys politely, gesturing for them to sit. After a fulfilling and silent breakfast, they bid the old man good-bye and left for a long drive to Florida.

*****

I wasn't sure if I was in shock or just so tired I was seeing them, imagining my three favorite boys sitting on the couch in my living room, looking up at me. Was I happy about them being in my house? I should have been. I missed them so much, but the truth was they were going to ruin everything. Sarah knew about Andy being my boyfriend, but she was under the impression it was just a high school thing and my feelings meant nothing for him. So how was I to pull this off? Jack wasn't supposed to be here with Derek and Lucas until the end of May, which was the deal. Lucas ran to me, lifting me off the ground as he spun me around, his long golden curls flying from side to side. I looked into his dark-green eyes as he put me down, kissing me on the cheek. What was I supposed to do now? I should be leaving tomorrow after school, but how would I explain that one. The only choice I could think of was to cancel.

My back pocket started to vibrate, and I knew it was Andy verifying our plans for tonight. I would have to cancel those, too. I took my phone from my pocket and read the text; Andy was so excited for tomorrow. I smiled at his message and the heart he left for me. I typed in I needed to talk to him that I would call him later and that I couldn't see him tonight, something came up. Lucas stepped away, his hand still grazing my arm. He looked at me then my phone then back at me. In the surprise of everything, I realized I had blown Lucas off, caring more about my text than him. After being away from each other for so long, I think he expected me to be more excited over his sudden arrival. But I had a lot on my mind, and the boys being here just made everything worse.

"Just a friend from school—her name is Kady. You'll get a chance to meet her later," I lied. "I really need a shower," I said, pointing to how dirty I was." I stink, but I promise we will catch up in a minute." I walked to my room to discard my soccer gear. I figured this would be the only time I could call Andy and explain things to him. It would also give me time to think about what I was doing.

Sarah stood in the kitchen making a fabulous dinner. The smells and sizzles filled the house. Jack and the boys were sprawled out on the couch channel surfing, making small talk about a much needed break after what they had been through. I stepped out of the bathroom, a towel twisted in my hair. I put on a pair of black leggings and a pink tank that fell past my hips. I fell down onto the couch beside Jack, laying my wet head on his shoulder. He smelled so much like home to me. I smiled at him, wrapping my arms around his right arm. I snuggled into his body, curling my legs underneath myself.

"So, baby girl, tell me what's been going on with you," Jack said in a deep dominate voice. Derek moved closer to me setting the TV on mute. I told them everything, from Kady to soccer. I didn't bring up Andy too much because I was scared my voice would give too much away. I only told them I was friends with a few guys from school and that they were pretty cool to hang out with but not as cool as my boys. I laughed as I told them about all the holiday stuff I got to do and how Sarah let me have a New Year's party here.

*****

I was really excited when Sarah suggested it after Christmas; Kady helped me plan every detail. Even her mom made time to help put things together since she was a professional party planner. The night of the party was perfect, and the air was cool enough to have it outside by the ocean but warm enough for me to wear a strapless black chiffon dress laced with silver specks that matched my eyes. Kady had bought it for me as a Christmas present. The dress was breathtaking, nothing I would have ever worn in my past. The top fitted tight to my small chest, showing off enough skin to flatter but not enough to look sleazy. The bottom half rested right above my knees and fared out. A rhinestone belt fit snug around my waist. I paired it with black flats and the gold necklace Andy had gotten me with two hearts intertwining. Half of the senior class had shown up including Amanda and her clones. Riker also made an appearance along with a few parents Sarah had gotten to know through our soccer games.

At a quarter to twelve, everyone headed inside to watch as the ball dropped in Times Square. As I started to make my way inside, Andy grabbed my hand and led me to the beach. The moon brightly shined in the water, scattering a blanket of diamonds across the ocean.

"Hey," Andy said as I looked out into the sky. I stood there, smiling, feeling the warmth of his hand wrapped around mine. He moved his hands to my waist, pulling me closer to him. Our magnetic force pulsed through my body as he touched my face. He brushed his lips against mine, pulling away right as I started to push closer to him.

"What?" I asked in a low voice as he locked his gaze on mine.

"Just, wait a minute." I moved my head to his chest, taking in his seductive aroma. He moved his hands to my hair, smoothing out my curls. I still didn't understand the undeniable passion I felt for him. Was it just emotional or physical, or was it something supernatural. My only explanation was it was because he was human and I wasn't. But it wasn't like I could ask Sarah why every time he was near me it was like my blood started to boil in my veins, or why the energy between us flared up like sparks on the Fourth of July. I couldn't ask her without giving my feeling away. I couldn't make sense of it—the urge to want him so badly it hurt, and the invisible force that pulled our bodies together. Was this what love felt like? Did I love Andy?

Inside I could hear the crowd counting down—ten, nine, eight, seven. Andy lifted my head, bringing my face closer to his.

Six, five, four, three. I brought my arms up, curling my fingers in his hair.

Two, one. Then his mouth met mine, slowly and softly at first but then with much more force. He tasted like a dream—a beautiful and magical place I never wanted to leave. My hands moved down his neck, bringing myself closer to him. The heat between us started to burn my skin, but I didn't want to move away from him. The pain seared through my body, causing my chest to tighten. I dug my nails into his back, feeling his reaction of pleasure. The feelings were far more intense than it had ever been before. He moved his hands down the opening of my back, finally pulling away. "Wow!" I said, trying to catch my breath.

"Yeah," Andy replied. His smile vanished. He tightened his jaw as if he were in pain. A serious look appeared in his eyes. Then he said something that knocked the breath out of me again, "I love you, Alikye."

******

I could feel Andy's lips on mine and still hear his voice in my head when he told me he loved me. I could still feel the happiness I felt when I said "I love you" back. But I didn't mention that last part to the others. I saw how much I changed in their eyes, how I went from this arrogant little girl to a free-spirited woman in a matter of months.

Jack and Derek were so consumed in my stories I hadn't noticed Lucas sitting in the corner biting his nails until he finally spoke, "Have you been keeping up on your training?"

"Yeah, Sarah and I practice three day a week and soccer keeps me pretty busy," I spat out.

"Are you sure that's enough?"

I couldn't believe the smugness in his voice, especially from him. "Are you kidding me…" I said, rising from the couch.

"Lucas, what the hell is wrong with you?" Derek interrupted.

"Sorry, just making sure you'll be good after all this. I didn't mean it how it sounded," Lucas said in a hushed tone.

I saw how hard it was for him to listen to stories in which he wasn't included in my life, or maybe after all these months being away from me, he finally realized how much better he was without me. Either way he was acting as if I didn't matter to him anymore, and it kind of hurt. I figured I would have the weekend to reconnect with him, so I just shrugged and accepted his apology.

Chapter 23

Sarah had me stay home from school that Friday. Andy didn't take my phone call very well. He sounded disappointed that we wouldn't be spending our first Valentine's Day together. But after an hour of apologizing, he finally understood how important it was for me to spend the time with my family. I think he was more disappointed in the fact that I didn't ask him to come by and meet my family.

Kady came by after school to drop off my homework. She walked into my house and embraced Jack in a hug, telling him how wonderful it was to finally meet him. After the initial shock, he smiled and hugged her back. Derek and Lucas came in a moment later from the backyard, water dripping from their shirtless bodies, their hair messy with salt. Kady's eyes fell on them, and for a moment she couldn't move. I started to laugh until she threw me an evil glare, shutting me up. I could just imagine what she was thinking being surrounded by so many beautiful people. I never noticed before how we all looked to the outside world; I was used to the beauty of my race. Even Jack and Sarah, who were in their late forties, looked like twenty-year-old models. Sarah with her long golden hair and golden eyes, her small frame, and defined jawline, and Jack, the spitting image of Derek but with the same eyes as Lucas, were a match made in heaven (pun intended).

"Wow, how do you spend all your time with them and not get distracted? Even Jack is hot for an old guy," Kady said. We were on my bed taking some time for ourselves, and I needed to talk to her in private about Andy. I shut the door and turned up the radio just in case they were listening.

"Is Andy pissed—I know he's pissed—I'd be pissed," I rambled, laying my head in her lap. She ran her fingers threw my hair as she tried to console me.

"I think he's more hurt about not being asked to meet your family."

I knew that would be the reason, especially after he made such a big deal about me meeting his family. He said it was a big step in becoming exclusive, whatever that meant. I never saw it that way. I didn't even want to meet his family, and there was no way he could ever meet mine. Plus my real family was dead; he knew that, so really he could never meet them. But I know they would have loved him. Sometimes I wished I still had my mom so I could ask her questions I couldn't ask Sarah. But then again, if I did have my mother, I would have never come here. I wish I could have both. I know my mom would understand my feelings because she would love me no matter what.

"Earth to Alikye," Kady said, snapping her fingers in front of my face. "Like I was saying, I will do what I can to keep him from here."

"Good plan."

By Saturday morning Andy had left me three voice messages and ten text messages. I didn't know what to say to him anymore. All I was doing was lying to him, and I hated it. I hated myself for what I was doing to him, but I couldn't stay away from him. So Friday night I told him I needed space. I told him we would talk on Monday. It was nothing against him. It was just the easiest way to protect myself. At least that was what I though until my phone kept blowing up all night. It took all my strength not to go see him so I could hold him in my arms and tell him we were fine, that it was just bad timing. But I needed this weekend to be with Lucas, to reconnect with him.

"Kye, come out here." Lucas yelled, his voice echoing through the house.

Lucas knew something was going on with me. How could he not—we were bonded to one another; I have known that since combat school. To him I was a prize, a Legacy who would one day have his children. He should have been the prize to me; he was stunning, like liquid gold, a vision of ecstasy. Michael himself would have a hard time describing him. He was a true definition of an angel, perfectly carved like a diamond. He was a slice of chocolate cheesecake that would make your taste buds tingle with satisfaction as it melted in your mouth. That was Lucas with his halo of golden curls; seductive eyes of green, darker than the jungles around the world; washboard abs; and sculpted chest and arms. But it was never about his looks. He was the most amazing guy, sweet and passionate. He loved everything and trusted every one. The complete opposite of who I was. But it wasn't enough for me—he wasn't enough. Not like Andy. Andy made me into the girl I wanted to be. He made me realize things that no one else could, made me see things about myself and the world that no one else could. I've kissed Lucas before, only a few times, but it never compared to the way Andy kissed me.

I walked into the kitchen where my family stood around picking at the mess of food spread out on the counter. And for the first time ever, I couldn't eat. My stomach was in knots from all the guilt I felt. Every vibration from my phone made me feel even sicker. I pulled myself up on the bar, swinging my legs back and forth, hitting the door with the heel of my foot and every so often kicking Lucas or Derek just to piss them off. The boys went on and on about their Nimphica they had killed. They even got a phone call from Anastasis herself. Anastasis was the head elder of the council. She was also the one who decided I could move to Florida or work side by side with her since I technically belonged on the council. But because of my age, I wouldn't get a say in anything, so I declined that offer. But it was a big honor when she took the time to make a congratulatory phone call. I just rolled my eyes and kicked Derek in the leg, making him jump. I had heard enough of their story. I knew I was being unfair to them, but jealousy got the better of me. I would have loved to been there when they defeated it, a creature no other Guardian had ever been able to catch. And I should have been the one who killed it.

"So what are the plans for today?" I said, interrupting Lucas

"Just thought we would all hang out here today, have a barbecue, sit on the beach, have some quality time together," Jack said, placing an arm around Sarah.

"Sounds good to me. I deserve a vacation after that Nimphica battle," Derek said, bringing his face inches from mine. "Huge, awesome battle. Best one I've ever been in," he bragged.

"Cute." I rolled my eyes while everyone just laughed.

The sun was bright, and an azure sky hung above . The salty breeze blew past me as I sat in my chair, my feet splashing in the water. The ocean was clam, motionless like looking in a mirror. Boats and Jet Skis were anchored in the distance on a sandbar a couple hundred feet out, and I heard the sounds of music and dancing. I let the sun soak into my skin, feeling the water roll over my body and then fall back leaving a salty foam in the wake of a receding wave. Sarah walked up to me and handed me a glass of sweet tea. The drink was refreshing as it hydrated my dry mouth.

Derek walked out of the house holding a small black box in his hand. My attention was elsewhere until I heard the vibration in his tight grip. My body jolted to life as if the lives of the people I loved were being threatened in front of me. In a split second, I was on my feet, sand spiraling out of control. I was at his side in the blink of an eye, grabbing the phone from his fingers. Accidentally I pulled too hard on his hand, breaking several of his fingers in the process. My jaw dropped in horror, and I sucked in a breath and held it for what seemed like hours. "Oh, shit," I blurted out. I watched as Derek's face turned bright red. He grunted a few swear words before turning his glare to me. He pulled his hand to his chest, straightening each finger back in place. I heard the bones crack under his groans and the blood rushing threw his hand. I curled my lips into a slight smile as if to say I was sorry without using my voice, afraid it would crack.

118

After a moment Derek said, "I was going to tell you your phone was ringing."

I knew my phone was ringing; it hadn't stopped ringing. I also knew who it was, and I was afraid Derek would get a glimpse of what was written on the screen. It was becoming a bit ridiculous on Andy's part, and I had to deal with him sooner rather than later. I apologized again as I ran into the house, almost slipping on the white tile. Sarah was going to freak out on me when she saw all the sand I was bringing into the house, but I needed to get to the front yard to have a private conversation without being disturbed. I took a seat underneath the large tree that stood in the center of the yard to the right of the driveway. I opened my phone, scanning through the fifteen messages that Andy had left for me. I wiped the sand from my body as I hit the call button. Two rings and Andy answered the phone yelling my name in the speaker.

"What the hell, Alikye? I've been calling you all day." I could hear his teeth grinding.

"This is the last time I'm telling you, Andy. I'm with my family, and I haven't seen them in months, so you need to stop calling me every five seconds because you're really starting to piss me off," I yelled back at him. I was livid, I didn't know why he was acting so obsessive and sure as hell didn't enjoy his attitude. I understood that he was in love with me, but if that was what love was about, I wanted no part in it. I just wanted to get through this weekend with no drama, but he wouldn't let it go.

"This is crap, Kye. If you won't talk to me, I'm coming over now," Andy replied. I could see it now: Andy running into my house, pleading his undying love for me while my nonhuman family sat back and watched, and Lucas hearing those words, words that should never be spoken from a human to a Guardian. That would definitely be bad. But how could I stop him from making such a rash decision? To save myself there was only one option, and it hurt to even think about it.

"Fine, I need to talk to you anyway. Meet me at our spot in twenty," I said, hanging up.

I loved our spot. Andy found it a few years back and never told anyone about it. I was the first. Tucked far back in the woods behind the beach was a small clearing surrounded by wild flowers. Palm trees overlapped one another, hiding the sun. A log that had fallen after a hurricane lay on the ground between two bushes.

I went straight to my room, throwing on black tights and a dark-blue blouse that fell off my shoulder. Without bothering to take a shower, I threw my hair into a messy bun and met my family in the living room.

"Hey. Kady just called. She wants me to help her with something. I'm only going to be gone for like an hour," I said, heading to the door.

"That's fine, sweetheart, and while you're out, would you mind picking up some basil and mint?" Sarah asked

"Oh, hey, some beer, too," Derek added.

"Umm…I'm sixteen, stupid, I can't buy beer," I said with an attitude, crinkling my nose.

"Well, then you're useless," he joked, throwing his head back in laughter.

I got to the clearing just as Andy was pulling into the parking lot, which gave me a few minutes to collect my thoughts and figure out exactly what I needed to get off my chest. I took a deep breath, watching as he walked to where I was seated, raising one of the overgrown palms out of his way. He looked tired; black bags hung under his eyes like he'd been up all night, and all I could think about was it was my fault that looked so distraught. It made me reconsider what I was about to do, but it had to be now and not five months from now. It would be easier now, easier to get over me. Maybe even find a girl whom he deserved, one that deserved him more than I did. I needed to focus on my family, on Lucas. I needed to fix our relationship and stop lying to everyone. Would I ever love Lucas the way he loved me? No. Andy was my world, but he deserved better.

"Hi," I said as he took a seat next to me on the log. He placed his hand in mine, intertwining our fingers together. I was about to pull away but at the last minute decided that it would be better to let him have it.

"What's going on with you? Why are you being so difficult?" he asked calmly, gripping my hand tighter.

Was he serious? I wasn't doing anything except asking him for a little space.

"Are you kidding me? I'm not being difficult," I said, pulling my hand away from his. I stood up from the log and watched his face drop. "What's going on with *you*? I told you I needed time this weekend. Damn, Andy, we don't have to spend every minute or every hour together. Did you ever think that maybe I just wanted quality time with them without the pressure of my boyfriend around?" I was starting to yell. "I understand this weekend was supposed to be special and, yes, plans change. I'm sorry for that, but seriously you're acting like a controlling ass, and to be honest I don't like it. "I stopped to catch my breath, I tried not to get angry, but my emotions became so strong sometimes that it was hard to control them. And by the way Andy looked, I probably went a little too far, but I didn't care. I couldn't care. My body was going numb, my emotions getting the better of me.

"Is that what you think? Well, I'm sorry, too, but when my girlfriend calls me up the minute her family comes into town and says she needs a break from me, something is a little bit suspicious. You're not telling me the whole story, and I think I deserve it—the real story, that is," he replied. He was right about everything`, but he would never get the real story. He couldn't handle the real story. My anger turned to tears because I finally realized the fault was on me and me alone. I couldn't be with him without hurting him more, same as Lucas. He had every right to be upset, but I wasn't about to admit it, because I didn't want to admit it to myself. That everything was my fault, and his pain and suffering was because of me. I knew I would have to leave him, and for reasons that I couldn't fathom, I let him fall in love with me anyway, knowing that he would soon have his heart broken. So I said the only thing that would ease his pain. I finally did what I came here to do, and it took every ounce of strength not to break down and lose myself.

"You're right," I whispered, tears running down my face. "I don't think we should be together anymore. After the school year is over, I'm leaving with my family."

"And let me guess, you knew this all along, so everything you told me about staying here, playing soccer next year, going to college with us—it was all a lie." He started to laugh, but the laugh wasn't one that was contagious. No, it was more like anger ran through it. "That's why you wouldn't meet my parents, because you knew this whole time and couldn't bear hurting them by hurting me." He was figuring out everything, throwing it all back in my face.

"It's not that simple, Andy. Yes, I knew I was leaving, but a part of me was trying to stay here, to stay with you. But the fact is you're leaving, too, so what's the point?"

"The point is we were supposed to figure it out together because we love each other enough to make us work after the school year." His face was blank, but his eyes showed all emotion like a storm brewing in the depths of his soul.

All my emotions were swirling around in my head like a twister out for destruction. I should have just left it at that, told him I loved him and walked away, salvaging what was left of us. But, no, my anger, my arrogance that I couldn't seem to control, got the better of me. I was back to being the girl I was when I had first arrived in Picture City. All my hard work vanished in that split second of hearing the truth that I didn't want to admit to myself. But Andy knew me too well and made sure that I knew myself.

I wiped the tears from my eyes, taking a deep breath. "I wanted to make it work, I wanted to love you as much as you loved me, but I couldn't. I still can't. I'm not capable of love. I never have been." I walked away before he had time to process what I said. Before he had time to stop me and realize it wasn't true, that I was completely in love with him. Before I realized I was making the biggest mistake of my life and ran back to him. I walked away from him, knowing that nothing could ever fix what I had just said to him. But I also knew I was doing this for him, for everyone.

Chapter 24

The night of my parent's death was the first time I had ever felt real pain. When I found them lying on the floor in a puddle of their own blood, I didn't want to believe they were gone. For hours I sat covered in their blood, screaming and crying, shaking them until I had finally passed out from exhaustion. It wasn't until the next morning that Jack had found me curled up to their lifeless bodies unwilling to let go of their hands. The pain was so unbearable for such a small child that I couldn't deal with it. So I did the one thing I could do: I shut off the part of my brain that registered pain, but in order to flip that switch, I had to turn off all my emotions. Years later when I was old enough to handle the pain, I gave myself my emotions back, but all at once I felt the pain change to anger. I was angry at my parents for leaving me. They were dead and never coming back. After that I wouldn't get close to anyone out of fear they would one day die, leaving me nothing more than an empty shell of my former self. Andy was different though. He was still alive, but the pain was similar. He was gone to me forever, and for the rest of my life, I would have to live with the fact that I was the one who left, not him.

I ran straight to the bathroom slamming the door behind me. I fell to my knees, my face planted into the toilet and puked my entire stomach contents. As a Guardian I had never been ill, never once had food poisoning even if the food was spoiled, never had the flu or anything else humans caught. The only time I had ever felt nauseous, it was caused by something bad happening, so it wasn't long before a knock at the door came and a voice asking what had happened. I knew it was Lucas coming to comfort me for reasons he would never know. For a lie I would have to tell him, because lately that was all I was doing—deceiving everyone I loved.

"Kye, let me in please," Lucas said in a hushed voice. "I know something happened—talk to me."

The only times I had ever been seen crying was for one reason, the one thing that kept me up all night hiding in bathrooms or small nooks in dark corners, crying my eyes out. It was the only lie no one would question. I crawled to the door, unlocking it, allowing Lucas to come in. He sat next to me on the floor, his back resting against the cabinet. I curled up next to him, hiding my face in his chest.

"What happened," he whispered, running his hand through my hair.

"I miss my mom and dad," I half-lied, but I wished they were here to give me advice because they, of all people, would know what I was going through.

Lucas sighed, knowing there was nothing he could say that would make me feel better besides sit with me and listen. Plus it wasn't my parents I was really crying for this time. It was a boy I was in love with while sitting in the arms of a boy who was in love with me, and all I wanted was someone I could talk to about it. But I had no one.

"Hey, kiddo, did I ever tell you the story about the day you were born." Jack's voice broke through the silence. I looked up toward him with puffy bloodshot eyes. Jack stood leaning up against the wall in the doorway, a look of grief on his face. I'd heard the story a million times; it was my favorite one about my dad.

"Can you tell me it again?" I said sniffling.

"Well, your dad was a lot like you, never scared of anything, but the day you were born was the first time I had ever seen a look of real terror cross his face. He was so scared to hold you, fearing you would break easily because you were so tiny. Finally when he did hold you, he would not let you go, not even for your mother. She would yell at him all the time saying he was spoiling you, that you would get used to being in his arms and never want to be alone.

Even when you slept, he always had you in his arms; you wouldn't have it any other way. You two have the same eyes, the exact shade of silver, and you have his strength. He would be so proud of the woman you're becoming, I know I am," Jack finished, pulling me to my feet and wrapping me in his arms. "Let's go, I have a great idea."

We drove five hours north heading to a small camp used for training and owned by the Guardians. A fifty-acre field was hidden behind a ten-foot brick wall, equipped with everything from weapons to training rooms specific to each scenario you could find yourself in. For hours I stood alone, reconnecting with my bow and arrow never missing my target. The distraction was nice, but often I was thinking back to my last conversation with Andy, wondering what he was doing now, wondering if he would call Kady or Greg and tell them everything, wondering if he would call Amanda and confide in her for his own distraction. I wasn't an expert on human behavior, but I had watched enough movies to know that's what someone did when they were hurting. In the loneliness of the field, miles from anyone, I fell to my knees and broke down, knowing time could not heal my pain, knowing nothing would but to escape to a place of darkness and nothingness, a place inside my head where nothing mattered.

Monday morning I woke to Kady standing over me, staring in shock. I furrowed my eyebrows, rubbing the sleep from my eyes, looking confused as to why she was in my room. "Morning," I said, stretching my arms over my head. "Um…Is there a reason why you're in my room this early?"

"Seriously, Kye, were you even going to tell me what happened? OMG, I was worried sick. Andy came to my house in tears." Kady's voice started to rise, echoing through my room. "He told me everything, and all I could think about was you and how you were doing. I called and called. Greg called, and even Andy tried to call to make sure you were OK. I drove by a thousand times but nothing." She sat down beside me, taking a deep breath. She lowered her voice and finished. "I thought you left without saying good-bye."

"Jack took me to a training center on the West Coast, him and the boys left this morning. I'm fine, Kady, trust me, and I'm not going anywhere for a while."

"So was it true what you said to Andy, that you never loved him? Kye, he's devastated. I have never seen him like that before. It was horrible. I made Greg stay with him all weekend."

I looked at the time on the clock, the green numbers blinked six o'clock. It was too early to have this conversation, plus it didn't really matter what I felt because at that moment I felt nothing for him or Kady. I would have told her it wasn't true, that I loved him more than anything. I would have asked how he was doing, but at that point I didn't care. My brain was fried. I was numb. The pain was gone, leaving an empty shell once again. I turned the switch in my head. The lights were off, the doors locked forever. In that moment alone on the field I decided to shut it all down, erasing my feelings for everyone, becoming nothing more than a true angel. The human part of me was gone, the part where my emotions were stored. I didn't want them anymore.

"Does it matter?" I said nonchalantly, turning over in my bed, pulling the covers over my head.

I walked into Riker's class expecting Andy not to be there. From what Kady had told me about his condition, I figured he would take the day off. But like me he was just as surprised. I heard his pulse quicken as I walked by. I took my usual seat next to him, not making any type of contact with him. He looked normal, better than I expected. He wore a dark pair of jeans with his black Reef flip-flops and a light-blue T-shirt that brought out the color of his eyes. He looked the same as he did the first day I met him, beautiful and confident. The class went on for what felt like eternity. Every now and then I would catch him staring at me but nothing else.

By lunchtime I snuck out the back and headed to my car in the parking lot, knowing that my presence would make the situation awkward. Days went by in a blur. I started isolating myself, ignoring all attempts of conversation. At practice I dominated the field, throwing all my pent-up anguish into my game. Kady tried to be my friend, but I wouldn't let her. I wanted her to forget about me just like I wanted Andy to. Weeks passed, and my attitude stayed the same. I finally got what I wanted—to be an outcast, the girl with no friends. A girl who would leave here and never return, never look back. I would take what I learned and become a better Guardian, one who would make her father proud. At home I acted normal, leaving from time to time so that Sarah wouldn't know anything was wrong. A few times I headed to the training facility and worked harder than I had ever worked then came home days later with no explanation. I walked around school like a zombie, passing teammates and teachers and acting as if they didn't exist.

"You know," Andy said, "it is one thing to want nothing to do with me, but your friend did nothing wrong but love you, and all you're doing is treating her like crap."

I closed my eyes sucking in a heavy breath. I stayed facing my locker wishing he would go away.

"I'm not leaving until you talk to me, Kye," Andy said, taking a step closer.

"Fine, then I'll leave," I snapped, slamming my locker shut. I turned on my heels accidentally throwing my shoulder into his and walked away from him. But this time he didn't let me leave so easily. The last bell rang, clearing the hallways of any students. Andy ran in front of me, stopping me in my tracks. We stood alone, staring at one another.

"No, not this time. You need to talk to me," he protested.

"What, Andy, what would you like to talk about, because the way I see it, there is nothing more to say," I barked.

"Kady. That's who we need to talk about."

I closed my eyes again remembering what it was like to be around her.

Andy continued in a calmer voice. "You say you never loved me. Fine, I get it, but what I don't get is how you could just shut her out like that? I know you love her, but right now she feels betrayed by her best friend." He took another step closer to me, clasping his fist to his side. The energy from his body engulfed me, sending tendrils of heat up my arms. My head started to spin, causing every cell in my brain to go into overdrive, automatically rebooting my emotions. Every feeling of pain and happiness, hate and love, anger and rage came back, and like the Hoover Dam opening its gates, everything flooded back to me at once, everything I had blocked out. I grabbed my head, screaming as the pain seared threw my skull, kicking open each door I had locked up. Andy caught me in his arms before I hit the floor, gently placing me on my knees as he knelt down beside me cradling me. I gripped his biceps, digging my nails into his skin, tears running from my eyes.

"Alikye, are you OK?" Andy asked in a worried tone. I couldn't do it anymore; I couldn't go on pretending he meant nothing to me. Memories flooded back. I felt our first kiss and the first time he told me he loved me. I felt the way he always made me feel. Being apart wasn't doing any good for either of us, and for the first time, I couldn't block it out. My brain wouldn't let me forget him.

"I never stopped loving you, Andy," I said in a hushed whisper as I kept my eyes focused on the ground. My head was lying against his chest. I breathed in his scent, he smelled like the beach and guy-soap mixed together.

"What!" he said, backing away from me, holding my face between his hands. The pad of his thumb swept across my bottom lip, soothing me.

I raised my eyes so I could look at him. "I lied when I said I never loved you. I just thought it would be easier for you to forget about me if you thought I didn't love you. I have always loved you—since the moment we met, it was there. My heart will always belong to you. It always has, and no matter what happens, it's yours forever. But there are things about me you'll never understand. There are things I can never tell you. I'm so sorry for…" Before I could finish, his lips were on mine, and at that moment all the pain and heartbreak were gone in a blink of an eye. In his arms I was safe from everything. It felt as if nothing had ever happened between us, that we were at the place and time we were supposed to be at.

"We will figure this out together. Just please don't ever do that to me again. I love you, pretty girl," he said cracking a smile. He wiped the tears from my eyes, kissing me one last time.

Chapter 25

I never thought much about college. To be honest I never thought much about anything that had to do with the outside world. My life was simply planned out, up until the day of my death (which I'm hoping won't be any time soon). But today was different, today the thought was stuck in my head. I knew there would be no way the elders would agree to college, but it was nice to fantasize about Kady and me getting a place together off campus.

Kady had brought the idea up many times. She had this thing about planning everything so far ahead of schedule, that sometimes I wondered how anything ever worked out.

Today was the day we were leaving for our weeklong soccer tournament. The idea brought up so many hidden feelings. More than I ever thought I could feel about sharing a dorm with Kady for an entire week. It was just Kady and me and really no adults to tell us what to do or where we could go. Sarah wasn't bad about telling me what to do, but sometimes I felt that she thought my recklessness would get me into too much trouble; therefore, she always had an extra eye on me whether I was with my friends or alone in my room. Trust was hard for her to handle with me, and I understood why. I never made her life very easy growing up, and although I had calmed down a lot over the past seven months, I still had a way of showing my true colors. But this week had nothing to do with her, and honestly I was hoping to get into a little trouble while I was gone. I really started to get a handle on this teenage thing, and to my knowledge raising a little hell was normal behavior (no pun intended).

So when coach Riker had assigned us as roommates, Kady simply said, "Do you realize if this works out as well as I know it will, then this time next year we will be signing a lease to our own place?"

"Kady, you know it's not that easy for me to just tell my family that I want to go to college," I said, a little confused about my reply. Did I really want to go to college? It was an idea that had been playing around in my mind for the past three months after a scout offered me a scholarship as long as I passed the SAT and played as well next year as I was playing this year. Kady had already sent out her application. It was a great school, too. Sarah knew about the offer but never brought it up once. She still expected me to want to leave next month and said my time here was done and once school ended I could go back with Derek and Lucas. I was not sure I still wanted it. Not sure if I still wanted that kind of life of fear and loneliness.

"Hey, you ready? We need to leave in like twenty minutes. We still have to pick up Greg and Andy then run by the school and meet everyone. Amanda said she'll be there waiting with Coach Riker."

I still hated the fact that Amanda wormed her way into my car. I know she did it on purpose just to piss me off.

It worked.

"Yeah," I said, walking over to my room. "Let me grab my things and get the car ready."

"Are you excited? I'm so excited about this week. I cannot believe the school is actually letting us get away with no work or make-up work this whole week, and I even heard those scouts are going to be there and even more, but promise—"

"Kady," I yelled from outside my door. Man the girl could talk a mile a minute. "Deep breaths, and I know I won't pick a school without discussing it with you. I still don't see this working but if it does, we are going to the same school, promise."

"Sor—Hey, how did you know I was going to say that? Please don't tell me you can read minds now."

I laughed at that comment even though it would be pretty cool to have that kind of gift. But, no, it's against a human's free will and an invasion of privacy so no gift that cool.

"I can't read minds, but I can read your face, Kady."

Sarah was sitting in the kitchen when I returned from my room and threw my bags by the couch. I had two bags, one for cloths and my soccer gear and the other one packed with weapons. I know I wanted to give up that life, but I still couldn't bring myself to leave my weapons when I went anywhere. Rule number one we learned, "Never go anywhere unprepared…EVER."

Kady shook her head in disbelief.

We had that conversation last night as she watched me pack.

"We are going on a school trip, Kye. Is that really necessary?" Kady asked as she sat cross-legged on my bed.

"Look no one will know it's in my car, but, yes, as a Guardian I can't just expect everything to go as planned. That's how people die."

"I understand your logic, but still, this is the human world, nothing bad is going to happen."

"Well, I understand your logic, but something bad always happens when you least expect it, and *that's* my world," I relayed, painting a huge smile on my face.

She just smiled, shaking her head.

A red cooler stocked with snacks and drinks for the trip sat on the counter. Sometimes I wondered if Sarah would be sad when I left. Well, I knew she would, being as her only girl was leaving, putting her life in danger every day. But I wondered if she would be sad that she couldn't play the normal house-mother any more and cater to me and all my friends. In the past few months, she had gotten really involved in being a team mom, watching my practices, planning special events, going out for the night with the other soccer moms. She had a good life here, a normal life, but like mine it would be short lived.

Sarah grabbed the cooler and headed out to my car with Kady and me.

I froze.

What I saw standing by my car couldn't be real. It was impossible. I looked at Sarah and saw her face drop. I was surprised she didn't drop the cooler, but she held tight to it, set it gently on the ground, and ran over to the man standing there smiling.

It was Jack.

And like two high school kids, she ran into his arms putting her lips on his. And like a grossed out teen watching her parents make out, I turned around, sticking my finger in my mouth and making a gagging noise.

"Um, eww, hello children in the area," I yelled still holding a disgusted look on my face. OK it's not like it really grossed me out, and, yeah, it had been months since we'd seen him last but come on.

"Oh, stop, Kye, its romantic," Kady said, still smiling at how cute she thought they were.

"You're only saying that because it's not your parents. Hey, I know, how about we go to your house and watch your parents make out?"

That would also gross me out but I got the reaction I was hoping for.

"Ew, Kye, that's gross," Kady replied, painting the same expression on her face that I had a moment ago.

"Exactly."

Jack came over to me and like always wrapped me in his arms so tight. And like always the smell of home came to me. I could have stayed like that for days, my head resting on his chest, his scruffy bread scratching at my forehead. I missed him so much.

"Hey, baby girl, can we talk?" Jack said, still holding me.

I looked down at my phone and realized we were already running late. But I couldn't just leave without talking to him. I would be leaving this place soon and had no clue when I would see him again. His dark-green eyes looked so tired. I noticed his hair had grown out a bit in messy waves of chocolate brown reaching toward his neck. Derek had so much of Jack in him.

I looked over to Kady, but she just gave me her megawatt smile and nodded. "I'll call the others. They will understand." Kady said.

That's why I loved her so much: she always understood me so well, and knowing my situation made it that much better. Over the weekend when my family was all together, I finally told them the whole story and how I had to tell Kady everything. The boys were shocked, even a little disappointed in me, thinking maybe I had not changed at all. But Jack just smiled and reassured everyone it was for the best. He told them that I had the best intentions at heart, and in the same situation, he would have done the same thing.

I walked inside the house with him, leading him to the couch. There was something so wrong about the way he was looking at me, or maybe he was just tired.

"So what's this about?" Not that I wasn't happy to see him, but like I said before, I hated surprises. "Are the boys OK?"I knew the answer to that—they were fine. I would have read it on his face if something bad had happened to them, but still I was very confused.

Jack took a deep breath before speaking, which made me even more nervous.

"Kady's a good friend, huh; she's keeping our secret very well."

OK, now he was really making me nervous. Why bring up Kady. Oh God, did someone outside my family find out the truth about what happened. I mean, no matter what she would be fine, and a lot of other humans knew about us, kind of, but that was only because we had saved their lives from demons. Some humans didn't buy our cover stories, and honestly I think they felt better knowing we were out there protecting them. But I had saved Kady's life from an accident not created by demons, and it was forbidden to intervene in a natural accident.

"Jack, is this about Kady? Did they find out what I did?"

He shook his head.

I let out a deep breath.

"Then what? I can see it in your eyes. Something's wrong."

Jack just laughed, scratching his beard. "You always had a gift for reading people. I talked to Sarah the other day about your progress here, to make sure you were ready to go back to protecting. I don't know what it is, but I see it to. You have changed so much over the past several months, and, well, I don't know. How are you doing here?"

I didn't really know how to answer that. I mean, I was fine, but what would drag him all the way here. I thought I was doing so well with everything—and then I saw it—I was doing too well with everything, with everyone. I loved it here. I loved being around my friends and playing soccer. I loved being with Andy.

"Everything's good, and I'm excited about next month, about fulfilling my destiny," I lied

"Alikye…"

I hated when he said my name like that, so stern like I did something wrong or like when I was caught in a lie.

Jack went on. "I know you're lying. Sarah got a call from your coach saying how happy he was you accepted your scholarship."

Damn, no one was supposed to find out about that, or something like this fun confrontation would come up.

"Look, I know you told him you were thrilled about the offer, and at first I figured it was what you were supposed to say to make him feel good."

"Well, yeah…" I tried to finish, but Jack just waved it off.

"But then I come to find out that in two weeks you are scheduled to take your SAT test and…"He paused for a minute, giving me a knowing glance. "You were the one to sign up without anyone telling you to. You and Kady both, since you want to attend school together."

Again *damn*…No one was supposed to find that out either. I could have come up with a stupid excuse for why I did it, but there was no point. He knew why I did it, and I knew why I did it. I wanted to keep my options open just in case I got permission to go.

"Look, Alikye." He did it again in the same stern voice, calling out my name like I did something wrong, but I guess in his eyes I did do something wrong. I betrayed everyone by signing up to take a pointless test.

Silly, really, if you think about it.

"I know you have been getting really close to your friends and playing soccer, but you know your destiny, and this isn't it. Even if I agreed to it, you're a Legacy; they will never let you throw away your skills to live with humans. They won't allow it.

His accusations I could take since they were true, but to tell me my life was not my own to decide—now that got me worked up. Shouldn't it be my choice what I want to do with it? I'm the one who has to live it day to day, and I was starting to think this was where my destiny wanted me to be. These were the people I was meant to spend my life with. I don't know, but at that moment I realized I didn't want to go back. There were too many rules and politics

"Look, I hear your concern—well, rather *their* concern to control me—but I have to go. I'm already late." I got off the couch and headed toward the door. I knew he would follow and protest my attitude and maybe even suggest that it would not be a good idea for me to go. So I said something I should have never said: "If you're going to ruin my life, then let me just have this one last thing." Without looking into those eyes, I walked out the door without another word to anyone.

******

I pulled up to the front of school forty-five minutes late. When I picked up Andy and Greg at Greg's house, I still didn't feel like talking. On the trip over, I told Kady what had happened.

"So what are you going to do then?" I knew she wasn't asking me that for her own benefit. I knew she was just implying it was my decision alone.

"I don't know" was all I could say.

Coach Riker was pissed at my arriving so late. Amanda just looked annoyed. I didn't care. Let her be annoyed. It was actually the only upside to this day so far.

"Because Kady called earlier and explained it was your father, and he's only on leave for the weekend." Riker said. "You're not going to get a lecture, but let me be clear, next time we will go without you." I turned to Kady giving her my best smile, well nice job to her, always a genius under pressure.

I knew that was a lie because school policy states if driving to a school function in your own vehicle, you must be accompanied by a teacher or staff member as long as both teammates and parents agree to not using the bus. But I decided to just apologize and nod my head like it would never happen again.

Coach Riker sat up front, sticking Andy in between the two of us. No complaints there. But behind me there were enough complaints to go home and call it a day. We hadn't even pulled out of the school yet before Amanda and Kady began to argue about the space in the back. For two small girls, boy, they took up enough room, leaving poor Greg squished in the corner behind me.

My head was still reeling about what Jack had said to me and even what I had said to him. What was I going to do? I only had a month to figure it out, and someone was bound to get hurt.

There was no easy choice.

The ride was long. The sun started to raise high into the sky, escaping the coverage of the clouds. The temperature started to rise as well, and sunrays coated my skin. The light breeze felt nice though, blowing through my curls as they brushed against my face and covered my right eye. With a small twitch of my neck, my hair tossed itself to my back. In my head I sang all the songs on the radio, getting lost in the upbeat tunes I had put together for the ride. I beat my thumbs on the steering wheel and tossed my head around as if I were the one singing on stage and making my debut. Andy just watched and laughed, telling me how much he loved the way I could get lost in myself.

Chapter 26

From up ahead lights flashed red and blue. Orange barricades were scattered all around the crash scene. The traffic began to back up, making it difficult to turn around and head the other direction. Something big was going on, but they were keeping the information away from the public. I looked farther into the scene, past the numerous cars. My surroundings became blurry. Everything froze. I watched as a sheet of colors danced in the heat, shimmering from the sunlight that slightly touched it.

I passed the cars.

Tied around four six-foot cement barricades was a thick grayish blanket of nylon walling. I couldn't get through it. Whatever it was, it was blocking my vision. I tried to move around it, but all I got was a glimpse of broken gravel, smashed cars and the smell of blood. I was snapped back to reality as I turned the corner. The world sped up, and the colors dissipated.

"Can we just turn around and go home? We can meet the team tomorrow," I groaned to Riker.

I knew there wouldn't be any way of passing, but I couldn't tell them that. I couldn't tell them I saw what had happened. The entire road was caved in, and some cars were lost in the rubble. People were hurt. Riker didn't look pleased, but he told everyone just to be patient.

Time passed and everyone started getting just as irritated as I was. The team would be expecting us at the game tomorrow, but that would mean waking up a dawn and driving another four hours to get to the exact spot we were in now and heading another two hours to our final destination. We would be restless and unable to give 110 percent, which we would have to in order to win the title. Andy looked over the map. He was seeking another way to go, but there were no other roads. We were trapped in a one-horse town heading to another one-horse town in the middle of the state with nothing even close to a major highway or interstate until we would finally reach the city.

"You know," Amanda's voice rang out over all the noise from horns and sirens, "if you would just get into the twenty-first century and get GPS, we wouldn't be stuck here looking at an ancient map that I know Andy stupid ass can't read. I'm just saying."

"Amanda, shut up before I make you walk home. You are giving me an effing headache and pissing me the F off," I yelled as I turned around to face her. I clenched my teeth, scolding her as fire flashed in my eyes. It was getting too hot to deal with her sarcasm. I needed her to give me a moment to think.

"Girls, knock it off, and, Alikye, that is not nice to say to another teammate."

Was Mr. Riker kidding? All day Amanda had been crying over this and that, and no one would say a word. All day she complained and mocked me. All day she criticized me and my car. No one said a word. But the moment I say something to shut her up, to put her in her place, to let her know she had no right to speak to anyone like that, I get yelled at. Sometimes I wish I could tell Amanda what I really was, or tell the whole school that I was an angel hybrid that fought demons and monsters every day. I wish I could let them know that if it wasn't for my race they would be slaves to the darkness. Maybe I would get the respect I deserved. But as Sarah would say, "We do this because it is our destiny. We do this because we are the only creatures who can. We do not do this so humans can worship us." Sarah always got into my head to point me in the right direction, even when I didn't need it or ask for it.

"Sorry, Riker, I'll be nice." That was all I could say while imagining beating the crap out of her and watching her cry, which I would never do, but thinking about it made me feel better. I threw her a hateful smirk when Riker looked away for a split second, sending Andy and Kady into a fit of giggles under their breaths. They got my mental picture just not as violent; well, at least Andy didn't get the full picture. Kady did, knowing what I was capable of. It was her own little defense if ever needed. She felt safe around me, and it made me feel good to have a friend like that.

After sitting for about forty-five minutes, Riker was out of my car and walking toward the police cars. I guess he was getting as impatient as we were. We all wanted answers.

The sun climbed higher into the sky, escaping from the coverage of the clouds, sending full solar flares our way. The sun soaked into my skin, and sweat dripped from my body giving me a wet shimmery glow. The water was gone, and the only hydration I was getting was salty.

The others began to get antsy, rubbing wet cloths down their arms, around their necks, and across their faces. It was getting too hot to stay comfortable. The air became thick from endless exhaust that spewed out black poison and combined with the humidity, causing my lungs to burn and my head to spin.

Andy's hot flesh stuck to my naked arm, sending chills down my body. His sweaty hand lay flat on my knee, causing my blood pressure to raise and speeding up my pulse. In that second he knew what was going on as he felt my body tense. He locked his gaze on mine, laughing. I gently bit my bottom lip, smiling at how cute he looked with his hair windblown in his beautiful face.

"Get a room," Amanda said hard, scrunching her nose at me.

"Screw you," I snapped.

Amanda was about to say something back, ready to strike like a snake. I was ready to strike back. She was playing with fire, and with no adult around, she was about to get burned. But we both saw Mr. Riker walking back to the car and closed our mouths. "Another time for that," I said under my breath. Riker looked frustrated, which for me was not a good sign given it was my fault we were trapped. But what was I supposed to do—not see Jack after months? Not give him the hug I had been waiting for since he left. He was the only Dad I knew, and I missed him. I missed my old life, but I didn't know how to let go of this life. I didn't know how to walk away from Andy or Kady now. I started to get frustrated over something I still had a few weeks to figure out. It still wasn't long enough but that wasn't the case here, I would have to think about it, but we had to get out of this mess first.

"Good news or bad news?" Riker said nonchalant.

"Bad first, that way good seems even better," I said trying to lighten the mood, but that was not happening, so I just backed into my seat and stayed quiet.

"I talked to an officer, and he said that the road collapsed due to rushed road work, and they have people on it now, but it's going to take at least twenty-four hours to make it safe enough to pass."

"Good then," Kady said before Amanda got the chance to make a smart remark about everything being my fault.

"He said that a mile down the road is a turnoff, and up five miles is a town that is not on the map, but they do have a motel and a diner. If we get there now, we might not get a room due to I guess some kind of festival they are having, but it's a good shot, and we will be on time to our game and well-rested."

"Whatever. Fine. But it better be nice with a pool," Amanda said.

"Amanda, it's a motel in the middle of God knows where. It's most likely gross and filled with bugs," I said, laughing to myself as she flinched, thinking about sleeping with bugs. I have to say it was entertaining until I got yelled at again by Riker for reading a book by its cover, as he put it.

I wasn't happy about staying, but it meant not driving home. It also meant an unfamiliar place, and unfamiliar places made me paranoid. This whole situation made me paranoid, but then again I'm always paranoid.

The turnoff was well-hidden, and the only way to spot it was to look for it. No one could have guessed there would be a town in the middle of a thick, plush forest. The dirt road made it hard to drive faster than fifteen miles per hour, and it took a big toll on my little classic car. Every bump we hit impacted her very old frame, making me worry about the unnecessary damage to my beautiful vehicle.

But I soon took a liking to my surroundings and admired the breathtaking beauty. Large oak trees outlined the path of the road, blocking out the sun and all of the contaminated pollution the world put off. Bushes of wild exotic flowers painted colors all around. The plethora of smells gathering together created an overwhelming pleasure of one new scent filling my lungs with purity. The crisp cool air blew through my curls, flushing away all the heat from my body. It felt as if we had driven threw a black hole and turned up in a forest never touched by humans or any of their diseased machines. This world was pure and natural. Every blade of grass that grew was clean and healthy. Every plant dispersed plump, juicy fruit and veggies. On a hot day of ninety-eight degrees, this place stayed at a comfortable seventy-two degrees. It was paradise.

A ten-foot iron gate stood between us and the small Old English town. On both sides the gate stopped at two very odd looking trees. The thick, cream-color trunk twisted and twirled around itself, it's long branches spreading eight or nine feet out. The light-green leaves covered every inch of every branch. They did not look native to this state or this country, but I couldn't quite put my finger on where they originated from.

In seconds an old short man walked from the forest to my window, staring me up and down. To stay alert I opened my senses to him. He smelled human, old and dirty, but the smell was human.

"Welcome to Hidden Falls. You are just in time, children. The last of the rooms stay open for your presence. Two are still available, and all the information you need for the fun festivities are at your beck and call. The fun lasts from dawn till dusk...enjoy." Without saying a word, he motioned to drive through the now opened gate. He didn't bother to leave us with any kind of direction, but this town had only one main street and a basic route to the motel.

At first glance you would think you were in Disney World. Red rustic cobblestone bricks covered every inch of the street. They had no cars, so the needs for sidewalks were absent. Bike racks replaced parking spots. Each one-story building was painted a different pastel color, creating a postcard of places you would see in Norway, separated by an inch or two. The street was short, maybe a foot less than half a mile. Everything needed was all together. The grocery store was small, only handling items needed by the town's people. Next to that an open building sat, three walls in all stocked with the biggest and freshest fruits and vegetables, most growing out of season or impossible to grow in Florida, period, but they managed to grow it here. Best guess they had a well-supplied greenhouse somewhere. The coffee shop and book store shared a building after someone had apparently torn down the wall that separated them. Outside, iron flower-inscribed tables and chairs flowed outward, inviting the town folk in to read and relax. A drug store, a doctor's office, and an outdoor redneck store were across the street. Next to them was a run-down bar lit up by beer signs. A funny looking man posted in the front, a big sombrero tilted down covering his face, got a defiant laugh out of me, and by the looks of him, he wasn't real. To the end on my right side, a well-packed diner opened the doors; the smell of grime and grease erupted in my hungry stomach, making my mouth water. The town was cute and quaint, a family's perfect dream.

At the end of the dead-end road, past the only turn that would lead us to the motel, was a building that looked to be from the sixteen hundreds. The two-story town hall was old and brittle, reminding me of a plantation in the southern states; six white pillars framed the outside, a balcony wrapped around the entire building with two sets of French doors standing noticeable at the front. In the middle of the circle driveway was a twelve-foot statue ten feet around made of marble. Three lovely older women, all holding different items, made quite an impression. From the left the first woman cradled a book in her arms, holding it to her chest and protecting it. The next held a cane between her bare feet, both hands placed on top of the oval aqua-green stone; it was no taller than her waist. The last woman held a box secured in both hands but away from her body as if she wanted to give it to me. It was stunning, carved and crafted well. The details made me think of the Statue of David by Michelangelo.

It took me back to a time when I saw some of his work in Italy one summer. His beauty created stories of the past living in the future. I imagined one day going back to share the beauty with Andy. Feeling the warmth of his hand tightly intertwined in mine as we walked the streets of Florence or sitting together curled up against one another in a gondola while slowly being taken away on a journey through Venice. I would give anything to create our own memories of love and passion as we spend a romantic weekend away just the two of us.

If only—

"Yeah, it's great, but can we keep moving? You turn here." From out of my daydream came Amanda's voice yet again demanding me to do something.

"I was admiring the statue," I said through gritted teeth. "Chill, dude, we are going."

Chapter 27

We drove up the steep brick-paved hill about a half a mile. We pulled up to the back of the one-story motel. The bare cream wall had no way of entry. I looked around confused. Everyone else seemed just as confused over what appeared to be the motel but was just a single plain wall, definitely not as inviting as it should be.

"The front is just around the corner." A tired old lady appeared out of nowhere, one wrinkly crooked finger pointing in the direction of the small driveway that led to the back…well…the front of the building. "Please come this way, child, you will find the accommodations to your liking."

"Why does it feel as if she wants to cook us in a large pot and make meat pie out of our bodies," Andy whispered to me loud enough for the people in the car to hear but quiet enough to escape the woman's hearing.

I should have responded to that comment with a slight laugh or a cute smile. If not for my conscience screaming it could definitely be true. If it weren't for the smell of human she let off, I would have figured her to be a hag. A creature who appears to be an innocent old lady to draw in young children for dinner, meaning they would be her dinner.

"Hansel and Gretel, wow. Aren't you a little too old for fairy tales, Andy. I guess leaving me for her," Amanda pointed her manicured little finger my way as she finished, "really put a damper on your manhood."

Andy did not look pleased with the childish joke. I could tell he thought it was his right to protect me or maybe it was his ego, but he was ready to lash out. His face began turning red, and at that moment I had to do something.

Andy seemed to really react to any comment about him and me being together. I, for one, didn't let that bother me. I loved him, and I knew he loved me. We got together after he had already broken it off with Amanda. But Andy hated being seen as the guy who betrayed one woman for another, and if I didn't watch my back, he would do the same to me when the right opportunity came.

Andy grew up with three older sisters and parents who were well-known in the local church. They drilled it into his brain that the worst thing you could ever do is disrespect a woman. They always asked how he would feel if a man treated one of his sisters badly and if he could live with himself if he treated his sisters badly. Andy took pride in being a good guy. He may sometimes act like he's a big jock who could get anyone he wanted, but when push came to shove, he would never act on those impulses.

I jerked the car as hard as I could to my right, slamming on my brakes, causing a push-pull reaction when the car came to a stop in front of another ten-foot iron gate.

I smiled because it got everyone to stop and give me a moment of silence until I could park. I drove through and pulled into a fifteen-car parking lot. All but one spot had been occupied in the far back. From behind me the five-hundred-pound gate slammed shut with a clunk, locking automatically. For such a hidden town, why would they feel the need to own two large iron gates to protect absolutely nothing worth any real value? The whole perimeter was enclosed from road to road with a seven-foot brick wall. The place, if I didn't know any better, seemed more like a prison, and I didn't do well in an entrapped environment.

Around the many cars was a smaller gate leading to the courtyard in the middle of the circular motel and the only door leading to the outside world.

The courtyard was blanketed with patches of sweet northern green grass. A large two-hundred-year-old oak tree spread its branches wide enough to give shade to most of the eight-hundred-square-foot area. Three wooden picnic tables were placed five feet from one another. A garden filled with tulips grew to the far end, complimenting the pink office door.

The old woman pushed us on our way, showing us to the last two remaining conjoined rooms.

"I do not advise for the girls and the boys to be sleeping together. This is an old fashioned town, and it seems that no one here is currently wed to one another."

"Thank you, ma'am, and I assure you that the boys will be in one room and the girls will take the other," Riker chimed in, complying with the woman's demands.

At least any kind of paranoid feeling I was having had now been banished with the realization that I would be sharing a room with Amanda.

"Great," I said under my breath.

I wanted to take a look around the town and survey my surroundings. I needed to check the sanity of this place before I got comfortable about being here. I knew everything would be fine, but as a Guardian we were trained to check, no matter what we saw. Andy and Kady agreed to go with me, but Riker thought it to be a good idea for the whole group to go and get some food.

The old woman had arranged for us to be picked up by a golf cart. I asked if I could just take my car, but she made a valid point when she asked where I would park it.

"What an odd way of life," I said out loud to myself. "And seriously, this place, it's almost like their little Utopia, which is not possible." On and on I spoke to myself, not noticing that I had drawn the attention of all my peers. The confused looks on their faces said they'd heard it all. Except for Kady—she looked nervous because I looked nervous. I turned and gave her a smile, reassuring her we were fine, and that I would tell her otherwise.

"Weird much," Amanda said.

147

I jerked my head toward Amanda, my silver eyes locked on her hazel eyes, but not one word came from my mouth as I rumbled through my brain trying to speak.

"Hello," she said. "Did you, like, go insane—well, more insane then you already are?"

"Oh, sorry. Have you guys noticed how odd this place seems," I asked to no one in particular, ignoring Amanda's stupid comment, or maybe she was right, and this time I cracked. I wasn't alerted on any awkward smells or demonic creatures. The humans seem to be using their own free will. Maybe I was going crazy.

"You know you do this all the time, talk to yourself?. Do you live in a whole different world in there?" Greg asked, using a knocking motion toward my head

I guess you could say I do. I looked over at Kady. She smirked at me, knowing it was true. Greg did have a point. I was always getting caught speaking to no one about nothing. My brain reeled a million miles per hour, and being able to store everything in it didn't help much on the sanity front. If I needed something important out of it, it took a second to go through everything, and that caused me to talk as I looked. Andy always thought it was cute and would watch me for as long as it took. He would sit quietly waiting for me to be done.

Before I had a chance to answer Greg, a cart pulled up driven by who could only be the mayor. His appearance reminded me of Santa Clause, fat and stumpy, long white beard, and completely bald (maybe that's why he was wearing a baseball cap).

"Hello there, children. How about I give you a quick tour, and then I will drop you off at the diner. Oh, and by the way, I'm Frank Pullman, the town's mayor, but please just call me Frank," Frank said, holding his hand out to Mr. Riker in a polite gesture to shake hands.

"This town doesn't have much to offer, but, trust me, it will be a great experience."

"Yeah, right. And why does everyone call us children? Do I look like a child?" Amanda whispered to Mr. Riker.

Mr. Riker snapped his head toward Amanda, pressing his lips together and widening his eyes as if to say, *that's enough.*

I laughed as she rolled her eyes and tilted her shoulders back in agitation.

"There is no service." I slid my cell phone back in my pocket. "Are there any landlines we could use to call our folks?" I asked.

"Well, as you can see, we do not have cell phone towers nor do we have Internet. We are in no need for those kinds of technologies, and I'm afraid with the road collision, our landlines were knocked out. We are lucky we still have electricity."

"No worries. The team's assistant coach will let your families know—I called him while we were still on the road," Mr. Riker said.

With a very jolly and polite giggle, the mayor finished, "OK, then, let's go." A large smile was plastered on his face.

He started on the tour with a history lesson, giving us a layout of the land. He went through dates and times and generations of families still living there, enough to put anyone to sleep, which I could have sworn Andy and Greg were.

"So what's the story behind the statue? It's beautiful," I said.

"I'm glad you asked. The annual festival takes place every year. You children will enjoy all the festivities, and it's to *die* for."

Chills ran down my spine, and all the subtleties I was feeling went back to paranoia.

There was something wrong about this man. He kept a smile on his face, but it didn't look endearing. He looked scared and coached and a little creepy to be honest. He looked like he was hiding something.

I didn't want to think the worst, so instead all I could think of was that this town was probably being used to smuggle in illegal substances. And the arrival of so many new faces caused the town to become unsettled. It would explain the iron gates. Thinking about all the crazy things that might be going on put a smile on my face and warned me I should stop watching all those crime shows on TV because my imagination was going haywire. But it was better than thinking the truth, that maybe there was something going on—my gut told me to believe the truth.

"I like the first idea," I said to myself.

Kady looked over at me, her eyes squinting. I didn't want to be rude and interrupt this man while he was talking, but he was beginning to put me to sleep.

"Dude, you think this place is a cover-up for like drug trafficking or maybe money laundering or both, or maybe they are trafficking weapons of some sort and our being here is putting a damper on their activities," I whispered to Kady with excitement in my eyes. "Alikye, you have gone crazy. Lay off your crime shows, but it would be cool, right?" She laughed, shaking her head.

We laughed together, causing Greg and Andy to look at us in wonder. We shook it off and kept it between us.

"It is to honor our three founding families." We pulled up to the statue. The mayor looked toward the chiseled women as if he wanted to kneel and pray.

We all sat in silence for a few seconds.

"These brave women came to the new world with nothing but a dream. Together they built this wonderful town, and that, my children, is the reason why they will never be forgotten."

"Then, of course, we will be there. It sounds delightful," I said. During my daydreaming I had missed half of what he actually said but figured I should at least pretend I had been paying attention.

I made a gesture to part ways. The diner was not too much farther, and it was such a nice clear day. A walk would be perfect. I started to walk with the others, trailing in front on my own, when I spotted the most angelic little girl in a pink dress skipping up to the mayor. All I could think was she was adorable with her light-golden-brown hair put up in pigtails. She was humming a sweet little tune.

She came up closer and her golden-brown eyes sparkled at me. She smiled.

I froze.

In less time than it took for me to blink, her angelic face turned gruesome and hideous. She was old and wrinkly. Her teeth were dirt-brown, and her eyes, black as night, locked on mine. All I could see was death. Crows took to the sky, hissing and screeching, circling the demon that stood in place of the little girl. She smelled of sage and lavender.

I was, for the first time in a long time, scared. I wasn't prepared for this, and by this I meant I had no clue what I was dealing with. Just as I saw her true self I knew what she was in theory, but worst of all she knew what I was. She read me the minute I saw her.

She winked at me and skipped over to the mayor, still humming her sweet tune. *There went my trafficking theory.*

Chapter 28

A sick feeling caught me by surprise. I steadied myself, trying to keep down what little I had in my stomach, and my hands twitched and tightened. I was terrified; this was supposed to be a simple trip, a simple place to spend the night until the morning when, for the next week, I could live out my life as a normal girl until it was time for me to get back to situations like this. Not now, not here, and not with my friends by my side.

The air around me grew cold and damp. To the others everything was just the same. To me at that moment I felt the true town and smelled the stench of death and decay. It might have all been in my mind but not that little girl—she was real, and I was in trouble.

Everyone saw that my demeanor had changed. My body language had shifted to a more negative sense, and I had gone back to the safe place in my head, shuffling through all my memories as if I were reading a book lain out in front of me. I turned through the pages, vividly seeing everything I had written down, trying to come up with the right information about not only this town but the humans who inhabited it. I was walking and in a deep concentration when I felt the warmth and security of a hand slide gently across my waist, knocking me out of my trance.

"Hey, you OK." Andy looked over at me, bringing my hand into his.

"Yeah, I'm just hungry," I lied, my words shaky, unsettling.

If something supernatural was going on in this town, the worst thing that I could do would be to panic. I couldn't alarm my friends, and stressing me out right now wouldn't help anything. I took a deep breath and cleared my head.

"I will deal with it later. Right now we are all safe." I tried to convince myself. Over and over I kept saying it. I was still hungry, and until I had a chance to slip away from everyone, there was nothing I could do but act as if nothing was wrong. "But how," I said under my breath.

How was I supposed to stay in this town, eat their food, and rest in their jail-like motel when I knew it was my job to do something, but was it? I was, after all, normal. For now I was out of the game, and lately I had been considering getting out altogether.

"That's never going to happen, and this is my problem. This is who I truly am."

I liked it better when I thought this place was smuggling drugs or something. That wasn't helping. It wasn't funny anymore.

The diner was coming up on my right, and the smell of grease made my stomach rumble. I was hungry, but I didn't realize I was that hungry.

Food would be good now. Maybe she didn't recognize me. Who was I trying to kid? She knew who I was just as I knew she wasn't human.

I made sure this time to keep all my thoughts to myself; it wasn't a cute laughing matter like before. I wanted to burst, scream, cry, something—not just casually walk up to a diner and sit and eat while we all have small talk about whatever, ignoring the fact that at any time something chaotic could occur, and I'm by myself and unprepared. I needed Derek and Lucas, and for once I could admit to myself I needed them more than ever. No Internet—no problem. The greatest thing about being a Guardian was that our technology was so much better. With a small device, we Guardians have Internet everywhere by using the earth's satellite systems we stole from the government. Not one soul noticed, all these years. It was pretty much like Mi-Fi, the same size and all, except our device reached out to the entire world, not just cell towers. That made me feel a little better. I wasn't stranded with no way of communication. I had to get back to the room, but I had to eat first and act normal.

The diner was small and quaint. Nothing new to this town—everything was small and quaint. Fluorescent lights illuminated the room. A large table-top bar sat adjacent to the kitchen where cooks would yell out their orders, calling for one of the three waitresses to pick up. Five booths lined the brick wall, and six tables sat in between them and the bar. One large circle booth sat next to the only large window in the diner.

I noticed when we walked through the door, all the townsfolk stopped what they were doing and stared at us with great big smiles. The only people to ignore us were the out-of-towners who looked miserable for the same reason we did: we were stuck here by force. They sat at their tables, face pressed to their plates, shoveling food into their mouths, wanting anything but to be trapped here.

The server ran to us, greeting us with a perky "Hello" and a jolt in her step as she brought us to our table, a large booth that fit six. Kady and Andy sat next to me. Greg sat next to Kady, and Amanda next to Andy. Mr. Riker sat at the end of our round booth, next to Greg.

"Mountain Dew, please, double veggie burger, extra cheese, fries and barbecue sauce on the side, and a dessert menu also." Easy enough. I ate the same thing every day, and as predictable as I was, Andy was the exact same.

"Water with lemon," Andy said. "Grilled double chicken breast, plain, and veggies as my side."

As he said the words, I sat in silence, mouthing them. Kady laughed.

"How do you eat all that crap and stay in perfect shape? Have you ever gained a pound?" Greg looked at me as my plate hit the table, and before I took one bite, I ordered my dessert, knowing I would finish every last morsel of food.

"Greg, you never ask a lady those kinds of questions," Riker said.

"Good thing she's not a lady," Amanda interrupted as she started to pick at half of a ham sandwich and a house salad with no dressing.

"Amanda, that's enough," Riker scolded her, after I gracefully swiped my hand in her direction indicating I did nothing that time.

"No, not a problem," I snapped, glaring at Amanda. "She just wishes she could eat like me, and, no, Greg, I don't gain weight. High metabolism I suppose."

"Yeah, a bathroom maybe," Amanda said.

"Jealous ah," I finished.

"Girls, enough. Just finish eating. We have a lot to go over when we get back to the room; this may give us a chance to go over some moves. We also may be able to practice in the courtyard," Riker said as he started on his burger and fries.

Amanda was just jealous. Any girl would die to be able to eat anything and never gain a pound. I guess my genes just burn more calories than a human's, or maybe my body works differently in that department. I mean, I eat a lot and yet nothing. My fat percentage is five, and my muscles stay lean and fit whether I work out or not. Since I hit puberty, my weight has always stayed at 105. My complexion is also perfect. I have never had a pimple or a blemish. Just lucky, I guess.

We got back to the rooms as the sun slowly started to set, bringing the cool air rustling threw the trees. I excused myself from the group, saying I needed a shower and that I would catch up after. As I mentioned that, I saw Andy's eyebrows shoot up, indicating a question of whether or not I was hinting for him to join me. I shot him an irritated look, smiling so he wouldn't think I was serious.

"Oh, so now you're taking a shower, princess? Great, let's all wait for her to take forever," Amanda snapped.

"Twenty minutes, I promise. I just need to relax," I said, assuring Riker I wasn't skipping out on practice runs even though I was the best on the team.

"That's fine. You know this stuff anyway."

"Thanks." I turned to Kady. "Do you mind if I use your stuff. I forgot mine?"

"No, it's in my bag. Go for it," she replied.

"Do you need some help, pretty girl," Andy said, winking at me. The heat from his body came crashing toward me. That undeniable passion between the two of us never ceased to amaze me. Sometimes I never knew what to make of it. I heard when you're in love with someone, your whole life changes, but I didn't think this was the same. I wanted to say yes. I knew it was a joke, but that urge to say yes was on my tongue—just like the times he's pushed to have sex. It's always there, that feeling of wanting him. But, as always, it's a no. I just couldn't go that far—sleeping with a human—not until I figured out my own choices in life.

I drew a smile on my face.

"Andy, not appropriate," Mr. Riker yelled, unhappy with the joke.

Andy threw his hands in the air in surrender. "Dude, just a joke. Alikye, I'm kidding, love."

"Yeah, OK, babe." I laughed, and for a moment all my problems had disappeared as the whole room laughed, and just like a shooting star, the happiness was gone and the problem was back. Who was that little girl—what was she?

I ran the water while I sat on the cold hard floor typing in the code to access my account. I scrolled down to Lucas's e-mail address and typed in 1404, which was our code for HELP.

I waited for one of the boys to do the thirty-minute check we do in case of an emergency and we need to have face time on the computers.

Five minutes till six.

I waited anxiously.

Chapter 29

The anticipation of Alikye coming back made Lucas jittery and overexcited. The past months had not been easy for either of them, and now, only a month away, they would all be together.

Lucas lay on his bed in the home of another Guardian he had been staying with, awaiting orders for a mission he had been working on with Derek for the past month. Derek had gone out with Tanner to investigate while Lucas stayed in, researching on his computer and making random calls to the elders. Tanner was a hard-looking kid. Young in age, but after the death of his partner and mate, life took a toll on him. He had light shaggy hair that was never tamed and sparkling blue eyes. He was small and lean for a Guardian, but he was fast and had a lot of skills. Dark shadows took to his eyes most of the time, and he was always quiet.

Lucas looked at the clock.

"Six o'clock. Time to check my e-mail, and hopefully Jack got back to me on this." No one was home, so Lucas realized he was just talking to himself. He typed in his codes and rummaged through his 152 e-mails sent in the last twenty-four hours, most of which he'd read but never erased. He had to be careful not to miss a beat in case of an important message he was liable for that could be a life-or-death situation.

One-four-zero-four—what's this all about? Lucas thought as he clicked on the link to the video chat, waiting as the computer loaded.

"Luke, are you up there?" Derek yelled from downstairs. His voice echoed through the almost empty wood-frame home on the outskirts of Nashville.

"Yeah, dude. I got a—"

"Luke, get down here now!" Derek shouted, startling Lucas.

"OK, on my way. What's up?" Lucas started walking down the stairs, forgetting about the urgent video chat Alikye sent him.

******

"What the hell!" I was staring at a blank room. The walls were dingy green, and patches of wallpaper were falling to the ground. In the corner of the room was Lucas's signature army-backpack. He was there a second ago but just walked away, yelling at who I'm only guessing would be Derek. That's just like them to start yelling at one another and completely ignore me; at least not much has changed. Unless one of them was in the same area as Lucas's computer, they would never be able to hear me. And if I yelled my friends would know something was going on in here. I had to just wait.

This was just my luck in the midst of the most dangerous thing I could think of. Now that I had learned a thing or two about being levelheaded in my newfound change, I was by myself. I would give those boys five minutes, and then I was going to sign off and try to contact Jack.

I needed to hear their voices again. It had been so long since we talked. They thought it to be in my best interest to give me the space I needed after they came to see me at the start of the New Year—we had not talked since.

I loved Andy with every ounce of my soul, but Derek and Lucas brought out the real and true me. They were *home* for me, even if we never really had a real home. Being with them felt perfect. But being with Andy felt safe.

"What the hell are they doing, and what are they yelling about?… What?" I started to laugh so hard tears fill my eyes. Derek was reaming Lucas out about something with his car. Lucas was the worst driver ever, so I could only imagine him crashing Derek's Toyota Tundra into something and covering it up.

"We don't have time for this boy's life or death—that's what one-four-zero-four means, damn." I rambled on and on to myself, starting to get agitated.

****

"What the hell did you do to my truck, Lucas, and when were you going to tell me." Derek's face turned red. He loved that truck. It was fully equipped with everything you could want and then some.

Derek had noticed the truck pulling to his left when he and Tanner took it out. He checked the frame and saw that the left tire was crooked Lucas was the only other person to drive it in the last couple days, and yesterday morning, before Lucas borrowed it, the truck was fine.

"Dude, I didn't do anything, and we have more important matters than your stupid truck, Al—"

"Stupid? You want to see stupid. Look in the mirror, Bro, and also you will see bloody after I break your nose." Derek had steam coming from his ears, and veins were popping out of his forehead. He clinched his fists tightly, placing them to the side, waiting for Lucas to make some nonsense excuse.

"Dude, Alikye's in trouble. She needs help," Lucas finally blurted out.

"What? What are you talking about? She's with Mom and Dad."

"She sent me a one-four-zero-four video chat."

Hearing that Alikye needed help, that she was in trouble, made Derek forget all about his truck. With Lucas at his heals, he ran upstairs in hyperspeed, entering the room within a split second.

They saw Alikye sitting on a bathroom floor, staring up at the ceiling, biting her fingers, which she only did when she was really stressed.

"Kye, what the hell is going on," Derek said, catching his breath.

"Finally! What is wrong with you two—screaming at one another about a stupid truck when I have been sitting here for ten minutes? If it wasn't important, I wouldn't have written one-four-zero-four. You know—the code word for *help*!" she yelled. Alikye was always feisty when she was angry.

In a more relaxed voice, Derek surrendered his ego and started, "All right, we are here now. What is going on? Are Mom and Dad OK?"

"Yeah, they're fine, but I figured I should call you before alarming them."

"You're not with them?"

"No. Anyway..." Alikye started to explain.

Lucas and Derek sat back, letting her explain everything from the soccer trip to the road collision. She described the town and the people in the town and what she saw when she ran into the little girl.

Derek started to get nervous; he didn't like not knowing all the facts and being so far from Alikye when she was stuck in a bad situation. He always felt as if he needed to be her protector even though he knew she was fully capable of protecting herself and anyone else around, but this was different. There was so much they could be dealing with, and they didn't have any idea what this was.

Alikye explained to them about the humans she was with, and when she got to a boy named Andy, her voice changed to a softer pitch. Lucas didn't react. He either didn't hear, which Derek knew he did, or he was denying hearing it, which Derek knew he probably was. Regardless, Alikye was attached to these humans—even if she did try to play it off as just feeling obligated to save them.

Derek and Lucas bid their farewells and gave her orders to stay close to her computer until further notice; they would contact her after they made a few phone calls.

"Be safe," Lucas said softly.

"I will. I love you guys," Alikye said before the screen went blank.

Without skipping a beat, Derek was on the phone with Jack, telling him all he knew as Lucas, now accompanied by Tanner, went over all their notes.

From one call to another, hour after hour, they were no closer than when they started. The sun had already set and night took to the sky. Still nothing.

Derek started to get frustrated. Tanner's new partner, Haden, had joined the search, but just like the others, she was getting nowhere.

Haden was a beautiful girl with long, straight brown hair and hazel eyes and a slender body with defined curves. She was a few years older than Alikye but not as skilled as her. Her parents, like most, were killed a couple years back. She teamed up with Tanner after his former partner was killed by a rogue demon. They worked well together, and having each other helped with their grieving period. Now they were back on their game and ready for action.

"What about the Brits? They have more information than we do," Haden suggested after a period of silence.

"It wouldn't hurt. I'm on it," Derek replied.

Derek walked out of the house and took a seat on the front porch as he dialed the number of one of the oldest elders still alive.

Anastasis was one of the elders for Europe. She was approaching 150 years old but didn't look a day over forty. Her long black hair and ruby-red eyes accented her curvy body. She spoke more from the eighteen hundreds and carried more information than any other elder. And like Alikye she also was a Legacy.

Derek felt uneasy speaking to a Guardian of her standing, so his words came out shaky and unsteady. Anastasis laughed, reassuring him there was nothing to be nervous about. That didn't make speaking to her any easier.

"I will do my best, young sir. You will soon hear from me. Good day," Anastasis said, hanging up the phone.

Derek took a deep breath, gathering up all his confidence before entering the room. "She is calling me back. She said not to worry, she will find the answer," Derek said

What only took thirty minutes seemed like days to Derek, and when the phone rang he was up in seconds preparing himself. Derek grabbed the phone with no struggle from Lucas. "Hello, Anastasis," he said nervously.

Back and forth he paced while Anastasis explained what she knew. Derek's face dropped from nervous to dead terror. Lucas knew this was bad, really bad. He waited patiently for Derek to hang up.

His heart pounded through his chest.

The phone clicked shut, and tears filled Derek's eyes. He placed his hands over his face. It was far worse than any of them had expected. Far worse than any situation Alikye had ever been in, and for a minute Derek didn't see any way for her to get herself out of there *and* save her friends.

"We need to go now." They grabbed their things and were out the door in seconds.

Chapter 30

I was still wet from the quick shower I jumped into before leaving the bathroom. I threw on boy shorts and a worn T-shirt then lay on my bed, collecting my thoughts.

"They will know what to do. They will call Jack, and everything will be fine," I kept telling myself as I lay in the quiet room. Laughter came from the other room; I could hear Andy and Greg ganging up on Amanda about a play or two she came up with. For the first time ever, I heard the sound of Amanda's sweet voice laughing.

"Maybe it would be better if I left. Everything seemed good when I wasn't around, and I never heard Amanda laugh before." I indulged myself in self-pity. It was true: if it wasn't for me, they wouldn't be in this situation. They all would be on a bus already up north. "I don't know what to do. Please, someone help."

"What do you need help with?"

I jumped to my feet faster than it took Kady to blink, my wet hair wrapping around my face, causing me to spit out a few of my dead ends. "You scared me."

"How? You always know when someone is coming, and by the way I wouldn't do that. What if someone saw? It definitely looked unnatural."

"I know. I don't know, I'm just stressed. I don't like being so trapped in a place like this."

I didn't want to alarm her. Everything about my life made her feel uneasy, not me but the demon thing did. She assured me she was OK with it all, but who was she kidding? No normal person could be OK with it.

"Something is up. You have been jumpy ever since we left the mayor. What's going on? Is it one of *your* things? Should I be worried?"

"No, I'm dealing with it. I'll tell you more when I know something. Let's just go into the other room," I said as we walked to the door.

****

Night fell on the small town, blanketing the sky in diamonds and gems. Everyone had gone to bed early giving me a chance to sneak out and do some proper investigating. I threw on a sweatshirt and a pair of sneakers and slipped out the door. I hurdled over the wall in one shot, clearing the top. I landed hard on my feet on the other side. I walked alone down the brick path, heading for the town hall and keeping a lookout for anything out of the ordinary.

It seemed irrelevant, but even being human I couldn't trust them. I kept my eyes peeled for any suspicious humans. This place had a strict curfew of ten o'clock, and it being almost midnight would draw attention my way. If the little girl did in fact know who I was, it wouldn't be long before the rest of the town knew, and until I knew what I was up against, I had to take serious precautions. I wondered if the town was involved or if they were being forced to act as slaves to the little girl. Was she powerful enough to do that or were the people the powerful ones who kept the supernatural trapped under their key for their own amusement? It's not like I had never seen it before: a person who knew enough about demons to enslave one as their personal bodyguard, but that would take a lot of dark magic and a very sadistic human.

Under the cover of trees, I crept around bushes and down the long hill finally arriving where I thought would be the best place to start looking for evidence. I stood beside a large tree that was posted in the back of the town hall. The lights were on in the room upstairs and shadows paced back and forth. The sounds were muffled, but I could clearly hear the voices of four men panicking.

And it was about me.

I needed to get up there. A steel pipe that ran from the ground to the balcony on the top floor was my best shot. The pipe was cold and smooth, but it wasn't impossible for me to climb it. As silent as a mouse, I used every muscle in my body to scurry up the pipe. Every step I made, I lost two more, but in five minutes I was pulling myself up onto the wooden railing. I stood at the French doors, waiting for the room to clear and give me a chance to search the area. The room emptied, and to my surprise the doors were unlocked.

"Well, yippy for their trust in the town." I laughed at my own premature joke.

From the hallway I heard the voices of more men and women discussing the festival. Some of the voices I recognized: the mayor, the gatekeeper, and the motel keeper. They seemed nervous about my arrival. The little girl finally spoke, and from the sudden silence of the room, it was clear to me she was in charge.

"How could this have happened—a Guardian in my town on the night of worship?" The girl spoke sternly with so much anger and rage in her small voice.

"Azaria, we didn't know. We gathered as many sacrifices as was asked. She came in with other normal people. It doesn't add up," Frank said, and he sounded terrified.

"Whatever. She is very lovely. I may have need for her after all. No need to worry, children, you did well," Azaria said, comforting the others."

My heart dropped. This was bigger than me and bigger than anything I had ever been up against. I listened as the meeting started to adjourn. This was going to be an epic battle, and there was no way of hiding it from the others. Sacrifices, century-old rituals, worship—it had to be some kind of witch, but no witch possessed that much power. What in hell could it be? I knew the ulterior motive, but now I had to be sure about the creature.

I crept quietly down the same pipe. My body trembled at the thought of telling the others; how would they look at me after this? Would they even want to? I mean, that's if they believed me. But now I knew their life was in danger, and I had to get them out of here, but how? I could leave now by myself, and grab backup.

No, Azaria would be looking for me and would use my friends as bait, so that wouldn't work. Could I protect them? It was only five miles to safety. Would they be able to last that long, that deep into the forest? That would be the better option. They had to believe me first, had to trust me. At least I had Kady—they would have to believe her.

The sound of footsteps startled me. They were coming from up the hill slowly toward me. The rhythm was poetic, like the person was looking for someone.

Maybe me I thought, but just then the scent hit me like a bag of rocks to the face, triggering my pulse to heat up uncontrollably. I loved what he did to me. The feeling was intense, and full of pleasure. I stood behind the old bar in the alleyway, waiting for him to pass. His scent consumed me.

More footsteps, and the smell was different this time, dirty and seductive. He was coming fast from the opposite side. Inch by inch Andy came closer. I watched as he looked around. His face lightened in the moonlight, and his blue eyes sparkled.

Out of the shadows, I grabbed him by surprise, pulling his body close to mine. I put my hand over his mouth, using the other to place one finger on my lips.

"Shhhh," I whispered, looking down at my watch and then to the shadow passing by.

His body felt warm pressed up against mine. I felt his breath down my neck, my heart started to race.

"So since we are already breaking the law, you want to make out," Andy said, grinning. He cocked his head and smiled, waiting for my response.

"You are such a dude."

"That's why you love me," he said.

I pressed my lips on his, causing a meltdown in my brain. He wrapped his thick arms around my waist, pulling me closer to him. Harder he kissed me until he was unable to catch his breath. I pulled away, smiling at him and wondering if this was going to be the last time he would ever kiss me like that.

"You know I love you, right? No matter what?"

"Yeah, I love you too, pretty girl," he said, gently kissing me again.

****

"Shut the hell up. I'm doing everything I can do, just drive," Lucas yelled at Derek.

They had been fighting since they got into the car. You couldn't blame them, they both were under a bit of stress, and with Alikye MIA their stress was doubling.

"I know, I'm sorry, dude. She had orders to stay put. That girl never listens," Derek said apologetically to his brother.

They were already in the car heading due south to Florida, but it would take hours. Derek knew that Alikye was fine. She was a mess of a girl, and mischief was her middle name, but she was fine. He did think that after so many months of being away from her life, she would have settled a little, but it was in her blood to take charge. "Can you keep your thoughts to yourself, she's going to be fine." Derek snapped, Lucas, wouldn't stop rambling on and on to Derek about how he needed more time to make things right. Lucas kept saying it wasn't fair and they were going to be too late to save her. Derek couldn't take it anymore; Lucas's negativity wasn't doing anything but pissing him off. "That is until I get to her, then I'm going to kill her for worrying me."

"This isn't the time for jokes," Lucas spat

"What else are we supposed to do, drive ourselves insane?"

They had tried to contact Alikye the second they were off the phone with Anastasis. Alikye never got back to them; it had been forty-five minutes. They couldn't understand how she could walk off, doing God knows what, when she was in so much danger.

Maybe nothing has changed with Kye after all, Derek thought to himself.

Derek knew what she would be up to, always investigating on her own, but he couldn't imagine why she was acting so reckless. Never mind that he could, but this was her, and it was the main reason she was sent away.

This girl is going to give me grey hair before I turn thirty, Derek thought to himself. He looked over at his sad faced brother who was researching everything known about pagan gods.

"What's it saying?" Derek asked.

"Nothing good. But Anastasis is making more calls about it."

"She'll know what to do; it's her job to know."

"I hope you're right," Lucas finished.

He didn't know what else to say to Lucas so he just drove, watching the dark road turn into nothing. On any given night, this would be his favorite part. He loved the peaceful sound of the wind whipping over his truck. The calming effects the night brought to the world, illuminating the true nature at its peak. He found it all therapeutic, and in this line of work, sometimes that's all you needed to stay sane.

He watched as the moon streaked across the empty wheat fields. And then it hit him—how did he not think of this before? He would have kicked himself in the gut if he was able to, so instead he swung the truck off the road and slammed it into park. Lucas jumped out of the trance he had put himself in and looked at his brother in shock, gripping the dashboard.

"We can send someone to check up on Kye. Give me your phone," Derek said, almost hyperventilating.

Lucas knew right away who Derek had in mind, and for the first time in days, his beautiful green eyes lit up with joy, and all he could do was smile.

"She's not going to like this," was all Lucas could say as he handed over his phone.

Chapter 31

Andy and I made it back to the motel around one thirty in the morning. The light in the girls' room was on. I forgot about my computer; the boys were probably hysterical. I had been gone for well over an hour. Kady's eyes locked dead on mine as we entered the room, she looked tired.

"Your e-mail keeps beeping. I tried to look in it to shut off the alarm, but I didn't know your password." She yawned.

"Sorry about that. Andy and I took a walk. You can go back to sleep. I'll deal with it."

I bid goodnight to Andy as he kissed the top of my head. I watched as he went into the next room. He stopped and turned giving me one last look. I headed to the bathroom, my computer in hand. Amanda was sound asleep with her eye mask over her eyes and her iPod blasting in her ears. She looked so peaceful and serene when she was asleep—if only she could sleep forever. I turned the lights off in the room and settled down on the cold floor. I had forgotten about all the danger and Azaria but was well reminded when I hit video chat.

"Alikye…what is wrong with you?" Derek yelled.

I knew what I did was foolish, leaving without an explanation, but I was doing what I was raised to do. I might have been doing the wrong thing, but I did it for all the right reasons.

"I got a name. I know what she is planning to do," I whispered to my screen. "Her name is Azaria, and she is some kind of witch. She's planning on sacrificing the guests of this town for a sacred ritual."

Derek's face softened. "We know what she is, and it's not a witch; she's a pagan god, and, Kye, you need to leave now."

Derek's words shot through me like an arrow. My body felt cold and numb. Azaria couldn't be killed, at least not to my knowledge. The only thing that could kill a pagan god was an archangel, and they couldn't step foot on this planet.

"What am I going to do, I can't do this myself."

"If you want to save the others, you have to get them up now and get going. Ten minutes. Whether they believe you or not, it's your job now to get yourself out alive."

"How?" I asked

"I've sent help. He should be getting there in the next minute—you disappeared and gave me no choice. I love you, kid." He finished and then the screen went black.

I ran out of the bathroom, slamming the door so hard the wall cracked down the middle. I placed my computer on the dresser and flipped on the light. Kady was up right away rubbing the sleep from her eyes. She knew something was up. I didn't have to say it—she just knew.

"What is wrong with you freaks?" Amanda grumbled from her bed. She ripped off her mask, throwing it on the ground. "It's not even two in the morning, and you freaks are making a shitload of noise." She jumped out of bed, heading toward the light.

I walked over to her and blocked her way. I was done keeping quiet. For months I had been letting Amanda boss me around, but no more; things were going to change. The pathetic weak girl I had been pretending to be was gone, and she was going to get what she had been asking for. I brought my hand up to grab her arm before she could reach the light switch when a knock on the door turned both of our heads. I prepared myself for the worst, expecting Azaria to be at my door playing a game with me. She wanted to keep me alive for a reason, but what could that reason be? I was of no use to her. My free will was unable to be penetrated, so she could not keep me as her slave. It did not make sense. I told Kady and Amanda to stay put as I walked toward the door. My hand shook when I wrapped it around the handle.

"Seriously!" I smirked when I opened the door. My body relaxed.

"Well it's nice to see you, too, love. I've missed you, "Shasta said in his sexy accent as he pushed his way into my room, shutting and locking the door behind him.

Kady and Amanda stared up in shock as the handsome stranger standing in front of me smiled.

"Hello, girls, I'm Shasta, Alikye's friend. You must be Kady and Amanda. Nice to meet you." Shasta was gorgeous. At six feet two, he had raven-black, messy hair, and his eyes were the color of ice. He had beautiful evenly toned olive skin. He spoke with a European accent and only looked to be in his late twenties. His ripped biceps and slender muscular torso fit perfectly in his turn-of-the-century combat armor, and double-cross leather sword holsters were secured to his chest and back. He wore tight jeans, laced leather boots, and a plain cotton tee.

"How do you two know each other?" Kady spattered out. "Are you like *old* friends?" She delicately asked him if he was the same as me without raising suspicion to Amanda. He stayed silent, waiting for me to respond.

She knows everything, and she is the only one. Shasta could read my thoughts.

Shasta was not really human nor was he a Guardian. He possessed special gifts, like mind reading, that came from his father. His father was a demon, and his mother a human. In the early fifteen hundreds, a dozen demons broke out of hell and ambushed a small village in Europe. They killed all the men and children and kidnapped and impregnated the women with demonic children to walk the earth. What they didn't expect was for the human in them to keep their souls intact until they took the life of an innocent. Shasta was found when he was two by my ancestors. His mother gave him up, knowing it was the right thing to do. He learned the lessons of the Guardians and eventually was able to live out his life as a Guardian. For centuries he fought alongside my real family and proved to everyone he was good. Most still didn't trust him, but he was always loyal to my name. My whole life he had been a big part of it, but our relationship was complicated, and we butted heads on everything. I think it was because we were the same in every way. Last time I saw him was over two years ago when he went on a hunt with me and helped me kill the demon who killed my parents.

"Family friend, but we don't have time for this. Where are the others?" Shasta demanded

"The other room." I pointed to the conjoined door, bringing my head toward the floor.

He walked over to the door and banged on it, surely startling everyone. Within minutes three tired, grumpy boys walked through the door, confusion all over their faces when they saw Shasta standing at my right.

Riker was the first to speak, taking charge of the situation. "Is there a problem, sir? Did the girls do something wrong?" His eyes moved from me to Kady then to Amanda.

"He is *her* friend—don't look at me," Amanda said, now sitting on the bed with her legs crossed.

"Thanks, dude." I had no easy way of explaining this, but I was glad Shasta could read minds so I could tell him to let me do all the talking.

Everyone looked at me. I had to just tell them, no more stalling.

"What's going on, Kye," Andy said, walking over to my side. I put up my hands asking him to stay where he was. Shasta turned his body toward mine possessively but still faced the humans. He was so close his arm grazed mine. Andy caught Shasta's movements and became uncomfortable, worried. Andy took a step back.

You have to say something, love, Shasta sent to me.

"Look, I understand this is confusing, and trust me when I say no one was supposed to learn the truth like this, but now I have no choice but to tell you." I stopped to gather my train of thoughts. I had one chance to explain this situation very delicately. But I didn't get the chance.

The door slammed open, and black smoke clouded around me.

PART TWO

Chapter 32

With Shasta at Alikye's side, Lucas was feeling a bit better. He would have preferred to be in Shasta's place protecting her, but only Shasta had the ability to teleport. Lucas stayed on the phone with Jack explaining every detail while Derek drove expeditiously over the speed limit. Jack had already left, clocking the time to about two hours. He called everyone he could, coming up with a decent amount of help and feeling good that his friends were there for him in times of need. Lucas felt comforted by the turnout, but he was still unsteady and uneducated about how to kill Azaria.

Maya and Kayla beeped in giving their ETA of one hour and twenty-five minutes, and Jack had already grabbed two old friends who were nearby. Both men had jumped at the opportunity to save Alikye.

"Anastasis said she would have the information by now, but she hasn't called." Lucas snapped over the phone.

"Son, she will call. Have faith, but I still have some calls to make, so keep your head up. Kye is smart, and she knows what she's doing," Jack said, and then the phone went dead.

Lucas was feeling unsure about everything, and his faith was resisting. How could he say to have faith? He needed to pull himself together and get his head in the game. Complaining would only make things worse, and Derek was becoming fed up with Lucas's pity party. His computer, hot in his lap, lit up with an urgent message from Anastasis; Lucas's eyes fell to the screen.

"Read it aloud," Derek urged.

"Lucas, I ran through all that I know, coming up with one option. It will be difficult and the journey will be long, but with the help from my trusted friends, you and Derek will make it on time.

"The legend says that in the time of great suffering, pagan gods were sent to earth as neutral parties to help in secret. They were not made like us, pure and wise; they were made with many flaws and free will of their own. In order to keep control, four archangels were given special weapons made by their fathers, but over the centuries the weapons were lost for they were never needed. Four swords pure of heart were left on earth and protected by their protectors.

"A blue sword sculpted in the name of Michael himself and used only by him was buried deep in the oceans, never to be found until the day came when fire rained on the sky and a soul was lost to the depths of despair. The legend was soon lost. Centuries ago a new legend was created in secret, and the sword was said to have been moved to deep inside the earth. Hidden in the caves off the coast of Maine is a pathway to where the sword is now being kept. The only clue I have may not be accurate, but it may be helpful.

"The light will paint the color dark.
The open shall appear.
The pain means you still exist.
But you should walk in fear.
At the mouth of the beast, he will bare his teeth.
And there you will find what you need.
Beware of the knight.
For they must awake.
They hold the key."

Lucas noticed the coordinates of their new destination that Anastasis had set up for them. They were headed to North Carolina to an elder's home where they would then take a jet to Maine. They needed that sword if there was any hope for Alikye's survival, and the risk had to be taken. The others had orders to meet up and wait at the gate until Alikye gave word. It was a rule to never risk the life of another Guardian if the one in need is proclaimed dead, and with Shasta's arrival with somewhat of a plan. Alikye needed to get out first before the message would be sent of her survival.

Anastasis also had the knowledge on rituals. They had been going on for centuries all over the world and in different ways, but they were basic, and in the end the tragedy was all the same. In this case with an abundance of research, news articles, and interviews, whatever was going on in Hidden Falls, had been going on since the early nineteen hundreds to their knowledge. Around the same time, every seven years, a handful of people around the area went missing after informing their loved ones of an accident and a town they had to spend the night in. Then they were never heard from again. The human rescuers would send out search parties and helicopters, but this so-called town had never been found.

Human stuff, he thought to himself. *People disappear all the time for no reason. Why would we think anything of it?* Now he was feeling guilty for letting this go on for so long and angry that no Guardian had ever taken the time to investigate such a disaster.

"So what do we know about pagan gods?" Lucas asked his brother, trying to sound more positive now that a plan was under way, and the means to kill her was at his fingertips.

"They are usually used for good: protection, health, wealth, and a lot of witchy stuff," Derek joked.

"OK, but all that health and wealth has to come at a price. The worst of the bunch may use human sacrifices, and in this case Kye overheard them say that the guests would be sacrificed. And with all the disappearance, they have to be dead. So my guess is she is killing innocent victims to atone for the town's debts."

"What about the townspeople? They are human—we can't kill humans."

"Yes, but maybe they have no choice but to obey her, or her price would be their own lives," Lucas defended

"That still makes them guilty by association, and the older folks wouldn't be able to learn any differently. They are already tainted by evil."

"Let's just agree to disagree until we know all the facts."

"Deal," Derek finished.

"It's hard to imagine that your whole life you could be controlled by such an ugly and evil force. That every minute you are frightened about making a mistake that could cost you your life. Always looking over your shoulders and knowing your children would be seduced by this evil, and that when your life was freed, you would be tainted forever." Lucas rambled aloud not asking for a response.

Derek figured as much and only responded, "Yeah."

Chapter 33

The door hit the wall with a bang, mangling the wood to pieces. The wall cracked and splintered. Azaria, the pigtail angelic girl, skipped in with three of her demonic guards close at hand. On instinct I ran to protect the others but was suddenly interrupted by an invisible force holding me right where I stood.

"Humans, if you may so politely step into the other room, I have business to discuss with the Guardian and her pet," Azaria said with the sweetest tone to my friends who stood in shock not trusting themselves to move. "And, Henry, sweetheart, if they give you any problem," her voice sang threw the room, so peacefully, "kill them!" She sneered at my friends and her people, barking orders.

They were stricken with fear, scared to even breathe. I couldn't imagine what they were going through. I never wanted this for them. If I would have known my company would have put anyone in danger, I would have backed off from the beginning before a friendship could ever have had a chance to build. I couldn't move, couldn't help my friends. I was as weak as everyone else, and Shasta stood in the corner, unable to move also but not for the same reasons I couldn't. He knew if he left, the only thing left for me was my pathetic demise. I watched as Andy was being shoved into the other room, hoping he wouldn't take that chance to try to save me. He would be killed instantly and right in front of me. I couldn't bear it, and then relief blew through me as he walked through the door with the others. I was alone, trapped in a nightmare of fear I couldn't escape from.

"Azaria, I should have figured. But what I don't understand is your smell. I couldn't detect it," I said, trapped in the middle of the room. I knew my *Arcus* was under the bed, but from where I was, and with my new disability, it felt as if it was a million miles away.

"As you know I was created not for evil. Free will made me evil. Power made me evil. Your disgusting humans made me evil. I don't quite understand what you see in them and their filthy habits," Azaria sneered.

Shasta was able to lighten the hold on me, giving me a chance to break free. Over the centuries Shasta studied the art of magic with some of the most prestigious witches and warlocks all over the world. He picked up on a lot of information, both black and white.

I had one chance to get to my *Arcus* and get a *Sagitta* straight through Azaria's heart. I knew it wouldn't kill her, but it would give me a window to save the others. Before she had time to finish her uninspiring speech, I ran in hyperspeed to the bed, falling to my legs and sliding like a baseball player stealing home base. My hand slid through the cheap carpet, and it burned the tips of my fingers, then instantly my body healed each rug burn. I felt my energy pulsing from my hand to my *Arcus,* just barely commanding the object to obey me and connect to me. But as it brushed against my fingertips, I felt a force more powerful than anything I had ever felt grab hold of my body, throwing me into the back wall, knocking the breath out of me. I hunched over, my hands to my knees, gasping for more air; my lungs were on fire. Azaria wrapped her mind around me, pinning me back against the wall. My feet dangled six inches above the floor. Azarie stood seven feet from me, laughing as I lay helpless. Her guards stood by the wrecked door, keeping their eyes on Shasta, ready to strike in second's notice.

"Do you know the reason for all this—the reason why I stay in this inferior town when I can be out in all the world manipulating humans to do my bidding, controlling demons to love me more than their master, or just sitting on the beaches of Bali being served as the goddess that I am meant to be?"

I wouldn't give her the pleasure of answering, and my breathing was still uneven. I didn't need her to hear my broken, shaken voice when I spoke. I stayed silent, watching as Azaria's face became impatient.

"I will tell you then. In the beginning of the new world, Columbus was said to be the first to discover it, some say Ericson, neither is correct. Three sisters discovered it—my sisters—not by blood but by witchcraft. I was their goddess, and they worshiped me. The Protector of Witches and the Goddess of Witches, I was once called." Azaria took a deep breath. "They came to make a new life where witches were loved and treated equally, and they fled from their homes in Europe after watching hundreds of their friends and families burned at the stake all across the world. So they came to the one place that was not run by kings and queens pretending to be their own kinds of gods. Please!

"America was uncorrupted at this time. The natives signed a treaty with my sisters allowing them to stay and make a home for themselves; they could practice white witchcraft (and as you know the natives had their own kind of beliefs in magic and practiced it regularly). If they never brought harm to humans, they were free. And anyone who wanted to join their village was free to do so.

"Years went by, and the sisters built this town. They built a life, and they fell in love and had children—everything was perfect. I would come in and out every so often to check on my ladies—but nothing ever stays perfect.

"Men came one night after days of spying, after days of watching them. They came in the night with fire and rage. They burned the town and killed the native men who had become fond of the sisters. They raped and tortured women and children until they finally killed everyone but the three sisters and their five children: three girls as beautiful and flawless as the sisters were and two boys as handsome as gods. They prayed to me asking and begging for my help, but I was far away, out of your world, and didn't get the message in time. The sisters would not turn to black magic to save their own lives, keeping their promise untarnished. They fell to their knees and wept for their babies.

"I made them a promise that I would punish those who did them wrong, and, hey, you can't blame me for being so creative. The greatest punishment was to not kill them and to keep them as my prisoners. I decided to take charge of the small burned down town and control those who were involved by not only punishing them but by also punishing their families for all eternity."

Azarie's smug smile made a sick feeling erupt in my stomach. How could she justify what she was doing? Maybe I would agree with the murderers being punished by death but not their families and certainly not the innocents who had nothing to do with this.

"Why the innocents then? Why kill them? You're just as guilty as those men," I spat.

"I gave them the choice: their lives or someone else's life they didn't know. They chose to kill the innocents, and they are being punished for killing innocents. It all fits; I'm doing my job even if you find it twisted."

"The choice is kill or be killed. That's not exactly punishable."

"Let just agree to disagree, and now it's time for you to be punished."

A ripping sound came from my body, and it took a second to realize she had torn threw my ribs with such force that blood sprayed all the way to the bed. I screamed in agony, my skin and muscles being torn to shreds. The seals of my markings were being broken.

Azaria tilted her head back, her eyes changed from mocha brown to a midnight black. Azaria's form shifted from the little angelic girl to her beautiful breathtaking goddess form. Her golden hair fell down her bare back, and her skin appeared flawless and untouched by her age. Her warrior-princess leather attire fit to every curve of her body with a large amount of her pale skin showing. She was magnificent. She spoke to the skies in Latin, and black smoke rolled over the ground like waves hitting the shore.

Blood ran down my body, staining my clothes and skin a dark red. My head became light and fuzzy, and I was becoming fatigued.

Finally the pain subsided but not because of my healing abilities; Azaria had cursed me with black magic breaking all ties to my healing power. I was going to die. I could feel it. Death was knocking at my door, but I didn't want to answer it. She held me in midair, using nothing but her mind to throw me hard against the dresser mirror, shattering the glass. The agonizing pain shot threw me once more, causing my entire body to tremble. I rolled to the ground, bleeding from numerous areas of my body. I tasted the sweet, metallic, thick liquid in my mouth, My organs were shutting down slowly. If I were human, I would have been dead where I lay, but I wasn't, and I would suffer for a long time before my death.

They are distracted, I sent to Shasta.

Shasta pulled his *Gladius* from his back strap, jumping from his position to the back of the demon, thrusting the single-edged sword across the throat of the monster. The demon screamed, attracting the attention of Azaria and her other demon. In flames of fire burning green and blue, the demon exploded into ashes, crying until there was nothing left. Shasta jumped from the fire, obtaining both swords in hand. In that same second, Henry, the handsome six-foot-one, two-hundred-pound demon, ran into the room. His light colored hair was slicked up with grease, and his glassy bluish-green eyes stared in shock. He had pale skin with scars down both his forearms.

At first glance I hadn't noticed him, but after gazing into those eyes, the right eye with the small brown freckle, I remembered. How could I have forgotten? It was me who had given him the scars; I had sliced open his arms from wrist to elbow before he had the chance to send me flying across the room a year ago. He was my first level-one demon and strike-one that led me to move to Florida. Like Shasta, Henry was also a half human, but he took the life of an innocent to become what he was. He wanted to be powerful, but for reasons I couldn't fathom, he was now a goddess's lackey.

He ran to the side of his master, protecting her right flank but leaving the left side vulnerable. Deciding I was no longer a threat, they all went after Shasta. But he was too quick for any of them and was able to subdue the weakest man.

I crawled over to my bed, and with one word I summoned my *Arcus* and *Sagitta* to me. I ran my fingers down the thread of the *Arcus*, feeling the texture of my old friend. I was weak, but my Legacy gave me all the power I needed to roll onto my side and ready my *Sagitta*. I watch as it obeyed my voice, shooting straight through the heart of the God. With a loud scream and a massive explosion of black smoke, Azaria and the demon vanished from the room, leaving only Shasta and I with a mess of blood and ash.

Shasta barricaded the door and ran to me, picking me up in his arms. My skin was pale and cold to his touch. He felt warm to me, and he smelled like the ocean. I was going to die in his arms, and at that moment I was at peace with it. I lay my head against his chest, feeling the beat of his heart against my temple; he pulled me tighter to him, cradling me. The pain was gone, but the taste of iron filled my mouth. This was the end; this was how I was going to die.

A minute later I felt Andy at my side, the warmth of his body being pulled toward me. I felt his skin on me, and his hand was inside mine. He spoke, but I couldn't hear him. His gaze locked on me, watching as my life was fading from my face. I couldn't say the words I needed to say. All I could do was smile a bit, hoping he knew how much I loved him.

Then I fell into darkness.

Chapter 34

I lay on the bed in nothing but a sports bra and shorts, my body covered in my own red blood, my insides pouring out of me. I lay there in agony, screaming and cursing Shasta as he pried his hands into my opened wound. Spell by spell black smoke rolled out of me like a river of darkness. I felt every minute of him ripping my insides apart and sewing each internal marking back together. Shasta re-broke four of my ribs and reset them properly. I cried as he pinched and pulled my skin back and forth until he finally was able to stitch me back up as if I were humpty dumpty that could be put back together slowly and painfully.

I lay basically naked on the bed with ten sets of astonished eyes on me and dried blood plastered to my skin. When he was done, all my markings covering my body blushed a brilliant blue of Persian indigo. I didn't have to hide them anymore, they were all going to find out the whole truth anyway.

After I wiped off what I could of the blood, I was coming into my full strength. My healing abilities came back, mending what was left of my wounds. Physically I was feeling a hell of a lot better; mentally I was livid. I wanted Azaria's head on a platter. The next time I saw her I would be ready. I made the mistake of worrying about everyone else but not next time. Next time it would be her and me, one-on-one, and I would win.

"We should call the cops," Riker yelled toward Shasta.

No one would come anywhere near me. They were all afraid.

"Sorry, mate, that's never going to happen," Shasta said, helping me off the bed. "Plus she's fine—good as new."

"But how…" The words faded from Riker's mouth as he sat back on the bed with a look of defeat on his face. Kady ran toward me, handing me wet cloths to wipe up.

"You OK?" She whispered, so no one could hear.

"I'm fine. Please go to him." I didn't have to say who, she knew. He was on the bed, shaking, too scared to look me in the face. I didn't blame him.

I started to get dressed, putting on my fight gear. Dark-blue skinny jeans and my old plated leather knee-length boots that for years had gotten me through some fun times. The smile on my face was sinister, and I was sure everyone noticed. I put on a tight-knit cotton tank, covering it up with my cuirass leather upper-body armor with two matching forearm bracers equipped with small latches to hold silver Chinese stars. I grabbed my bag from under the bed. I paced silently around the room, gathering the rest of my belongings. I dreaded the explanation I would have to give regarding the incident that had just occurred.

They all sat patiently, waiting, wondering, and not willing to make the first move. The only sound in the room was the clock on the wall slowly ticking. I looked at my friends, wanting to say something, my eyebrows squinting. They looked at me, attention drawn on me like I was about to give them the answers to who killed JFK. I turned, still not ready. Shasta stood stern in the corner by the broken door like a soldier on high alert, arms locked behind his back, only moving his eyes and slightly reading the thoughts of each human. They were terrified.

I strapped a leather band across my chest, securing my quiver to my back; I unlatched the wire of my *Arcus* and hooked it to my belt. I stuck my iron dagger in my holster that I strapped to my boot and put my silver dagger on the other boot. I loaded two guns; pulling back the barrel, listening as the Glock 34 clicked, pulling a bullet into the chamber. One I strapped to my right thigh the other to my left thigh.

"OK, ask," I turned, facing my peers. "We might as well get this over with." My face stayed bitter with no emotion. Today was beginning to suck, and my ribs were still a little tender.

I knew Kady wasn't going to say anything—she knew every-thing. Kady looked more concerned while the others looked con-fused, except for Andy, who looked betrayed.

"What are you?" Amanda was the first to speak. She finally got rid of her attitude and asked with curiosity

"I'm a Guardian, my people and I. We protect humans from demonic beings. What you just saw were demon hybrids, and the girl, a pagan god." I explained to them the severity of the situation we were in. I spoke every word slowly and sincerely and told them they were going to go through the worst possible supernatural sce-nario. I was never prepared for this kind of fight, never wanted to have anyone I cared about go through something like this. They were my friends, and now they were all in danger. The reality of this was after we were all safe, they were never going to look at me the same way—everyone except Kady, she never had a problem with any of this.

"Are you even human? Because that shit that I just saw is no way human," Andy spat out viciously.

Ouch. He had so much anger in his voice. He stood up and took a step toward me.

Shasta took a protective step toward him, blocking his way to me.

"Not exactly," I answered.

"What the hell is that supposed to mean?" Andy snapped.

"She is still the same person she has always been, just a little dif-ferent. She is still Alikye," Kady interrupted, scolding Andy.

"Wait! What…? Did you know about her?" Andy asked.

Everyone turned their heads to Kady, wondering the same.

"Yes, of course. She's my best friend," Kady snapped back.

It was the first time I'd ever heard bitterness come out her mouth, and I almost laughed. I loved when she said that. I had never really had a best friend, so when she stuck up for me, it felt good. I was relieved.

Kady finished, "The car accident. How else do think I survived? She saved my life. I've known for months now."

"Well, I knew there was something off about you, but, whatever, let's say you're not crazy, what now? What the hell are we supposed to do? And who the hell is he, because I'm guessing he's not human either?" Amanda asked.

I rubbed my hands over my face, counting silently to myself. "No, he is not full human either. He's a demon hybrid, but he's not like the ones you just saw; he's different." I took a deep breath. "I can save everyone, but I need you to trust me. This is big and the most dangerous journey you will ever experience. If you listen and do what Shasta and I say, you will live to see another day."

Shasta started to get a bit antsy. Time was being wasted by just standing around talking. We needed to head out.

"We have to go now," I said.

Kady was the first to follow me. Eventually they all did.

The bathroom had a small window that led to the outside, but it was barricaded by steel bars. Shasta took one look at it and laughed. He teleported to the outside (jumping is what I like to call it) and grabbed a hold of the bars, yanking them out of the rock with a loud crash. Cement fell to the ground, making a bigger hole for us to crawl out of. Going through town would be suicidal; the woods would be a clear cover to our risky escape.

We got over the wall with little noise. As I did before, I scaled the wall in one jump, sat on top, and pulled the rest up over it. I didn't even break a sweat. Once we were all safely on the other side, it was my job to come up with a plan. I asked Shasta to jump around and secure a safe exit, and like that he was gone, leaving me with too many betrayed faces. Everything seemed clear for now, and the plan was to just walk, staying alert to any noises. Shasta had left me with two tranquilizer guns in any case we ran into humans. It would be the best way to subdue them, silently without innocent blood on our hands. I had my own skills to deal with them.

Early on when I was still a student at combat school, we had to learn how to fight without killing. I never understood then, but I guess this was what they meant. Sometimes you would be in a situation where the best way was to incapacitate them. Not kill. I was just worried about the others being unarmed in a dangerous situation. I gave one to Coach Riker. He was the oldest and most mature, and I felt the need to have someone responsible holding the gun. He took it with a stern look on his face, one that said we would talk later, but for now he would trust me. The other one I gave to Andy, maybe for my own satisfaction. Knowing he would be safe would put me at ease. He might hate me for the rest of my life, but I would always love him. To know he was alive and existing in the same world as I was gave me the only peace I would ever need. So he took it from my hand, not once making eye contact.

This is not the time, Shasta's voice rang in my head.

Until Shasta returned I gave the order to stay put. Shasta would be able to check the entire perimeter, which would allow us a clear passage to the main highway where my people would meet us and bring my friends to real safety. I knelt down to secure the rest of my weapons, I needed to double check that I was prepared for even the worst, when out of nowhere a small prick to the neck grabbed my attention. Without any warning everything went fuzzy then black again.

Chapter 35

The light summer breeze blew through my tangled curls, and salt dried on my sun-kissed skin creating a shimmering coating that highlighted in the sun. I took a step into the ocean, and the cool and refreshing water was perceived as astounding after a short nap in the warmth of the sky. Andy stood next to me. His hair looked lighter than usual, his eyes bluer then the ocean we were staring at.

He smiled.

I turned to him, my face only inches from his; I placed my hand gently on his warm cheek. His skin felt soft, and my fingers grazed the outlines of his face. I touched every wrinkle, every crease, thinking of the stories he would one day share with me. Andy's hair fell in front of his eyes. He was the most beautiful boy I had ever seen, and he was mine just as I was his. He tilted his head, kissing me gently on my neck and moving up toward my lips then my forehead. He wrapped his strong arms around my almost naked body. Water rolled down my stomach being absorbed by my bathing suit bottoms, and his board shorts stuck to my legs, dripping more water on my sandy bare feet. His hand moved to the small of my back, sending goose bumps all over my body. The other hand brushed threw my hair, getting snagged in my curls. Andy and I did nothing but stare at each other then at the wide open ocean. He pulled me closer to him, meshing our bodies as one; he kissed me again, but this time much harder and with much more passion. My breathing became uneven and heavy, my head a mess of *nothing but how much I loved Andy. He moved his lips from my mouth to my ear, and his warm breath tickled me.*

The bright sun started to set in the mist of mystery, disappearing over the horizon, leaving nothing but the faint shadows of the day. The sound of nothing but the wind and the crashing of waves simulated a calmness of amour. Our love was engulfed in a safe bubble that evil would never penetrate. I turned my head back toward Andy and saw that the beautiful boy was now a handsome old man, tall and strong, but fragile and weakened by life experiences. I saw I had changed, too, still stunning, but wrinkles covered my soft, flawless skin. My body felt human, weak and old. I looked and smiled at Andy watching children running in the water, children that resembled us. I saw a woman yell from the porch of a different home, our home. She resembled Andy to the tee but with my eyes. She was our daughter, and they were our grandchildren. I saw that my life with Andy led to happiness that I was able to grow old and watch my family grow. I saw that no evil would ever stop me from having the life I now wanted, but I also realized in this world of beauty it was not real. It was a dream I never wanted to leave. Andy bent over to me, securing my body in his arms, and with a soft smile whispered in my ear what I needed to hear: "Forever."

I looked up at the black open sky, the stars scattering through the heavens. My head was pounding; it felt as if I was hit hard over the head with a two-by-four. It hurt to keep my eyes focused—everything was blurry, I wanted to go back into my dream. I wanted to sit on the beach with Andy, old and brittle, listening to the laughter of our grandchildren as my daughter ran to our side and wrapped her arms around my shoulder, smiling. I couldn't make out the faces staring down at me or the shadows of people. The voices were slow and raspy. The darkness came into focus, and the aroma of freshly cut grass filled my nose. Where was I? What just happened? I couldn't get the words to come out; I couldn't get my voice to work.

"Where the hell am I?" I managed to mumble.

"Amanda shot you; Shasta said the effects should wear off soon, quicker than on a human," Kady's voice broke out of the darkness. Everything was coming back to me. The mission was seeping into my brain, and the realization of betrayal hit me hard. They all hated me. They left me to die at the hands of evil after knowing what that evil did to me and would do to them.

"Where is she? Where is everyone?"

"She left. Greg and Riker followed, trying to get her back. Shasta went out to find them. She had a twenty-minute head start before he came back and saw what happened."

"Where's Andy?" I knew he would leave at the first chance. He saw me as a monster and couldn't understand that the supernatural was real. I was created to protect them. I should understand. I should not blame him, but I did. He was supposed to love me no matter what, and now that he knew I was different, I would never be good enough for him. Kady understood. She didn't hate me. She wasn't scared of me. She didn't feel betrayed. Andy knew me, and I never once lied to him about the real me. I just never told him the whole truth. I mean, better he found out now than years from now if I chose him.

"I'm still here. I wanted to leave, but I couldn't." Andy's voice was hard, emotionless.

So he did stay. That's a start, I guess, but it would have to wait.

"We need to move. Shasta will find me," I said.

"You need to rest," Andy replied coldly.

"No, I don't. Like you said, I'm not human. I heal quickly," I snapped.

Andy walked close to me, taking my hand. The warmth of his touch was still there, and the electric pulse of our skin together never left. He helped me to my feet, which I accepted even though there was no need for his help. We began walking through the lush forest. The pathway was small, not an easy road to walk, and the thick bushes and tall oak trees surrounded us. The ground was covered in flowers and clovers, and layers upon layers of grass and weeds spread throughout the forest. The trees rustled in the wind, telling stories of the days that came and went. The night never impaired my vision, but I could see that Andy and Kady were struggling to walk. The moon gave little light to the world—not enough to comfort them. We walked for a while with no kind of distraction. It all seemed a little deviating, and I had to think.

The silence was amiable, and I enjoyed it. It put me at peace and gave me clear pictures of what was around me. I preferred the silence, but I could see that the others were distressed. Mostly Andy who looked so sad; he walked with his head to the floor, whimpering as he kicked the dirt with his foot. I couldn't stand it anymore.

"So what, you hate me now? The truth is not what you wanted to hear," I whispered looking at Andy. I know. I told myself to wait, but I couldn't. It just came out. It was not the time, but since it was out there, I wanted answers.

"What?" he said.

Oh, so now he wanted to play dumb, like I wasn't even worth an explanation. His eyes turned dark as he glared into mine with so much pain, like the sound of my voice was more like a knife to his heart. I didn't think the truth was that bad. Yes, I'm not exactly human, and, yes, I lied about my identity, but would he be throwing himself a pity party if, let's say, I was in witness protection and the people after us were normal psycho killers?…No, he would be forced to understand. This was the same situation. "You heard me," I barked.

"This is not the time, Alikye," Andy argued.

"Yes, this is the time."

Shasta jumped back in, and Kady ran to his side, pulling him away from us. They walked a few feet in front of us, giving us some privacy but still in plain view of me.

"I could have left, but I stayed. You lied to me—everything about you is a lie. How can I love someone that I don't even know?"

Well, that was harsh. I guess it would be better for him to be mad at me. I would leave soon, get back on the road, back to missions. It would be easier for both of us. I could one day make myself fall in love with Lucas like it was supposed to be. I still had fourteen years left before our wedding and children soon after. I had till I was thirty. Every Guardian did. At that age it would be time to settle down and start a family. Eight years later we would live together in our family home, raising our children until the day we sent them off to combat school, and after that we would team

198

up and begin to fight again, or fight on our own. It all was clock-work, all planned. Until now I never second-guessed the plan, but what if I wanted a different plan for myself? What if I chose to live unharmed for the rest of my life? "No, it's better this way." I didn't have the energy to argue. I didn't have the patience to explain myself to him.

I froze dead in my steps, and at the same moment so did Shasta. Fifty yards away a twig snapped in half, and bushes were disturbed. The others didn't hear, but I did, and I smelled who it was. I grabbed Andy, placing my body in front of his, shielding him from the hostile area.

As we stopped, they stopped. They knew, we knew.

Eight, love, Shasta sent to me with a smile in his thought.

I know. Why aren't they attacking? I sent back.

The wind started to pick up, and soft, thin clouds coated the starry night. The moon stayed bight, untouched by the earth's atmosphere. Footsteps fell closer on both sides of us. We were clearly outnumbered *and* had two humans to protect, and they obviously had the home-field advantage, so why were they taunt-ing us. They were hunting us but not attacking. They were ordered to stay close. They were bay dogs trained to look and find but not catch. They were herding us like cattle to our deaths.

We kept on walking at a steady pace; their unseen footsteps terrified the others. Kady trembled with every moment that passed by. I couldn't tell if she was cold, scared, or both. They were never trained for this kind of mission; I was barely trained for this kind of mission. They weren't ready for this nor did they ask for it.

Amanda, Greg, and Riker were still missing. They were some-where alone and scared, not understanding. I found Greg valiant for protecting Amanda, knowing I was capable of doing the same for Kady. I also found him absurd for leaving unprotected. The plan seemed so easy, but I guess if it were easy, it wouldn't be real. I tried to catch Amanda's scent because her aroma was the most distinctive and it carried among crowds. Like an animal on the hunt for prey, I stood motionless, my head tilted toward the wind. I cleared my mind and concentrated. For a split second, her scent fluttered past my nose, and a hint of her pressed against my cheek. She was there, still alive, two miles due east. She wasn't traveling; she was staying in one position. I gave Shasta the coordinates to Amanda's whereabouts. He went into my head, pulling out all the information he could. He traced her scent. Shasta jumped out.

"Why doesn't Shasta just pop us to safety," Kady whispered.

She seemed to be feeling a little better about this nightmare she was in, we all were in. Andy kept a secure arm around her shoulder, keeping her calm. They walked closely ahead of me. I walked keeping one hand on my bow resting near my hip and the other hand around my arrow, ready to strike.

"Human biology could never withstand teleporting. Your cells would not remember how to rebuild themselves into a solid form. Jumping out would cause sudden death."

"Can you jump?"

"I can, but I won't—" I began to say as Shasta jumped back in, worry all over his face.

"They are trapped in chains of magic, guarded by demons. They are all alive and well and have not been harmed. The humans seem to be staying away, but there is something else, and you won't like this," Shasta said, running a hand threw his dark hair.

Shasta sent the images into my mind, showing me everything I was up against. It all seemed too much, though a little flattering. All this trouble for one teenage Legacy? It was going to be a hell of a fight, and one I was bound to lose.

"That explains the hunters," I said aloud, causing Andy to look over at me, confused. I guess having private thoughts with Shasta and then speaking aloud to answer random questions did lead to confused humans. "It's a trap. Azaria knows I won't let innocents be killed by evil forces, and she knows I will come for them. She also hired some hellhounds to finish me off," I explained.

"Like the big dogs that protect hell's gates, like in that movie?" Kady replied.

"More like hellish dogs with super strength and speed that can also turn themselves into phantom creatures. They are big and scary and not fun to play with." I pointed to the four scars that ran down the right side of my face. One was almost impossible to kill, and now I had to deal with four.

"We need a plan," Shasta said.

"We need to first kill these hunters," I replied.

Chapter 36

They heard me. Their hearing is impeccable. The threat of being killed intrigued them; it would be the only way to lure them out of hiding. Demons are reckless, stubborn, and stupid. They are trained to hunt and take orders, but when the rage and hatred kicks in, nothing can control them. If you start a game with them, they will play, with pleasure.

I steadied my hand; Shasta pulled Kady and Andy away from me, placing a tree in their way. He came to my right flank, his hand securely around his sword above his back. I looked into the woods, and the yellow of their eyes lit up. I pulled back my *Arcus*, eyes focused on my target. I was ready for this. I had been waiting so long to get back into the fight. All my training gave me the strength I needed to kick ass.

The *Sagitta* came alive at my bidding, and the ancient scripture lit up in the moonlight. I felt the power of my bow climbing threw my body like a rush of adrenalin. I aimed, my thumb resting on my cheek as I took a deep breath and let go. The *Sagitta* sliced through the air, twisting and twirling, passing each tree and bush. Unannounced and unnoticed the *Sagitta* stabbed deep into the heart of the demon, releasing its poison. The creature was then submerged into a ball of blue fire, screaming in agony before turning into ash. My arrow disappeared from its victim returning to me.

One by one the brigade of demons circled us like hungry sharks in a tank. They came at us fast. I reached behind my back, pulling out another arrow. I gripped tight to my bow in my other hand, standing side by side with Shasta. Shasta stepped away from me, slowly taking four of the demons with him. I was left with three. Sensing there was one behind me, I quickly spun to my left, dropping to my right knee. He didn't even see it coming as I thrust the edge of my bow up thru the demon's chin, piercing a hole through his green scale-covered face. The demon's thick, dark blood cascaded down my arm. He was a pile of ash in seconds. Without hesitation I was back on my feet, waiting as two more came at me. Shasta seemed to be doing fine only taking one or two hits but not hard enough to knock him off his feet. I glanced over for a split second, giving the third demon the opportunity for a right hook to my jaw. Face-to-face and no time to ready my weapons, I twisted my arm in a corkscrew-like motion just before impact as I threw a left jab, automatically being in position to throw a straight right. Trying to regain balance, I had enough time to finish off the demon with an uppercut, causing him to let go of his weapon. I dug my knees into the earth's soil, taking control over his weapon as it burned like fire in my hand. I plunged a knife into the fallen demon's chest sending him to his grave. Unexpectedly I was hit hard over the side of my head. Startled I toppled over, rolling to my back. This couldn't be it—this couldn't be the end. I had to think fast. The demon was on top of me about to put a knife through my chest, his solid body crushing my spine. He pushed down with all his might on my arms, which were blocking the weapon from my heart. The tip grazed my skin, cutting a two-inch gash across my collarbone. The dagger burnt through me like fire through paper. I gritted my teeth, only allowing a little sound to escape while in my mind I was screaming for help. My arms shook ferociously, and every muscle tightened as the demon pressed harder and harder.

It was no use. He was too strong, and it was only a matter of time before the knife would finally pierce through me. I thought about Andy and how scared and helpless he looked as Kady held him back. He wouldn't be able to do anything; the demon would snap his neck in a second and still have the time to kill me. Shasta couldn't get to me; he was busy dealing with his last demon. I tried withering my way from his grip, blood and dirt smearing my skin. If I was going to die I at least wanted to see Andy's face one last time. Our eyes locked and it was then I knew Andy was about to do something stupid. He pushed Kady out of the way, taking the gun I gave him earlier out of his belt. He lifted it, shooting the demon in the neck. It was in a split second that the demon was off of me heading toward Andy. The effects of the needle did nothing to slow him down. I jumped to my feet putting myself in between Andy and the demon, forcing Andy out of the way. But I wasn't quick enough to protect myself. The demon took an arrow from my quiver, screaming as the metal burned through his hand. As I turned to face the demon to finish him off, he jabbed the tip of the weapon into my stomach, pushing it harder in me until it went up into my ribs. My body stilled as the pain shot through me. The demon dropped me to the ground expecting me not to get back up, but little did he know, I couldn't be killed by my own weapon. It just hurt like hell. I yanked the arrow out of my belly, getting back to my feet. The demon was headed toward Andy again. This time I was ready and so was he because as I advanced on him, he jumped out, jumping back in behind me.

"Andy, do not move!" I screamed. "You're not helping me. And all you are going to do is get us both killed!" I spun around throwing all my weight into the demon, knocking him to the ground but at the same time falling alongside of him. In the matter of a split second, we both were on our feet at the same time circling each other, eyes locked on one another. He looked so human besides his skin and mouth, which were full of rows of sharp teeth. He had long blond hair pulled back in a ponytail. He was tall and muscular with washboard abs. Everything was familiar except for those eyes. Eyes like a wild, hungry animal hunting its prey. He laughed viciously, backing away from me.

Step-by-step I watched, bewildered by his actions. I slowly lifted my arm, rubbing my palm against my hair, flexing my fingers out toward my arrow. It had to be quick; my bow was five feet away from me, way out of reach, so it was up to my throwing skills. But before I could get close enough, a hard pain came from my upper arm between my elbow and shoulder. I grunted loudly when I noticed he had read my mind and done the same thing. But instead of throwing his dagger, he jumped to me and stabbed my arm. The fire spread across my arm, locking my muscles, paralyzing any chance of moving it for minutes. Before he had time to jump back out, I called to my *Sagitta*, locking my fingers around the end and twisting my wrist outward. Like a Philadelphia baseball player in the World Series, I threw my *Sagitta* at my target, striking him in the throat. He froze like a statue, grabbing the arrow as he gasped for a final breath of air.

I pulled the knife from my arm, feeling my blood running down it. I looked into the empty forest, pausing to catch my breath; Shasta had finally killed his last demon and was making his way toward me. Behind me a branch snapped, causing me to jump back into position and spin around on my heels in hyperspeed. I stopped, the blade barely touching his throat; he froze.

"Not smart," I said, my voice raspy.

"I thought you were hurt," Andy said, worried.

"That was a stupid move you made. You could have gotten yourself killed," I said referring to his earlier actions, "But I'm fine," I insisted.

I wasn't, I was badly beaten, bloody, tired, and soar. The battle was over, but the war was just beginning.

Chapter 37

I looked down at my watch; it was already 3:56 a.m. We had been walking for forty-five minutes. Kady and Andy looked exhausted. They were dragging behind. But the night finally stayed quiet, and the hunters were dead. No others would risk their lives coming after us.

We need a plan, I sent to Shasta.

How did I get myself into this? How did I get my friends into this?

I'm sorry, Kye, but we should just cut our losses and save these two. After help arrives we can go back for the others, Shasta sent back to me.

I wouldn't leave the others to die, to endure the hours of torture Azaria would put them through until they begged for their own demise. I wouldn't let them suffer like that. It wasn't their battle. They didn't ask for any of this. I didn't ask for any of this. I didn't want any of this anymore. That was the truth.

I looked back to see Andy, his arm wrapped securely around Kady protecting her. His hair fell in front of his dark-blue eyes. I loved when his hair did that. I loved how his eyes sparkled in the moonlight. It made him look so handsome. He walked with his head down, not looking my way. He was still not talking to me or looking at me.

I thought of a plan…my life in exchange for their lives. Shasta couldn't understand that—he might be good, but he was still a demon and that meant he still carried that part inside him. The trap was set for me and me alone. I could bargain and bribe Azaria. I was the most important thing.

I was a Legacy.

I could turn myself in and suffer the consequences and somehow figure out a way to escape without worrying about the others. They would be long gone, and Shasta could protect them. I would stall until backup; they would come for me as long as I was still alive. Azaria might go for that. The greatest sacrifice to her little town she would ever make. It was kind of flattering really—her wanting me that bad. She's gone through so much to make sure I would come. She was right. I would come, there was no other question.

I looked over to see Shasta in tune with my thoughts. His icy eyes squinted, and his perfectly rounded lips tightened. I took a deep breath, closing my eyes.

What else could I do?

"Well, for starters you could stop wallowing in self-pity and be the girl I know you are," Shasta said, cutting the silence like a steak knife cutting butter.

He always thought he knew everything, but not this time. He wanted to leave and just let my friends die. At least I had a plan, and I *wasn't* wallowing in self-pity—I was constructing a rational strategy.

Sure you are, Shasta sent

"OK, then, demon boy, tell me."

I stopped to see Andy now looking at me but not the way I wanted.

I continued, "You know what we are up against; you know nothing can change the situation we are in. What other choice, besides allowing that bitch to kill them, do we have other than me?" I took a step away, and sat on a stump. I put my head in my hands to think, and then added, "If I am going to die, let me at least do it my way…fighting."

I saw Shasta considering it, not that he would actually agree. But he let me think he would only to give me the satisfaction. He took a moment to think over what I was telling him. He listened carefully, replaying the strategy in his head. Shasta was true to his kind. He was hard to his core, always making sure no emotions slipped out when none were needed. We were like two peas in a pod. Two people trying to be good even though deep down we had a dark side. For years he was always around me, showing up unexpectedly to give me pointers that were forbidden at my school. Mostly magic both black and white. He said I would need it even if the Guardians said I wouldn't. They said magic was seductive, and if used too much a Guardian would rely on it and that it was never a gift given by the angels.

"Again with your recklessness, ah," Shasta said.

I smiled at him knowing exactly what he was thinking about. He would never let me kill myself; he would always be the one to save my life.

******

My first kill was a Kyro demon, a monstrous creature that made its home in the deepest depths of hell, and it just so happened to be the creature that killed my parents. I studied it for years, learning it's every move. It was a hunter, an assassin out for the blood of Guardians.

It took me weeks to track. It moved like the wind, never staying in the same place for more than a night. I went on my own. I had to because they would have never understood. I took off the night after graduation, the night I should have been preparing to leave with Derek and Lucas. I snuck off in the middle of the night with only the clothes on my back, my weapon, and a little cash. I left them a note saying I would only be gone for a little while but not to worry, I would be fine and not to tell the council. If they found out, I would have been stripped of my duties, but I knew they would never tell.

I was fourteen.

It was last spotted in LA where it took the life of two Guardians. It ripped out their hearts and mutilated the bodies. My school had found out the news, and trained Guardians were on the move to catch it. They didn't have the knowledge I had about it. They never took the time or spent sleepless nights learning. It was my only chance, and I took it. Washington State was the first place I started tracking it. The others, the more experienced Guardians, were still in California hunting it.

I knew better.

From Washington I moved south to Nevada. The demon was always two steps ahead of me. I needed someone I could trust to help, someone who wouldn't stop me, someone who wouldn't turn me in.

With not one question, he met me in an old run-down motel in New Mexico. A week had already gone by since I'd run off on my own.

The last time I'd seen him was when I was thirteen and he came to train some of the advanced students at school. We spent the whole semester together. He told me stories of my mom and dad. He told me stories of the Kyro demon. All the information I had was from him. So when I told him what I was doing, he was not surprised one bit. He actually seemed intrigued by it.

"I was waiting for the moment when you would ask for my help with this. I just never expected it to be this soon," Shasta had said in his strong European accent as he came to my bed and sat next to me. His warm hand lay on my knee, steadying my shaken nerves. Shasta was always the one person I could count on who would bend the rules for me. He was also the one person who I knew would want this as much as me.

Every other Guardian would have considered it reckless. And although it *was* reckless, it was something I had to do.

"So are you in?" I asked, still not sure what his ulterior motive was. I knew how much he wanted this. I also knew how much was at stake. Shasta was still looked at as a demon amongst most Guardians. They all waited for the day he would turn, and some even prayed for it to happen so that everything they believed in about demons and angels, good and evil, was never tested. Shasta was always the exception, and they didn't like that, but because my father was a Legacy and my family trusted him, the elders could not touch him. But this could be where they drew the line. This could be the turning point. Shasta was obligated to turn me in. It was his responsibility to be the adult and save me from an irresponsible decision. He was as reckless as I was, so when he said he was in, we were out the door and back on the road.

"You ready for this, love?" he asked as he drove past the state line. His beautiful ice eyes burned into mine, and his black hair was pulled back in a rubber band, and like usual he wore his gear: his upper leather body armor; leather straps across his chiseled chest; two swords on his back; dark, tight jeans; brown boots; and a weapon holster strapped to each thigh. Shasta was the picture of a true warrior god, more beautiful than any human alive.

I locked my stormy metallic eyes on his and smiled. "I was trained for this."

We spent the next two weeks on the heels of the demon, Shasta went through every connection he could think of, and finally the night came when justice would be served. We got word of a family of Guardians residing in a small town in Alabama. The hunter was on the move to destroy them all.

"Are you sure your guy is good? I mean demons do lie," I said as we pulled up to the house across the street, parking behind a cluster of trees. The neighborhood was beautiful, a great place for a normal family to raise their children. The homes were all two-story, wooden houses, and large trees lined the road. There were sidewalks on both sides, and most of the homes had variety of flowers planted in the front yard. It made me think of my home, safe, quiet, and full of night-blooming jasmines.

"Not when they're afraid. Remember what I taught you about Kyro demons?"

I nodded.

"Kyro demons are nothing more than scum; they don't do anything without orders from their masters. They don't think for themselves—they can't. They are not the brains of this operation; they are only muscles. Word is, this is the next target."

Two days earlier we'd hunted down a level-four demon, and with help from Shasta, we were able to restrain it for questioning. For hours we sat, with little to no answers. I thought it was hopeless, that this guy would never speak. But after a day, he started to talk for reasons I never want to relive. We finally got him to spill everything. After killing him we took off in the direction we were given.

Without Shasta I would be dead.

****

I jumped back into the present, looking over at Shasta who was reliving the past with me. He smiled at me, silently telling me he would always be there on my reckless journeys to watch my back. We must have been locked in each other's gaze playing that memory over and over for a while, because Andy loudly cleared his throat, staring between the two of us.

"Who said anything about dying? That's not much of a plan," Andy said, walking toward us, crossing his arms over his chest. The look on his face told me he was serious.

"That's how this game works, Andy. I save you, but I die. You don't get a say."

The sadness in his eyes took over the anger, but like the snap of a finger it was gone and back to anger. "Like hell I don't," He spat.

Fire flickered in his eyes. He was not about to let me say a word. He grabbed me by my arm, pulling me up to my feet. If he was angry before about the truth, Andy was even more pissed now and was making hell look like a child's playground. I walked with him guiding me into the thickness of the forest. Pinning me to a tree, he forced my arms to my sides, his hands wrapped tightly around my wrists. I stared in shock. I had never seen him so aggressive, so sexy. His eyes changed into a deep royal blue. My entire body tingled with heat. Our magnetic force pulsed even stronger than it ever had. I stood frozen, locked in his trance. I wanted to wrap my arms around him. I wanted to bring my mouth to his with more force than I knew I had. Like a hungry animal, I wanted our clothes to be torn off so we could make ourselves into one, skin on skin. I was turned on more than I had ever been. So much control and confidence made Andy irresistible. He didn't notice my hungry eyes.

"You think this is a game, Alikye? You think I could just let you die? After everything, do you really think that low of me?"

I opened my mouth to protest. This had nothing to do with him. But he wouldn't give me the chance to speak.

"You lie to me, fine. I'm mad, but I'll get over it. I'll even understand everything there is to know about you. But to lose you...No! I won't let you. I won't live without you. I know you feel it, too. Every time we are near or every time we touch. Some kind of force draws us together, and I won't just let it be ripped away."

Andy was right about one thing. From the moment we met, I felt it, the energy that bound us to one another, and over the months it grew stronger. For the longest time, I denied it. I was prearranged to another man. But it kept getting harder and harder to fight. It was one of the main reasons I allowed myself to give in, to be the person I was supposed to be. He was the main reason I wanted to stay. Because like he said I, too, couldn't stand to live without him. Andy's face lightened up, and his eyes went back to the midnight blue I loved so much. This time when I wanted him, all I wanted was to feel safe in his arms, to lay my head on his chest and listen to the sound of his heart beating for me. More importantly I wanted him to want me first. I wouldn't make the first move—it was his choice.

"OK, you win" was all I could say, my words lost to the night. I had a reason to fight; I had a reason to live. And it was Andy.

He pulled me close to him, wrapping his arms around my waist. I lay into his body, feeling the rush of energy go from him to me and back to him. A bright-blue light engulfed us both, and my markings glowed brighter than they ever had, appearing across my body. He stared in amazement, running his fingers down my arm, tracing each marking

"Will they ever go away, like before?" Andy asked, looking down at me.

"If I will them to, yes, unless my emotions bring them out again." The light finally dissipated, leaving blue symbols across my skin. "I would prefer to let them be seen though; they are a part of me."

"They do make you look more sexy," he joked, giving me his award-winning smile, showing off a mouthful of perfect teeth. The smile I had been waiting to see all night.

"Sexier," I corrected his grammar.

"That, too," he brought his mouth to mine, gently kissing me, then pulled away still smiling. "I love you, Kye. Forever."

Shasta and Kady were wrapped up their own conversation by the time we returned. I could see how intrigued Kady was with Shasta, asking him more questions than she asked me at one time.

She talks a lot, Shasta sent.

I laughed.

Kady turned to us smiling and looking a lot better than she did before I left.

"So, again, we need a plan?" Shasta asked flatly.

"Yes, Shasta. My plan to kill myself—it's now out of the question, so, yes, we need to come up with something that doesn't get any one killed," I replied sarcastically.

We went back and forth throwing around half-assed ideas, getting nowhere. Twenty minutes passed by, and we were still at the beginning. We began to argue, getting louder than we should have.

I yelled, "Hell no, that—"

"Umm guys…" Kady said, trying to interrupt

"But that's our only—"

"I said no, Shasta. No—"

"I might…" Kady said.

"Then what?" Shasta argued.

"I don't know, but so far they all suck, and we are wasting time."

"I might have a plan!" This time Kady yelled.

We all froze, turning our heads to Kady, who was innocently sitting down on a log, smiling. Without asking, Shasta jumped into her mind scanning her thoughts. As he did that, he was also sending them to my head. I was impressed. She was good, better than I would have given her credit for.

Yeah, that's good. But can you do it? I sent to him.

Hell yes! He sent back.

Chapter 38

The plane was small, only six seats in all and two of them for the pilot and copilot. They didn't need anything bigger. The smaller, the faster, or at least for a Guardian plane, it was faster than any other aircraft for reasons that can never be explained.

Derek was the first to step off the plane. The air was thin and wet with a light drizzle that soon fell harder and harder. The temperature plummeted from a humid night in North Carolina to a freezing, storming night in Maine. The late-spring air cut threw Derek's skin like ice. He pulled his jacket tight against his body to find warmth. Lucas stood next to his brother, shaking his head back and forth.

The car, the elder had scheduled to pick them up, was waiting on the landing strip for them. Down long and twisted roads they headed to the coast.

Both Lucas and Derek were scared. For the first time in ages, they were truly scared. This whole situation was way out of their league, but it had to be done. This had to end, and once they had the sword, they would bring the fight to her. It would be legendary. But first they had to find the sword, and that was the tricky part. They were instructed to find the cave that sat on top of the water, which Derek couldn't make sense of. They edged themselves to the cliff, looking down at the ocean lapping against the rocks. It was a sixty-foot drop onto jagged boulders. There was a small area of sand no bigger than the size of a bedroom surrounded by countless caves, which most sat below the water. The climb down was easy besides the occasional slip. At about ten feet to go, they both jumped off the rocks, dodging the uneven surfaces. They made it down and planted their feet into the wet sand. Thick clouds formed a heavy overcast sky, and ice rained down on them soaking every inch of their clothes.

Derek couldn't think of a worse situation. It couldn't just be as easy as finding the sword on the ground and picking it up. Or finding it in a stone and being the one knight on a mission to release it. No, it had to be something difficult. Everything in his life was always difficult. Everything that had to do with Alikye was difficult. He would never resent her, but she was always getting him into trouble, always doing shit without thinking. One of these days, she was going to get him killed. He would never admit it though, never to anyone, especially Alikye. His brother, on the other hand, could never really see all her flaws, and Derek knew she had many. But Lucas couldn't see it. Yes, it was Lucas who suggested sending her away but only for one flaw. She had many though. It was getting exhausting for Derek, but he would never give up on her.

Ever.

There was no determining which cave it was. They didn't have time to search them all, and with high tide they didn't have time to wait for the morning to bring the tide back down.

"Maybe the meaning is cryptic. We are not actually looking for a monster-looking cave," Lucas said, turning to his brother. Lucas was the genius. He could tell a person anything they wanted to know about, well, everything. Derek was the pure warrior; his ability to fight was godlike. Together they were…No words could explain them. They should be Legacies, but it didn't work like that. Add Alikye in that mix, and they were unstoppable, but they were also each other's Achilles' heel.

"So what do you think then? This is out of my league, genius," Derek joked, bringing a simple smile to Lucas's face. Something that was uncommon for him lately. He loved to see his brother smile again. But the smile soon faded as the realization became hopeless.

Derek started to the other side of the beach, but the caves all looked the same. He ran his hands against each rock, feeling the difference but finding them all alike. Just as he turned his back to the ocean, making his way toward Lucas, the moon danced from the clouds casting a shimmering stretch of light upon the caves. The golden, salty rocks glistened in the moonlight, all but one. One cave stood out like a brunette in a crowd of blonds. The blackened rocks ran beneath the others protected by smooth algae-covered boulders in a foot of below-zero waters.

"In low tide this would be a walk in the park," Derek said aloud to himself. "But like everything else in my life, this was never made to be easy."

The cave was a good fifty-foot swim around numerous boulders that in the night couldn't be seen underneath the black water, and with each wave crashing heavily onto the shore, for a human the odds would be sudden death.

Derek and Lucas stood silently peering out toward the ocean. As the world froze and colorful light danced in front of them, they could see the outlines of each hidden rock. Together, without a word, they drew out a path in their minds that would be the safest route.

They dove into the water, feeling the cold rip through their skin, like knives cutting the flesh off their bodies; they clenched their teeth, fighting against the inevitable pain. They pushed through the water, gasping for a breath, but taking in sharpening discomfort.

Finally the numbing feeling started to take control. The feeling of loss and sleepiness seeped into their heads as their hearts started to give way. But as their organs started to shut down and their markings glowed to a brilliant crimson, they both felt their bodies repairing themselves. They climbed to dry land, feeling the warmth of their blood run through their bodies. Within a few minutes their energy and determination kicked into full gear.

The front of the cave was small, six feet high and four feet across. The walls were like daggers, tearing flesh from the arms of both boys. They crawled slowly through the cave, feeling the cold spray on their backs. Up ahead like a large mouth engulfing them, the cave opened. All around, darkness drank up any hope of finding the sword, as they came to a dead end.

"No sword appears to ever have been here," Lucas said. He fell to his knees, gripping handfuls of sand.

Like any cave would look, the room was small. Dagger-like rocks made up all three walls. The damp, stale air was like breathing in fumes. Water dripped from above wetting the ground of sand as did the waves running through the mouth. Lucas groaned helplessly, placing his waterlogged hands over his face, while Derek ran his bloody hands along the jagged walls, feeling for any kind of secret latch or doorway. Derek had one shot at saving Alikye, and he would never give up, never leave empty-handed, and never give up the chance to kill a pagan god. He was determined, although like Lucas, he was tired, bloody, and cold; this was part of being a warrior. Lucas, on the other hand, moved to his back, sand clinging to his wet skin like a parasite to its host. He propped his right hand over his head, stretching out his body. Without thinking his hand slammed into the wall making his reaction catlike, but it was too late as his hand ran across the surface. Waiting for the pain to shoot through his hand as the rocks tore off his skin, he jump up and put his injured hand inside his other hand. But there was no pain, no blood, nothing. Lucas had hit smooth surface but didn't realize it till now. He turned to his stomach, wiping away the sand from the wall. Markings were sketched into the stone, markings from a Guardian.

"Derek, I think I found something." Lucas's voice echoed as he yelled for his brother's attention.

"What is it, dude?" Derek replied.

"It's markings from our people, but these markings remind me of Alikye's, ancient and Legacy markings," Lucas started. "Centuries old, maybe even longer. I'm not sure what it says. We were never taught this language."

"It's not our language to know. It's Legacy. How do we open it?"

The instructions were there, in plain view. It said how to open the door and how to solve the rest of the riddle to obtain the sword. The only problem was this was the wrong language. Guardians had two different languages. Like Spanish and English, the languages were very much different yet both very important to learn. Legacies were required to know both. Other Guardians were only allowed to know one.

"I have an idea, give me the *Mucro*," Lucas demanded, using the daggers Latin name.

Derek took his dagger from his leg holster, laying the handle inside Lucas's palm. Lucas clenched tight to the *Mucro*, running the sharp blade against the smooth stone. A bright Persian-indigo light lit up an outline of a doorway. A large crack ran down the outline, separating the smooth rock from its wall. With a loud rumble, a door appeared and opened to reveal a small hidden room.

The circular room was lit up by torches and soft, dry sand covered the ground. They stepped into the room and breathed in the fresh air. The door slammed shut behind them, molding back into the wall.

"What do you seek from me?" A loud voice echoed around the room.

Derek and Lucas both jumped, spinning in a circle. Eyes wide with fear, Derek was the first to speak. "We need the sword of Michael. We were sent here by Anastasis, the Guardian elder and a Legacy."

"You have no business asking for something you have no right to," the voice roared, almost godlike.

"We need the sword to kill a pagan god. She trapped a town full of innocents, and if we don't get there soon, they will all be killed," Lucas said, his voice unsure.

"For the sword you must pay the price. A test. If you pass, it is yours to borrow. But if you fail, your journey ends here."

Before they had time to answer, the walls around them shook. The ground moved with such force Derek and Lucas were both brought to their knees. The fire around them exploded into a blazing inferno of green light.

As they scrambled to find their balance, they began getting lightheaded. They started gasping for air, but there was no air left in the small room. The oxygen was being sucked out. Their lungs felt dry, their vision became blurry, and their bodies went weak.

They fell into the sand, and everything went black.

Chapter 39

Maya and Kayla sat in their pickup awaiting the arrival of the others when out of nowhere Maya caught a glimpse of a vehicle's headlights coming up fast. Maya and Kayla were identical twins, one as beautiful as the other. Dark glossy black hair cascaded down their backs in soft waves. With their Asian background, their caramel skin and dark eyes made them breathtaking.

They stood armed in their hunting gear and out of sight in case of danger. The newly painted black four-door Jeep came roaring to a stop just inches from the girls' green Chevy. It took only a split second for them to recognize the three older men stepping out of the Jeep and onto the plush grass sprinkled in dewdrops. After the worst call of his life, Jack called his two closest friends, Nathan and Frank. He was proud to know his trusted friends would come on such short notice when they heard his beloved daughter Alikye was in danger. Even though they knew what they would be up against would not be easy and may lead to a casualty, if not two. Jack stood for a minute by his car, away from the others, as he watched two young inexperienced girls and two old mature men working well together discussing new and old tactics. Together they gathered their weapons, compared the hot new devices, and waited patiently for word from Shasta.

This case really hit home for the three older men. Nathan and Frank had grown up with Alikye's father. They were all friends in school, and as time went on, they all kept in touch. From time to time they would even team up on the bigger missions. All together their children were born one after another, Derek being the first. Frank then had Kyle a few months later, but tragically Kyle lost his life two years ago. Laura, who was Frank's only other child, partnered up with Nathan's two girls, and together they made an unbeatable team. Lucas came next, and then Alikye. There would have been another Macayan child if not for the sudden death of Alikye's parents, but time ended too early for another child to be born. All the children, including Alikye, attended school together, yet Alikye kept a safe distance from having any attachment toward the others, always afraid she would be hurt. Jack never knew how to deal with it, and now with the bond she finally built with her new friends and her new life, Jack felt like a horrible father having to rip her away from it all. This would be another time in Alikye's life that she would lose everyone she loved. And it was all because of rules that Jack now felt should finally be broken before Alikye was the one to be broken.

"We have a plan," Shasta said, suddenly appearing out of nowhere. Everyone jumped back in shock, readying themselves for an attack, grabbing the nearest weapon they could find. "Hey, no need for that. I come in peace," he said with a chuckle, jumping in and out to avoid a blade to the throat.

"Shasta, son, you know better than to just appear out of nowhere with no warning, especially now when everyone is on edge," Jack said, placing a hand on Shasta's back and shaking his head back and forth.

"Sorry, mate, didn't mean to rattle your cages, but I bring good news and bad news."

"So start with the bad," Kayla's voice rang through the forest.

"Well, to begin, Alikye is safe with two of the humans, but I'm afraid with everything that has happened, three of them got away and were captured by the pagan god. She is using them to bait Kye into turning herself in. But as I said before, we have a plan," Shasta said, and then one by one he planted the plans into everyone's minds and waited for their response.

"It sounds like a good plan, but will there be enough time? Because if this doesn't go accordingly, then it's Alikye who will pay the price," Maya said with a voice just like her sister.

"Kye knows, and it's a chance she is willing to take. Besides I'll be there," Shasta said with a suspicious grin while running his hand threw his dark hair.

Chapter 40

Andy detested the first part of the plan. He couldn't understand that if I let him stay with me, they could use him as my only weakness and we would both end up dead. But I found it sweet that he offered to fight beside me, that in the face of danger, he stood strong for all the people he cared about. The first part of the plan was easy. Maya and Kayla would meet us all at the designated coordinates along with Jack, Nathan and Frank. But only the girls would take Andy and Kady out of the five-mile radius where the town's perimeter and magic would end. Once they were to safety, I would be able to finally focus on saving the others and not worry about my best friend and the love of my life.

We walked deeper into the forest, staying hidden in the thick brush and the dark shadowy night. All the while I listened to the million thoughts swaying around my mind and fought with my inner self about choices that needed to be made. This trip was supposed to be my week of normalcy that would determine my stay, but like always something that good could only be given to me for a price or for blood. I didn't want to risk either. I didn't even know how we would explain this to the rest of the team once it was all over. The tournament was out of the question, and together we would all head back to my house for a full day of debriefing, but that wouldn't be the hard part. The hard part was figuring out a way to say good-bye to Andy. I didn't know how Andy would take all of this. Our connection, our magnetic force was too intense, he said so himself. I didn't even know if I was capable of being apart from him, but I had to leave. But what if I decided to stay? Would my people accept me being a normal girl? Or would they turn their backs on me and shun me. I wouldn't tell them about Andy. I had to keep him secret, but as for college, there were no rules against being normal.

It made me think of a book I read in English class a few months before about an Amish girl who was given the chance to live in the real world to experience life in a different way. And like me she made a life for herself and fell in love with a normal boy. When the time came for her to make her decision, she could either go home to the comfortable and stable life she already knew, a life with her family and friends to one day have a man chosen for her, or she could leave everything behind and take a risk, start over and believe that fate would make everything OK and that the boy she was in love with was actually *the one*. I read that book over and over, knowing the end wouldn't change but hoping to find the answers I needed. I found out later the girl in the story was actually the author. She wanted the people to know her story. I wish I could ask her if she ever regretted her decision. If leaving everything was worth being in love.

You know, darling, you might want to get your head in the game, Shasta sent.

I snapped my head to the side, glaring at Shasta. He always got into my head without my permission, which never really bothered me before when my head wasn't filled with personal things. I just didn't want to hurt anyone, and either way I would be hurting someone. There was no way of having both lives.

Why do you worry so much about how everyone else feels? Why not do what makes you happy? It's your life, Shasta sent, running his hands through his beautiful dark locks.

Even if it means I hurt others for my own selfish reasons, I sent back, locking my gaze on Shasta's stunning ice eyes. Andy, who had been standing at my side with his fingers intertwined in mine, squeezed my hand when he felt my body stiffen.

It's not selfish. Someone is bound to get hurt, and you can't have both. You might as well do what you want to do.
What about you? Will you always be here?

Shasta stopped abruptly, turning on the balls of his feet. His face stood inches from mine. I could feel his warm minty breath on my neck as he placed a strong hand on my cheek, running his thumb along the scars over my eye. For a moment we stood in silence, no words being spoken in either of our minds. Shasta smiled. *You couldn't get rid of me even if you tried, darling. I will choose you every time until the day I die.*

Shasta had a forever debt to my family. Back when my ancestors Katarina and Sebastian first found him, they did everything in their power to keep him safe. Because by our laws my family name was second in line to the head council family, they allowed them to keep Shasta as long as he played by their rules. Later he became a big asset, but it took a long time for my people to finally trust him. Elina, daughter to Katarina and Sebastian, loved him from the moment they meet. She never once saw him as an evil being or a threat. They became best friends, and as the years went by, their friendship grew into a love so intense, she was willing to leave her future mate and family just to be with Shasta. But he loved her too much to ever put her in that kind of danger, and the night of his twenty-fifth birthday he packed up and moved to England to work side by side with Katarina.

Shasta kept busy at the council, doing anything he could to keep his mind off Elina. Every so often he would jump back and forth just to see her from afar but kept enough distance for her not to know he was near. He watched as she finally married the man who was chosen for her and saw the sadness in her eyes as she wished it was Shasta standing next to her. The day she gave birth to her daughter was the first time in years he allowed himself to be close to Elina. A year after their tearful good-bye, their forbidden love soon ended in tragedy with her death. Shasta felt it when the dagger pierced her heart, and by the time he made it to her side, it was too late to save her. Her last dying wish was a promise that for as long as Shasta lived he would always protect her family. Without having to think about his decision, he nodded his head and placed his lips on hers. When he pulled away, feeling tears soaking his cheeks she whispered, "I love you." and before her final breath, he sent *I will always love you...forever.*

I looked over at Shasta and saw a single tear roll down his cheek before he wiped it off. He sent, **If you want my advice, choose love over honor, because if you don't you, will spend the rest of your days regretting your mistake, like I do.** Then he said, "It's eerie how much you and Elina are the same, and for the first time in five hundred years, I finally have the chance to fix my mistakes even if it's not for my own benefit." Shasta said, leaving my gaze and staring directly into Andy's eyes.

Chapter 41

I felt their dark eyes on me as I walked past a large oak tree, moss covering the entire trunk. Two pair were watching, and the scent of wild berries fluttered past my noise. Maya and Kayla then walked out from behind a cluster of bushes, gliding through the grass like two Asian princesses. The twins were another bloodline of Legacies who, like me, also lost both their parents when they were children. They and their younger brother were the last of the Nehy Legacy.

They came heavily armed with a set of matching daggers, delicately cut and remastered from their family sword. They were forged by the purest of metals from paradise. In the hilt of each handle a priceless jewel was set, representing one of the archangels.

For Andy this was the first time besides Sarah that he would be meeting another Guardian. And the twins were by the book, true warrior angels. They would never understand the relationships I built with these humans or the feelings between Andy and me. I had to come clean to Andy about our love and how in front of the others, we had to act as our relationship was nothing more than friends, like Kady and me. I pulled him to the side along with Kady and sent Shasta a small message to stall.

"What's this all about?" Andy asked as I pushed them both behind the cluster of bushes the twins were hiding behind only moments before.

"You're not going to like this, but before I finish you need to understand this has nothing to do with how I feel about you and what we have together." Kady walked over to Andy, taking his hand and sitting him down on a tree trunk that had fallen many years ago. She knew exactly what was coming; she also knew this was something he wouldn't be able to understand.

"Pretty girl, you're scaring the shit out of me, what's going on?"

"You and I can't be together right now." Before he had time to speak, I placed my hand up, wanting him to let me finish. "I'm not saying I don't want to be with you, but in front of the others, it can't happen. Among my kind it's forbidden for a Guardian to be in love with a human."

He stood up and walked over to me. Only inches from my body, he grabbed both my hands. "Are we over then?" Andy asked in a hush whisper.

"You know that's not what I want; I just need for you to act like we are *only* friends, just while we are around my kind."

"Alikye, are we over?"

"No. Of course not," I whispered.

"Then we will figure it out, I love you...Forever," Andy said, placing a kiss on my forehead. I looked around to make sure the girls were preoccupied and pulled Andy into my arms, bringing my mouth to his. Andy wrapped me tightly in his arms, hardening our kiss. An electric pulse ran down my body as his hands moved to my waist, pulling me closer to him. I tightened my grip, intertwining my fingers in his soft, beautiful, messy copper hair. I pulled away, staring intensely into his dark-blue eyes, his hair falling into his eyes. I moved my hand, brushing his hair out of his face as he ran his thumb down my jawbone causing me to tense. *Holy crap!*

"And always," I said breathless.

I watched as my best friend and the only guy I would ever really love walked away from me, and for the briefest of seconds, I imagined what would happen to them if I didn't survive this, and how heartbroken Andy would be if I never returned to him. Not only that, but before they left with Maya and Kayla, I finally got the chance to talk privately with Kady about what kind of danger Greg was in. For the entire night, Kady had been staying strong for the sake of Andy and me, but now that she realized she would be safe, all her emotions rushed back to her. She broke down in tears when she told me she had a bad feeling about Greg, it was all I could do to comfort her. I promised her I would get him back to her safely. I wanted to tell her I would risk my own life because if it came down to it that's exactly what I would do, but that would only put her in more of a panic then she was already in.

I was alone with Shasta as I watched the last of their silhouettes disappear in the distances of the dark and eerie forest. This would be my biggest fight, and for the first time, I didn't feel ready for it. I knew now I had too much to live for. I finally understood who I was. I'd found myself, but I wasn't ready for the world to know.

And I wasn't ready to die.

Chapter 42

Nothing made me feel as safe as I did at that moment wrapped in the arms of Jack. It felt like a century ago when I said those horrible things to him, and in less than twenty-four hours it was as if nothing was said, and we were back to the days when normalcy never mattered. Jack gave me the hope I needed to get through this without any causalities. The plan seemed to be airtight, but we had to prepare for the worst, and after a plan B and plan C, I felt confident that I would soon see Andy. Jack, Frank, Nathan, and I had our parts covered. Maya and Kayla were to stay close to obtain the remaining humans: my friends. But unless we found ourselves in a tragic situation, they would stay out of the fight. Shasta had his orders to take out the hounds. He was the quickest and the only one who could see them in their invisible state.

I just wanted this night to be over, but I also knew with the end of the night the end of my normal life was inevitable. The fight I was facing now would be child's play compared to the battle I would face when I got back home and came clean with the decision I was sure I was going to make. It made me wish I could freeze time and forget about my problems. I mean, what's the worst that could happen? I had to keep telling myself to stop thinking about it, that I had more crucial matters to deal with.

We stayed thirty yards away under the cover of numerous trees overlapping one another. I watched as each warrior went back and forth, double checking the plans so there were no flaws. Shasta drew up a floor plan of Azaria's position and her men's positions. She couldn't be too happy that we had taken out so many of her minions. Although to her they were nothing more than the dirt on her boots, but it would make the situation more difficult if there were more of them.

Amanda, Greg, and Riker were bound magically to three trees, grouped together in chains, sleeping soundly. Azaria sat close by in a throne made of gold, waiting for my arrival. Her hounds lay almost touching my friends, and with one word from their master, there would be no time to stop them from tearing the humans apart. Her five remaining demons stayed outside the perimeter, weapons ready.

It all seemed too easy. Azaria was equipped with a lot of power, but I would think she thought better of me than to come alone. "I may be able to use this to my advantage," I said out loud to no one in particular. "She may not think I had time to bring backup, and with her trackers dead, she may be clueless to you guys being here. Besides Shasta she knows I have no one, and by our earlier encounter, she will think I'll run in half-cocked just to save my friends." I was on a roll. I felt my brain reeling with ideas. I thought back to soccer, a surprise attack to the heart of her defeat. I had everyone's full attention.

"Until the boys arrive with the sword, we need to take out the opponents and clear the way to the goal for the final shot. You guys stay back until you see the sign," I said pointing to Jack, Nathan, and Frank.

"Perfect, we can beat her at her own game. I can use a spell I learned to keep Azaria at bay just until we eliminate the others. At that point Alikye will be one-on-one with Azaria, and I have an idea to keep my darling girl alive and stall, giving the boys enough time to show up." Shasta said after reading my mind and interrupting me in the middle of my inspirational speech.

"I hate you," I said, shooting him a smug grin. He just laughed throwing a rock hard arm over my shoulders.

"Sorry about stealing your glory. Actually, come to think of it, I'm not since really without me the idea is a bomb, plus I have an idea of my own," Shasta said, raising one eyebrow and showing off his perfect set of pearly white teeth.

"Should I be scared?" I said with furrowed eyebrows.

"Darling, you should be terrified." He laughed.

Shasta and I headed out first, taking a ten minute head start, giving us enough time to do the spell. As we entered the hot zone, chills ran down my spine, causing a sudden swarm of butterflies to fly across my stomach. Part two of the plan: we needed Azaria out of the equation for ten minutes tops. Shasta taught me a spell that if performed right would make her believe nothing out of the ordinary was going on. She would see only what we wanted her to see while we took out her guards and dogs, giving us the time to get my friends to safety. Afterward Shasta's secret weapon would come into play. When the spell wore off Azaria, enough white magic would surround me protecting me against her biased tricks, and even the purest of black magic wouldn't be able to penetrate me. So the fight would be hand-to-hand combat or a bunch of nonsense, "I'm older and better than you...blah, blah, blah." The crap all evil villains like to say just to hear their own voice and because they think they're better than everyone else.

For now the first spell had to come from the object of the other person's affection, so I would have to be the one to say it.

"You sure I can do this? I mean, I've only practiced the basics of magic...unlike you."

"My darling girl, you need to believe you can do this. You'll be fine, and I'll be with you the whole time. You got this, kid. I mean, you had a pretty damn good teacher if I say so myself," Shasta said, arching his perfectly groomed eyebrows at me, his bright icy eyes burning a hole through my soul. I rolled my eyes, shaking my head. He just laughed at my childish expression.

I sat cross-legged in the damp grass, feeling the wet soil soak into my jeans. I closed my eyes, clearing my head and absorbing my natural surroundings. Since white magic comes from nature and all things pure and natural, the forest would provide an increasing amount of strength for my benefit, and since Azaria mostly uses dark magic, the forest would work against her for the time being. I called to my elements for support; bringing forth all four to work in my favor. Just then I felt the wind wipe through my hair, dissipating as suddenly as it appeared. Next the sound and smell of burning wood engulfed my senses as if for a brief second I was sitting next to a campfire roasting marshmallows again with my friends. Earth came next, and the smell of planting night-blooming jasmines with my mother came back to me, and as quick as a blink of an eye, I smiled, seeing her sitting next to me holding my hand. Last the sky opened up, drizzling ice cold drops of water down my face, hydrating my body. I called upon my elements, and like a moth to a flame, they came to me with a force of power so great I knew just then we would all be fine, and my journey up ahead was nothing I couldn't handle. I then called upon my own magic for the protection and guidance for balance and purity. And as my words came out in Latin, I opened my eyes to see a single thin silver string glide past me, gently sliding across my flawless skin as if it wanted to know my whole body. From my hands to my feet, the silver string embraced me with the magic I needed to help me win this battle and stop this evil. The string then left me, gliding effortlessly unseen attaching itself to Azaria. Around her body it engulfed her in a world she was lost to and was oblivious to what was to come next. When it grew to an uncanny size, a brilliant flash of light appeared, and we knew the spell worked, and like the sand of an hourglass, the glow slowly ran down the string.

Chapter 43

They never saw us coming; Azaria was lost in her own time of peace and tranquility. The four of us emerged through the thick brush. We took the demons by surprise as they waited for orders that would never come.

"My lady, orders!" Henry yelled. He watched his master sit in her chair while she looked out into the black endless sky, oblivious to her right-hand man yelling at her as the others stood dumbfounded and lost. Normally demons wouldn't care and would attack without hesitation, but Azaria had such a tight leash around them, they didn't want to risk upsetting her.

Shasta jumped in just as the hounds went invisible. They disregarded my sleeping friends and went straight for the threatening prey: us. But Shasta was able to cut them off in mid-attack, taking them out in one swift move, or at least that's what it looked like since all I could see was him fighting the air and red blood being splattered all over his body. All of a sudden, he snatched his swords from his back, bringing one down and cutting into the ground, and just like that a seven-foot, two- hundred-pound body appeared, slumping to the floor, and his nasty red-eyed head rolled a few feet away.

One down, and four invisible hounds to go.

I went for the demons, shooting one arrow after another, but they were quick and had the time to jump in and out, avoiding each arrow as I ran and gained ground on them. Henry ran for Azaria only to be thrown backward when he slammed into the force field. An electric current ran through his body, bringing him to his knees. I was handling my own, and out of the corner of my eye, I watched as Jack, Nathan, and Frank held their own, too, only being hit a few times and defending fatal blows to their bodies. And like the fight I was in only hours ago, numerous demons jumped in and out around me, but unlike the fight earlier, these demons were faster, stronger, and better trained. I swung at one with an arrow in hand, aiming for his heart but missing it as he blocked me then turned around and threw a hard kick to my ribs. I fell to my back and quickly righted myself before he delivered another blow to my stomach. Stunned by my rapid movement, I threw a kick to his chest causing him to stumble back. I grabbed my bow and watched as my arrow shot straight threw his heart killing him instantly. I turned to fight off the next one and froze. Standing in front of me, fury blazing in his bluish-green eyes, was Henry. He jumped in so fast, lifting me off the ground, throwing me twenty feet into a tree. I rolled onto my stomach and jumped to my feet, ignoring the excruciating pain to my ribs as they reattached themselves. For a second I stood in place, my breathing forced, knowing one of my rib bones pierced my lung. As soon as my breathing steadied, I ran forward and threw myself at a demon that stood in between Henry and me. I grabbed a hand full of icky greased up hair and pounded his skull into the ground but was rudely interrupted when I took the impact of Henry's body against mine. We rolled a few feet, Henry landing on top of me. He pinned my arms to my side with his legs, glared down at me, and smiled.

"So my little Guardian remembers me. How flattering," he hissed. Reaching around to my back, he grabbed one of my arrows and was burned by it. I laughed as he pulled his red scolding hand to his chest, seething through his teeth. With his good hand, he smacked me across my face drawing blood.

"So, sweetheart, I see where you get your kicks, hitting little girls in their faces. How manly you must feel right now," I hissed back, spitting blood in his face. "And, yes, how could I forget you. Nice arms by the way." I laughed, wiggling my brows.

"Stupid girl, when will you learn that humans are not worth it?" he said in a deep Irish accent.

"Oh, yes, this coming from a pathetic demon who takes his orders from a god. Wow, such a big bad boy you are. Are you sure mommy won't be mad if you kill me? She may take you over her knee and punish you." I giggled and got another smack to my face, leaving stars in front of me. Ah, that time it hurt.

I moved my eyes to see what was going on around me. Shasta was still having trouble taking out the hounds, and a few claw marks ran down his arm. His body armor was being torn to shreds, but being able to jump in and out was saving his life. The others were in full-force fighting mode. Jack was trying to get to me but was battling two demons of his own.

Shit. These things are difficult to kill. We were so not ready for this. Henry shifted on top of me and grabbed one arm with his hand. His other hand wrapped around a demon blade, the one thing that could kill me.

"Let's see if I can make you giggle again…sweetheart. Oh, what a pretty laugh you have." He took the knife and ran the tip down my bracer, exposing my forearm. "By the way, nice arm," he repeated what I said. He stabbed the blade into my arm, running it from my elbow to my wrist. I screamed in agonizing pain as blood gushed from my arm. My hand fisted as the feeling of fire consumed my arm. I closed my eyes, and tears ran down my face. I stiffened as I waited for him to do the other arm but felt the weight of his body being lifted off me. I looked up, my vision blurring. Shasta stood above me. He threw Henry clear across the empty space into a cluster of shrubs. I got to my feet, blood staining my arm.

"Give it a minute, it will heal," Shasta whispered in a hushed voice. I watched in shock as my wound, which should have bled me dry, clotted. Shasta wrapped a cloth around my arm to stop the remainder of my injury from bleeding. I looked at him bewildered.

241

"Magic, love, does a wonder, but we need to treat that as soon as possible before the magic wears off."

I ran to aid the rest. Only one demon stood, and boy he was fast. He had the upper hand on all three Guardians surrounding him. One look at his face and I saw he was enjoying himself, playing mindless games with them. I grabbed my bow and steadied my aching arm. I pulled an arrow back and took a deep breath, my thumb resting on my cheek. My markings came to life with blue light consuming my body and bow. I let go, letting the arrow fly right through their circle, and missing Jack by an inch, it hit its target. Shock fell on the demon's face when he comprehended what had happened, but before he could look down at the arrow piercing his heart, the arrow disappeared coming back to me, and the demon exploded into a cloud of fiery ash. I smirked at Jack, and he nodded, pride filling his lovely unshaven face. Shasta walked off to help Amanda, Greg, and Riker, and time was running out on Azaria. I signaled to the others to help Shasta with my friends, who were starting to stir, waking up from their spell. When out of nowhere, not only did Henry appear, taking Shasta by surprise but also a hellhound lunged at Frank, tearing at his arm and ripping it clear off his body. He staggered back in shock into Jack's arms. I grabbed an arrow, aiming it at the hound that was now invisible, taking a shot at the air. Nathan jumped out of the way as the arrow dug into the dog's left shoulder. It yelped and reappeared, turning its ugly glare at me and growling. Great, this was all I needed. It dug its front paws into the dirt like a bull readying itself to charge, and just like a bull seeing red, it charged. Just as it came at me about to throw its claws against my face (yes, there's irony in that), I jumped out of its way, doing a backflip around its body and landing on my feet at his backside.

"Grab my friends!" I screamed when I saw them start to get up, shocked at watching me fight. In complete awe, my friends stood frozen in place as I dodged the hound again, rolling to the floor, missing yet again another head shot. I picked up Henry's dagger from the ground. I plunged it deep in the dog's hind leg and twisted it as hard as possible. The thing yelped again. Nathan ran to my friends and helped them move around the perimeter of me and the dog while Jack tended to Frank and tried to stop the bleeding of his severed arm. Walking in circles around the hound, we glared at each other, neither of us making any sudden moves toward one another.

"Shasta, sword." He was in hand-to-hand combat with Henry when I yelled for him. Without missing a beat, he darted his eyes to where his swords were lying on the ground. I broke eye contact with the mutt for a moment and ran in hyperspeed to obtain the weapon. Finally the thing charged again. Amanda froze in her tracks when she saw not only how fast I ran but also how I grasped one sword in hand, kicked off a tree, and brought the blade down cutting its head off. I placed my hands on my knees panting before yelling for them to get out of here. Any second now Azaria would be waking up, and she would have complete control over anyone but Shasta and me. I waited until everyone was out of view then I turned to see Henry, his eye blazing fire, throw Shasta into a nearby tree. "Not this time traitor!" Henry yelled.

"Shasta...*No!*" I screamed. His head snapped back against the bark with a cracking noise, knocking him out. I ran to him, and in an instant I stood between him and Henry.

"Round two, baby," Henry said, smirking.

Using the magic inside of me, I created a force field around Shasta and me, blocking any harm that would come to Shasta. But using that magic I took away the force surrounding Azaria. My eyes moved to her just as she was waking up from her dream world.

Henry followed my eyes and saw the look on Azaria's face. He turned back to me. "My little Guardian, this will not be the last time we meet, and next time I will kill you. Well, that is if you survive this." He laughed and disappeared in front of me.

Oh crap!

Chapter 44

Derek and Lucas awoke groggy and gasping for air. Neither of them could remember what had just happened or how much time had passed by, an hour at least. Frantic and confused Lucas jumped to his feet only to be frozen by what he was looking at. His eyes lit up at the beauty that surrounded him. A hand reached for Derek and without thinking he accepted the help up. He stood astonished by the room and the man in front of him.

The room was oval. Soft red and orange rock covered the entire place, gold and silver specks glistened in the fire's light. Four golden high thrones sat at each corner on the top of three steps. Gems and diamonds outlined each. Treasures of the world lay all over the floor like it was nothing more than dirty clothing. Scrolls and books were stacked in a corner. This would be every treasure hunter's dream to be standing in a room full of the most beautiful crowns and jewelry this world has ever seen.

Men dressed as knights in metal armor and tights with a long white cape occupied three of the four thrones, swords hanging from their belts.

The fourth man, dressed like the others, stood motionless in front of Derek and Lucas, golden eyes digging deep into theirs. The man was ghostly white with long platinum hair cascading down his back. He wore his beard braided and well-kept. He looked to be in his late sixties but nothing like a weak and frail man.

"Is what you seek what you are certain you need?" His voice loud and strong startled Lucas. It was the same voice as the man in the other room.

"You could have killed us, dude," Lucas blurted out defensively.

The man placed his hand up, palm out. Fire flickered in his golden eyes. Both Derek and Lucas took a step back.

"Respect, my child." His voice boomed with such force a light wind ran through the boys' hair. "Again, is what you seek what you are certain you need?"

"Yes, we are certain," Derek said in a low raspy voice. He wanted to be strong, to show this knight he had no fear. But Derek was terrified. His body trembled, and he knew it wasn't from the obstacles he had just gone through. It was like staring death himself in the face and begging to be spared. Lucas was just annoyed that he couldn't see what Derek was seeing. They both saw the same person, but it wasn't the same energy coming off him. It was like the knight was testing them both in different ways, showing them two different faces. Lucas saw an old man getting off on playing games. The smile on his face was playful and deserving.

"The test, you have both passed. Your journey will still be taken," the man said, this time more pleasant. "The magic has read your hearts. In order to bear such power, to bear the sword, your intentions should be pure."

"A-Are you a Guardian?" Derek shuddered, still feeling uncomfortable by his presence.

"No, my child, we have no human in us. We live forever only to be awakened when we are needed. We are the protectors of the swords and of all power. We are not evil, nor are we good. We cannot die for we are already dead."

"Where are we? Are we still in Maine? Have you been hiding this whole time in a cave in Maine?" Derek asked.

"You are no longer in Maine? You are no longer anywhere. You're here, there, nowhere, everywhere. We exist somewhere that is nowhere. We have secret doors all around, and the test allows you to enter our plain. And don't worry about the time— time does not exist here. Once you entered through the doorway,

246

time stood still. Time cannot exist if a place does not exist or we do not exist."

Very confused looks crossed the faces of both Derek and Lucas. But the time thing gave them more relief.

"S-so can we have the sword?" Derek asked his voice low. He held his head down not wanting to meet the eyes of the man.

Lucas looked toward his brother, eyebrows lifted. He had never seen his brother so scared and couldn't figure out why.

In a much more confident voice and his eyes locked on the man, Lucas finished, "Yeah, we really need to be going. No disrespect."

The man turned his gaze from Lucas to Derek. Studying his face, Derek finally made eye contact.

"The sword is yours." The man pointed to Derek and only Derek. "TO BORROW."

He pulled the sword from his holster, and the sharp metal rubbed against it making a whooshing sound. The man held up the brilliant sword, tip pointing to the sky between himself and Derek.

The forty-six inch silver forged blade glistened with such beauty. Depicted in the golden handle were three famous stories of Michael. The first story was the garden of Eden: watching over Adam and Eve. The second was the battle between heaven and hell: defending heaven. And the final story was Judgment Day.

Twisting it sideways to where the tip lay gently in his palm, the man handed it to Derek, bowing his head in respect. Derek did the same before accepting the responsibility of the power.

"It can only be used by you alone. The sword chooses you. It made you see what your brother could not. It is your task now." The man placed a hand on Derek's shoulder. Derek then saw a gentle man, pleasant and friendly. The feeling of death was gone and replaced by life and hope.

"When your journey is over and the sword has fulfilled its task, it will then dissipate and return home to us. But be wise, my child. The power you feel is addictive."

Derek strapped the sword securely to his hip. He motioned for his brother then stopped and looked around. There was no exit. He didn't even know how they had gotten in. How were they supposed to get out? Before he had the chance to ask, the man replied as if reading his mind.

"The way out is through us, and to show our gratitude to our new friends, I will do you one better."

All four men walked to the center of the floor. One man picked up a gem as big as his fist. He tightened his grip around the gem, and all the men closed their eyes. Derek and Lucas stood silently watching, not saying a word. The men started quietly chanting something of a dead language.

Smoke burst through the room, engulfing Derek and Lucas in a cloud of grey and black. And like before, the world started to spin, and their visions blurred. But unlike the last time, they could breathe, and they had a calm feeling running through them. Like being in a plane during a hurricane, they felt as if they were being thrown back and forth through the fog of smoke. Grabbing a hold of each other's hands, they fell endlessly, like Alice falling through the rabbit whole. What felt like hours passing by was only minutes before they abruptly stopped, feeling the ground beneath them. But they were still being whipped around and had no clue where they were going or what was happening. They stood up, rubbing their vision clean until their focus came back, and standing before them, staring at the brothers with a bewildered look on their faces, were Maya and Kayla along with two human teenagers—one they recognized, the other they did not. The knight had sent them all the way to Alikye, and without a word they took off into the forest.

Chapter 45

Someone once said that right before you die you see your past play out before you in flashes of pictures and memories. Before I came here, to Florida, all my memories were of horror and death—not something I wanted to relive again and again. But in that moment it wasn't the darkness that appeared in my mind. The flashes were of the people I loved and the memories I cherished the most like my time with Andy. I saw his beautiful tanned skin and his tousled and unkempt hair falling over his sapphire eyes. I felt his lips on mine and tasted salt running off his mouth after stepping out of the ocean. I smiled at the memories, but my smile soon faded when my world came back into view. Shasta was still out cold, blood staining his raven-black hair. And standing in front of me, eyes blazing in fury, heat rolling off her pale, flawless skin, was Azaria, and words couldn't explain the anger she displayed. I stood up on shaky legs, steadying myself. The magic inside me was the only thing keeping me alive from all the blood loss. But when standing face-to-face with a pissed off pagan god, magic could only do so much to keep Azaria from killing me with her bare hands.

I had to stall; Derek could still be hours away or maybe five minutes away. There was no way of telling. I backed up a few feet, distracting her from harming Shasta. She kept her murky eyes on mine, emotionless. Cocking her head from side to side, she said nothing. My body trembled. I wanted to run, curl up into a small ball, and make her disappear. I took a deep cleansing breath. That was not me—that was never who I was. I closed my eyes, digging deep down for the girl I used to be. I needed her now more than ever. She would know what to do, how to handle this. I needed the girl who was fearless, who laughed at danger, who invited danger in for cocktails and small talk. I dug to the deepest part of my soul where the darkness slept waiting to be once again released, the darkness my body craved. I shot opened my metallic eyes, finding it easier to breathe. Azaria stilled for a moment, reading my face, and for a split second a tantalizing smile played on her face. She saw, in my eyes, the darkness coming out to play, and she was intrigued. She was enjoying herself and finally getting what she wanted.

The real me.

She raised her hand into the air expecting me to coil over, but when nothing happened, surprise shot through her eyes. I smiled.

"Hmmm…Interesting," she hissed, tightening her jaw.

In complete silence we walked around each other in a wide circle never once breaking eye contact. I was keeping her at bay for now, but how long could I hold her? I needed to come up with a better plan. I stilled my thoughts, reaching out to Derek, trying to catch his scent, but my mind was reeling and jumbled. He would have to be close in order for me to sense him. Keeping her talking would prolong the inevitable; she was sadistic enough that she loved to hear herself talk, but I also had to be careful not to give anything away. So what was there to talk about: life, the weather, my difficult choice that I had to make which would no doubt hurt someone in the end? No, she would have a field day with that one.

"We don't have to do this. Be reasonable. You can leave here, free the town, and go on to do what you want to do," I calmly said, keeping my voice soft and even like I was talking to a child.

She laughed, throwing her head back as if I were a comedian and had just told her the funniest joke in the world. "Oh…my darling girl, you're right. I *could* do that, but what makes you think I want to? That being here isn't giving me all the pleasure I need?" she hissed.

OK, this is working. Keep her talking. The boys should be here soon, I hoped, and then this night—or day—would finally be over.

I gazed up at the lightening sky as the sun started to peek its head over the horizon, striking it in lovely oranges and reds. Soft clouds drifted to the east, covering the last of the stars as they vanished to the unknown.

"You said so yourself. You said you would rather be the goddess that you are—sitting on a beach drinking Mai Tai's while men served your every need. No one has to die today, Azaria."

"I never said anything about Mai Tai's, but that's a thought. See, the only thing about that is I still can have all that, and the only person that has to die today is you." She took a step forward, closing our gap. Shit, Derek, where are you? No more playing nice.

"Damn it! I'm giving you a pass, Azaria," I hissed "If you don't take it, I guarantee you will die today, and all this" I gestured in a large circle "will be for nothing—just time wasted on this pathetic town with these pathetic humans." Anger boiled deep inside my belly. The thought of allowing Azaria to escape wasn't something I planned for, to have her wreak havoc on another town, but what choice did I have? She was itching for a fight, for blood—my blood, my life. If Derek couldn't get the sword or was running late, this was my only chance to ever see Andy again and my only chance at a life I wanted.

Azaria's smile faded as she considered my proposal. Did she know I had the sword in play and this could be her final day? There was no way she could know that. She didn't have the ability to read minds, only demons did, and I didn't think one was close enough to read what I had planned. But then I quickly realized she wasn't considering anything. She was taken aback by my outburst and what little respect I had for her. She didn't appreciate being challenged by a little girl, and that was exactly what I was doing.

That was a wrong move on my part.

She lunged at me, knocking me to my backside, but I quickly righted myself and jumped back a few paces out of arm's reach.

"You stupid girl, you can't kill me. I am a god, and nothing can kill me but another god, and I doubt you have one at your disposal since we loathe your kind. You are nothing more than an abomination of Michael's weaknesses. He should have killed his brother when he had the chance, but he couldn't, that coward, and it's caused all this." She swept her arms around, turning in a quick circle.

Ouch, tell me what you really think about my kind. Just then a sweet sensation swept through my body, and a smile played on my face. They were near, running toward me with so much power radiating off of them, which could only mean they had the sword. "Not just a god, Azaria." I gloated.

"What are you playing at, missy?"

"Oh...Azaria, you underestimate the intelligence of a stupid abomination. I do my research, and, you see, a little birdie told me that a specific sword, one belonging to a coward as you put it could *kill you*." I smirked.

She froze, widening her eyes in sheer terror. "Th—That sword has been lost for centuries." She stuttered, obviously calling my bluff.

This was starting to get fun. I didn't realize how much I missed my dark side. She knew how to play, and it was quite refreshing knowing that I could still bring horror to the deepest and darkest monsters around. I held all the power in my words, and now I watched as Azaria trembled, waiting for my next move.

"Yes...I have also heard that, but do you want to know a little secret?" I moved my finger to my lips, cocking my head to the side in the same manner she did earlier to me when she controlled the scene, but now the tables had turned. "I. Found. It." I finished in a hushed whisper. And right on cue Derek and Lucas came bursting through the thick vegetation, holding a stunning forty-two inch glistening sword. Azaria's face lit up in shock as she took a few steps back, finding Shasta's discarded swords on the ground, and as Derek ran to her, swinging Michael's breathtaking weapon, Azaria was able to block his first couple attempts.

Lucas ran to my side, taking me into his arms, kissing my hair, obviously shocked himself by my appearance. A wet bloody rag was tied to my forearm and a dried one to my bicep where a tracker demon threw his knife at me. My chest armor was torn, claw marks running down my side barely missing my skin. My lip was split open and there was already bruising around it and my left cheek. My auburn bangs were matted to my bloody forehead, and a deep cut ran down my right cheek just below my eye. I could only imagine how hideous I looked all broken and beat-up. Lucas kissed the top of my head, wiping off some of the dried blood with his thumb. "Are you OK, Kye?" he asked with a soft, loving tone.

"I'm fine....Help Shasta. He's knocked out." I looked up to see Derek and Azaria battling it out, metal to metal clanging as they made contact, neither backing down, and for a moment a pang of jealously spiked inside me because that should be me. I should be the one to finish this war, but all I could do was stand and watch as Derek stole my glory. I shook my head, realizing that was not what I should be thinking. He came here to save me, to save my friends. It was the dark side of me who wanted this, not me—not the girl I tried so hard to become. But my darkness wouldn't leave. She wanted to stay and fight. She wanted to play.

No...Not now.

I had to help, but how? A distraction. With all their skills and stamina, this could go on all night or day. All of a sudden Derek was knocked backward, taking the hilt of the sword to his head. He stumbled a few feet and dropped the sword to the ground at Azaria's feet. This was my chance. I ran in hyperspeed, sliding across the dirt, and claimed the sword to finish the job.

I froze. Out of nowhere my entire body heated up as if I was in a ball of fire. The intensity of the pain in the hand holding the sword was deafening. Inside I screamed in agony as the pain ripped through my hand and up my arm leaving bright red scorch marks in its wake. My eyes widened in horror as I threw the sword to Derek, who was now getting back on his feet.

The world froze around me as I looked up to see Azaria watching me in confusion as I clenched my burned hand to my chest. Then a spark lit in her eyes and a sly smile crossed her face as if she knew something I didn't know. I turned my eyes on my blackened hand, noticing a pattern edging itself out, and in a blink of an eye, the symbol was gone. Azaria kept her eyes locked on mine, and right then my world sped up, and as if the distraction

I needed had slapped me dead in the face, I knew what I had to do. Keeping her eyes on mine, I looked down at my hand, a sudden panic flashing by. Then, lifting my face, I smiled, and right then Derek came from behind and thrust the sword up through Azaria's rib cage, piercing her heart. She released her hold on me, moving her eyes to the silver object sticking out of her chest, and in an instant of silence, like smoke blowing in the wind she was gone. The sword vanished now that its job was done and was reunited with its keeper. I looked at my hand, still feeling the pain coursing through my arm, but the bright red scorch marks now faded into soft, pink lines.

Shasta woke blinking in the soft light. I ran to him, throwing my body on his lap, curling up to his chest. "What's wrong, love?" he asked, his icy eyes burning into mine.

"I thought you were dead," I snapped, smacking him hard on the chest, wincing after I realized I hit him with my bad hand.

"Oh, baby, you can't get rid of me that easy." He laughed, moving his eyes to my hand, grabbing it in his. "What's that?"

I shrugged. "Don't know. The sword burned me when I touched it."

He furrowed his brow then shrugged. "Must be all the magic. The power in the sword didn't agree with the power in you. Don't fret it, love, it's nothing," he said in a reassuring tone. He wrapped me tighter in his arms as I nuzzled into his chest, breathing in his musky but homey scent. Scents that always made me think of my parents. We sat curled up to each other on the damp ground as Derek and Lucas made a few phone calls to the others. I fought as my eyelids started to weigh a ton. "Sleep, love. The magic is leaving your body, and you're exhausted." And on his command the world went dark, and I drifted to a peaceful slumber.

Chapter 46

I woke with a startling jolt, blinking in the fading sun. I looked up to the dark cloudy sky wondering the time when suddenly everything came back to me like a tidal wave crashing on shore, and all I could do was wish for more sleep. Beneath me a solid form stirred, and I realized my head was resting peacefully in someone's lap. I was in the backseat of my car speeding down the highway, Shasta at the wheel.

"Morning, beautiful." His words hit me with a shock of heat and electricity. I smiled to myself taking in his warm scent. Andy shifted, taking me into his arms, and a sudden panic ran down my spine. Shit. Who else was with us? What happened while I was out? Did anyone know about us? My questions stirred around in my head aimlessly because honestly for the first time I didn't care who knew about us.

"You're fine, love. We are far from the others." Shasta answered my unspoken questions. I curled tighter in Andy's arms, placing a gentle kiss on his perfect pink lips. Kady and Greg who were sitting in the front turned around, smiling.

"How are you?" Kady asked sweetly.

"Well, not beautiful for one thing." I turned to Andy, who just rolled his eyes. "But I'm good now that everyone's safe."

"Honestly, hot would be a better description for how you look. Dude, you are like one of those sexy badass warrior goddesses,"

255

Greg added, taking me by surprise. Kady smacked him lightly in the chest, giggling, while Andy scolded him.

"Dude, not cool," Andy hissed.

"Are you kidding me? You should have seen her in action. Holy crap! One minute she was kicking and fighting some enormous scary dog, and then the next she was fading in and out, appearing out of thin air like some sort of superhero," Greg said, moving wildly in his seat, punching the air. We all erupted in a fit of laughter.

*****

We arrived back at my house just as the sun started to set, blanketing the sky with brilliant orange and red streaks. On our hour drive that I was awake for, Shasta took that time to explain what had happened after I passed out. At the time Jack had arrived, Sarah—along with Tanner and Haden and two other young Guardians—stayed in the town, controlling the delicate situation at hand, making sure that not only the townspeople but also the visitors were safe from harm. Once word got to her that Azaria was indeed dead, she and the other Guardians escorted the tourists out of town, letting them all know that the road had been fixed and they were clear to travel. The townspeople were given their freedom back with the choice to either stay or move on and start over, but without the protection and magic of a pagan god, the town would soon die. Shasta explained to me that there was nothing more we could do for them and justice would never be met in the aspect of the law, but growing up in a world they knew nothing about, the universe would have its own way to deal with them.

Frank lost his arm in the battle but kept his spirits high by bragging about all the new weapons he would come up with in place of his arm. It made me smile, picturing him telling people Wolverine had nothing on him now. The twins headed out with Tanner and Haden to help with a case in Ohio involving an old ghost story that appeared to be true. And while I lay unconscious, Shasta stayed busy playing doctor for me and was doing a horrible job at it. He laughed and told me once I got it cleaned up, he would be glad to take another shot at it to fix his handiwork. I imagined looking like Frankenstein's monster by the time he got done with me.

Sarah was soon to arrive with Riker and Amanda while Derek, Lucas, and Jack stayed behind to clean up the mess, like usual. They said they would be home in the morning, and the humans' debriefing would start then. I walked into the bathroom, welcoming the cool water flowing from the shower. I peeled off my grime covered clothing, discarding them in the corner to deal with later. Looking at my naked body in the mirror, I cringed when I noticed the dark bruising around my Enochian tattoos, which were still very much visible. My ribs, back, and chest were flushed with faded purple shadows, but they seemed to be healing rapidly. I peeled off the blood-drenched bandage, taking a better look at the ten or so staples stuck in my arm in different angles as if Shasta gave a staple gun to a six-year-old and told him to go at it with excitement. He would pay sooner rather than later for his rushed attempt to put me back together. I stood underneath the showerhead, letting the icy water run down my body, washing away the last twenty-four hours. I changed quickly into a loose tee that hung off my shoulder and black tights, letting my hair fall to my breast in thick wet curls.

Out in the living room, Sarah sat with Riker at the bar table trying to explain to him what all this meant but getting absolutely nowhere as he shook his head back and forth. He had a kind of defeated look on his face. Kady, Greg, and Andy sat together on the couch acting as if nothing had happened and the world was still normal. For Kady I understood why, but I was curious to know why the boys were fine. I would have to ask Shasta later to listen in on their thoughts. Amanda was the one who worried me the most; she sat alone in silence in the corner looking out at the ocean through the French doors, shaking her head slowly. I read so much sadness in her hazel eyes and wondered why she wouldn't be with the others for comfort. I planned to talk to her first but still had a small dilemma to deal with first.

*****

2222

222222

2222

"Ahh, shit, Shasta. This isn't funny." I grunted. Shasta was using pliers to take out the staples, and if I didn't know him better, he was truly enjoying himself.

Damn demon—always on my last nerve, I thought.

"Why don't you give her something? You can see she's in pain," Andy snapped at him while holding my other hand.

"For one, she's just being a baby. I have seen my girl handle a lot worse." Shasta giggled, showing off his boyish smile. "And two, her body doesn't take drugs the same way yours does. Her temperature runs too hot, and she will burn them off in seconds, leaving her stupid and unable to use her senses but still feeling pain."

It made me think of last year when I was in the hospital with Kady. The nurse gave me a sedative, and because I burned off the drug too quickly, it left me vulnerable and useless. That was until Andy touched me and counteracted the effects. I smiled, feeling his touch now and the way it always felt the same.

"Ahh, you stupid demon," I yelled again, shutting my eyes tightly. He just laughed, yanking each one out slowly. After he was done, he cleaned the wound and harshly sewed my skin back together. He then wrapped it back up leaving an unsettling sting in its wake.

"Done. Now bed," he demanded.

"Yes, Daddy," I replied sarcastically.

His eyebrows shot up in surprise. "Well, if you want me to be your daddy, we can always arrange something." My mouth fell open

"Excuse me!" Andy shouted. Shasta and I both stopped, turning toward him. "I have had enough of you," he said, looking Shasta square in the eyes. "Enough with the secret mind talking and intense eye staring and the pet names you seem to always have for her. She's my girlfriend, and I'm tired of the way you two flirt with each other all the time. I don't know what you two had in the past, but it's done."

I stared at him with wide eyes, and before Shasta and I could say anything, we both burst out laughing. I covered my mouth in shock, but I couldn't stop not even as tears welled in my eyes and my ribs started to feel sore. For years Lucas had dealt with the way Shasta and I acted toward one another and not once had he ever said a word. I knew what he was thinking though; Shasta never missed the opportunity to tell me the jealousy Lucas felt toward him. But to me the way we acted was normal, comforting even. I never thought much about outside parties witnessing it. But now, with Andy standing up to a five-hundred-year-old, magic-wielding, power-hungry demon, and by the look on his face, fear was not an issue. It was adorable.

"Ummm, fair point," Shasta said between laughing. "But trust me when I say, what we have" he said pointing to me, "is nothing of what you're thinking right now. It should be me telling her 'enough' because the only person that ever crosses her mind is you. The way your touch makes her feel, the way you kiss her, the way—"

"Yeah, OK, we got it. No need to spell it out, and stay out of my head, jackass, that's personal," I yelled, embarrassed. At that point we had the entire room's attention, excluding Sarah, and now Shasta was spilling out my most private moments. My laughing had finally dissipated.

"Really?" Andy asked.

"Like I said, nothing to ever worry about, mate. It's you. It's always been you," Shasta finished.

Chapter 47

"Where is she? I need to see her." I woke at the sound of a voice shouting in the living room. The blinds in my bedroom were shut, closing out all the light from outside. After our crazy fiasco last night, Sarah chimed in, sending us all to bed. Riker was the only one who stayed back, wanting to talk more about the whole ordeal. So Kady, Amanda, and I stayed in my bed while the boys made a bed on the ground.

"Lucas, let her sleep. She's exhausted and doesn't need this crap right now. You can talk to her later after she's had enough rest," Shasta hissed from outside my door. What the hell was going on now? Lucas didn't sound angry, just anxious. And why would he want to speak to me now? I looked over at my alarm clock; it was five in the morning.

"He is quite protective of you. If I didn't know better, I would have thought you two…" Amanda said in a sleepy voice, avoiding finishing the rest.

"He thinks he has to be. A long time ago, he promised someone very special to him that he would always look after her kin. He carries a burden that he thinks he can never repay. I've never know anything different from him. It's always been the two of us. He's my annoying demon protector," I whispered not wanting anyone else to wake up. "Why are you up? Are you doing OK with all this? It can't be easy."

"I don't know. I guess I couldn't sleep. I owe you an apology. I should have never run off. I almost got everyone killed because of my stubbornness. I just—"

"You don't need to finish. Trust me, this was nowhere near your fault. How could you not react that way?" I laughed trying to lighten up her mood. She smiled through the darkness.

"So what a world you live in, and yet the love thing is just as complicated. Who would have thought you would be the one with a list of guys chasing your tail?"

She caught me off guard with that statement. What did she mean by that? I mean, I think I had an idea, but how would she know that? I decided to play dumb. "What?"

"Oh, please, don't play stupid with me. Andy is head over heels in love with you, even more than he ever felt for me. Shasta is your hot protector that would die for you. And the really hot blond—I saw the way he looked at you when you were unconscious. What's that all about?" She had a playfulness to her voice that I found endearing. I never would have imagined Amanda and me talking about boys in my room. But here we were acting as if we were old friends.

"It's complicated. Way too heavy for five in the morning."

"I would love to hear this one, so please go on." I jumped to my feet so fast, I nearly threw Kady off the bed. In the corner, submerged in complete darkness, Andy lay awake. I was the only one who could see as clearly as if the lights were illuminating my room, so I was the only one who could see Andy's smug but playful face.

"You know I can see perfectly in the dark, so I don't appreciate that look on your face," I said joking. His smile widened.

"Dude, seriously, that's so cool," Greg said, sitting up.

"OK, if we are all awake, let's talk." I was hoping for my friends to get at least a few more hours of needed sleep, but then again how could they possibly sleep after everything. They were curious to know all about me, and they knew I would be the only one who would tell them. I explained earlier that debriefing was basically Jack telling them how to stay safe and what would happen if our secret got out. Unlike the movies where we could erase their memories and tell them a completely plausible story, the half-truth was all we could do for now. So in the car I promised them I would fill in the blanks before the morning.

"So let's talk complications," Andy said, now moving to sit next to me on my bed. Kady, still sleepy, scooted over, letting Greg take her in his arms. Amanda leaned up, sitting with her back toward the wall and her long legs crossed over each other.

"Andy, it doesn't matter and this is something you don't need to hear. It's irrelevant." How could I tell him I was bound to another man, that although I would never love him, one day I would have to marry him? How could I tell the man who carried my heart that I carried another man's heart? How could I stand to watch the hurt in his eyes when he found out the truth?

"Please, Alikye; I need to know…everything about you," he pleaded.

"Even if it means hurting you?"

"That bad?" His face fell. "I don't care—I need to know."

"OK, well, to begin let me tell you a story. Once upon a time, when my parents were teenagers, they were best friends and nothing more, just like Shasta and I are. My mother was in love with another man; she was in love with Jack. Her world began and ended with him. They were, as you say, star-crossed lovers. My father, too, was in love with someone else, another Legacy named Natalia. But unfortunately that wasn't enough. You see, from the beginning, to keep order, we abide by certain rules. Over the years those rules tend to change with the times, but one rule has been the same, and the council made up by the last nine remaining Legacy families, well, three are just fill-ins until the remaining three families come of age to take their place, they enforce the rules. To make life a little simpler and to make sure our race goes on, the council is responsible for arranging marriages. Back then, on the female's eighteenth birthday, her mate was chosen for her. My mother and father were bound together. Because no two Legacies can procreate, my father understood why he and Natalia couldn't be together, but he didn't see why my mother and Jack couldn't have their happily ever after. He pleaded to the council and to

263

my grandmother to choose someone new for him and to allow my mother her one true love, but they refused him, threatening to take his title if he didn't agree.

"Like I said, my father loved my mother, but their love was merely friendly, not passionate. I'm not sure of the whole story, but it seems because of a broken heart Natalia went dark, turned against her own kind, and worked with hell to bring down the council and all Guardians until her death. After that, the council, then run by my father, decided that the age of arrangement would be changed to thirteen—that way no one would end up hurt. That law passed." I eyed my friends, waiting for all that information to sink in, waiting for Andy to figure out the truth so I didn't have to say it out loud. And from the look on his face, he knew.

But it was Amanda who chimed in, thankfully. "So you're supposed to marry that hot Greek-looking god out there. I mean, you could have done worse."

Andy stilled.

"Thanks, Amanda, for putting it that way, but, yes, he was chosen for me a long time ago." I looked at Andy, trying to catch his gaze. His eyes burned with heartbreak, and my heart broke for him. "It doesn't mean anything; he doesn't mean anything to me."

"But you don't have a choice," he whispered, not looking at me.

I smiled up at him with a sort of mischievous look in my eye, which finally caught his attention. "I always have a choice, and I'm the last of my Legacy. They can't touch me. I'm not saying we can be together, but my heart belongs to you and you only. I'll refuse his proposal and go on with no attachments. My decision was made the moment I met you. I mean, I've already broken every single rule we have, why stop now?"

They all stared at me, to them I was this girl who couldn't possibly do anything wrong. Well, maybe at school and in this world I was well-behaved and a teacher's pet who always did the right thing, but in my world I was the black sheep that was always made an example of in school. Multiple personality disorder, a therapist would say—if I were ever sent to a real one, that is.

"Hmmm…" Andy raised his eyebrows.

"Where to start? Falling in love with a human: big no-no. Telling a bunch of humans the entire Guardian secret: again big no-no. Saving Kady from an accident not caused by demonic beings: well, we are not here to play God, they would say, so again big no-no. And then there are the reasons why I was sent here in the first place. Like I said, they see me as an uncontrollable, reckless adolescent who, if it weren't for my name, would have been given up on a long time ago. I'm a bad apple just like my father." I smiled thinking about how much alike we were.

"I still don't understand. I thought you were sent here because…well, I guess that wouldn't make sense anymore, so real story—why were you sent here?" Andy asked. Another story I really didn't want to get into, but I promised, and I wanted Andy to know the real me. The problem now was would he still love the real me? If he knew I was terrified, he wouldn't want me anymore. The fact that I wasn't human was enough to scare him the first time. But to understand the darkness that was a part of me would send him away screaming. I didn't want to risk it, but on the other hand if he gave up on me, my choice to leave would be easier, and some day he would be able to live a normal life with a normal girl away from danger and fear.

Tell him, love. He deserves to know, and I don't think anything will ever scare him away from you. There is something about him I can't figure out, but the two of you are drawn to each other. He will choose you no matter what.

Shasta was not one for privacy even if I was in the other room supposedly sleeping, but he would never leave me, and in the time of need, he was always in my head, which was kind of weird and creepy in a stalker-like way. From outside I could hear his erupted laughter, startling everyone in the living room, which made me start laughing quietly in my room, taking my group by surprise. They all stared at me as if I were insane, and to be honest if they had a demon in their head, I would think them insane, too. This made Shasta laugh again, which caused a slight chuckle from me again. I pointed to my head. "Shasta," I explained.

"So the real story. Let's see, before I came here and met all of you guys, I despised humankind—no offense. But in my case it was reasonable for me to hate them, to hate you." I stopped to collect my thoughts. "A while back I was on this case in Boston. A demon decided to make the streets his playground, hunting at night and mutilating human bodies. One night I caught its scent outside some run-down bar. It was on the hunt for another innocent life, but I was able to interject at the last minute, saving some drunken idiot's life. A few days later, I found out that drunken idiot murdered his wife and two young children. The papers said his wife left him and took her kids, moving them to Boston. He followed them there, and that night at the bar he was planning their murders. If I would have let that demon kill him and then killed the demon, those people would still be alive."

"That's not your fault. How were you supposed to know?" Kady asked, speaking for the first time. She knew almost everything I was telling the others, but this was the first time she was finding out the truth about my dark past.

"It doesn't matter. I could sense something off about him, but it's not my job to judge. I have so much power, but I can't use it to help the people that need it the most. After that I stopped caring. I didn't like feeling that kind of pain toward people I didn't know. And when I stopped caring about their feelings, I stopped caring about them all together. I didn't see the point in saving a world that would one day destroy itself with all its hate and greed and violence. So I fought because it was fun, like a game to me— who was the better man, so to speak. I fought because I didn't care anymore, and not caring made me reckless and suicidal. I put Derek's and Lucas's life in danger day after day. I put my life in danger every chance I got. The council took me out of my own game because I tried too many times to kill myself..." I trailed off, realizing the shock in their expressions—a human reaction to unstable people. I reworded my next sentence. "I didn't mean your typical human suicide attempts. What I meant to say was, not embracing my emotions turned me fearless, which made me rush in without thinking, causing fatal errors, which should have killed me multiple times." I pointed to my face where the claw markings stained my otherwise flawless face. No one spoke, too stunned by my revelation. "It's not the best idea to run into a hellhound's den without knowing it's a hellhound," I said trying to make a joke out of the situation but coming up with nothing. I continued.

"Anyway, I didn't know any better until I came here and realized that there is so much more to this world than what I saw: love, compassion, friendship. Having people in my life that truly cared for me before even knowing me, and then there is you." I took Andy's hand in mine, meeting his gaze. "The boy who turned my world upside down, who showed me whom I wanted to be, whom I could be. You brought the light to my darkness. When my parents were killed, I would not allow myself to love anyone. I couldn't deal with that kind of pain again until I met you and fell hopelessly and desperately in love with you. And for that, whatever happens in the future, knowing you're alive and happy is all I can ever ask for, and knowing that is enough for me to be happy."

Chapter 48

The day flew by in a blur. Seconds turned to minutes and minutes to hours. By the end I found myself alone in the backyard, looking out at the moon over the blackened still ocean.

Jack had gone through all the dos and don'ts as I stood in the corner silently. Every few seconds I'd catch Andy watching me, his sapphire eyes showing nothing but the love he felt for me. When Jack and the boys were finally done, they said their good-byes, and everyone wished them luck. I walked outside with them, telling my family I needed some time alone with my friends, knowing by Monday I would not be here anymore.

"So what now? This isn't really good-bye, is it?" Kady asked, pulling me into a warm hug. I could see tears forming in her eyes when she let me go, keeping me at arm's length. "I mean, we still have a few more weeks of school left," she sobbed.

"Kady, sweetheart, of course not. I'm not leaving yet," I lied. I didn't know what else to say to her. I didn't want to leave, but I had no other choice in the matter. But it didn't matter, she knew I was lying. She knew this was the end.

"Because you know if you want, you can stay with me for a summer. My parents are never home, and my place is big enough." We all stopped and turned toward Amanda, who was leaning up against my car, her arms crossed over her chest. "What, look, it's not a big deal. I probably won't see you much there anyway."

"Umm, thanks. I'll keep that in mind, but it's really not that simple," I explained. It was heartbreaking knowing this would be the last time I would ever see them again. I felt tears pricking at my eyes, and finally when it was time to say good-bye to Andy, I couldn't hold them in any longer. He wrapped his arms around my waist, pulling me to him as I wept in his chest.

"Baby, come on, don't cry," he cooed. "We will figure this out. I promise."

"How do we do that? I can't leave you, but I can't stay. How do we fix this?" I said, tears soaking his shirt. I looked up to see moisture in his eyes. This was just as hard for him as it was for me. He was the only man I would ever love, and because of what I was and who he was, we could never really be together.

"I don't know, baby. We just will," he said, kissing away my tears. With one last kiss, he was gone, disappearing down the street and out of my life. I didn't stop to talk to my family. I just went around back and stood on our little beach, watching the waves break on the shore.

Afterward they told me I had to start packing because I would be leaving my home. The only home I have ever really known would soon be a distant memory of pain and sorrow, just like it was for my last home. But even with all the pain and sorrow, my memories of happiness would surround the walls of my little two-bedroom house. I would say good-bye to my plain white room, a room I had spent so many hours in, gossiping about stupid normal teenage things that never mattered the next day. Or I would just lie in my bed with Andy, curled up to his bare chest, and listen to the thumping of his heart. I'd say good-bye to everything that meant anything to me, like the Florida heat that I hated so much but had grown to love the way it would kiss my skin with golden rays and the cream-colored sand that was soft to the touch but still found its way into every part of my body. I would miss everything about this life.

"Hey, sweetie. We are almost done with the house, and we will be leaving in the morning," It wasn't the first time today Sarah had reminded me we were leaving. She had come out here at least five times to tell me to start putting my things together.

"Won't you miss this, all of this?" I asked, sweeping my arms around me. "I mean, this was your home too."

"Oh, baby, of course, but it's just what we do," she said matter of factly.

"But what if we had a choice?" I had no clue where I was going with this, but I guess I was hoping she would comfort me with soothing words about doing what was good and not right. I was wrong.

"Don't be silly." She giggled. "This was never a life for us, just something temporary until you got back on your feet. It's getting late, so come in soon." She kissed my cheek before turning on her heels and heading back inside. I slumped to the ground feeling utterly defeated. I wrapped my arms around my knees, holding them close to my chest. Shasta jumped in just then, taking a seat next to me in the sand. I felt my tears staining my cheeks. He pulled me to him, resting his chin on my head as I buried my face in his chest. Finally after a while I broke the silence.

"If you could go back and choose her, knowing what you know now, would you?" I asked against his shirt. This was a hard subject for him. It had been over five hundred years, and still he carried the pain with him as if it had happened yesterday. Losing Elina almost destroyed him, and still to this day he won't talk about what happened after her death. The only thing I know was he was off the grid for nearly a hundred years.

"If I could go back, I would never again let her go. I think that's what hurts the most, knowing she would have chosen me. But I had something to prove, being a demon and all, and I couldn't risk having her hurt because of me. But I know if I did say yes, I would have gotten a couple hundred years with her." After that we sat for even a longer time in silence, listening to the ocean. "You know he knows, right?" Shasta finally asked. I knew what he was talking about. I knew Lucas knew how I felt about Andy, and so did the rest of the family.

"When did he find out?"

"He was listening to you guys talking in the room. At first I didn't know; his mind is really boring, so I tend to stay out of it—all facts and smart stuff and—"

"Shasta, get to the point please," I snapped, but he just laughed.

"Oh, right. Anyway I channeled into his mind after he sat staring at the wall for the longest time and realized then he was listening to your conversation. I tried to say something, but he stormed out of the house."

"I don't care anymore. I'm glad he knows." I sighed.

How do I choose between a man I have known my whole life and a man I fell deeply in love with in a very short time? How do I choose between a world I have lived in that makes complete and undeniable sense and a world that was full of new discoveries that made all the logic I had ever known seem expendable and misleading? Do I choose to break someone I love to make the other person happy? Am I able to make the best decision for myself? If I chose one path, I could never go back to the other. If I chose happiness, what price would I pay in return?

It would come down to a decision so elementary: real or fabrication. One path consisted of my fantasy world, the one where no one truly knew the real me and the sacrifices I had made. But it was a world full of love, comfort, and real-life drama. The other path was real. It was my absolute world where I never had to disguise the real me and what really made me tick. That life would allow me be the person I was destined to be. This was not a simple decision. It was the hardest choice I had ever had to make. I only had minutes to choose the right path, seconds upon minutes to decide what kind of person I wanted to be, what kind of world I wanted to live in, and what kind of man I wanted to love and spend the rest of my life with. Only *minutes...*

Whatever you choose, I choose you. But don't make my mistakes—all it leads to is a lifetime of regret, Shasta sent before disappearing with me in his arms.

Acknowledgments

First I would like to say Thank you to my family for always believing in me, to my mom and dad who encouraged me to follow my dreams. Thank you to my little brother Dominick, who has told me time and again as long as I wanted it I could have it. Thank you to my big brother David for being my biggest fan, you read everything I ever wrote and told me I was amazing and would one day be an Author, you gave me the courage to keep going. I love you guys forever.

Thank you to my best friends Tima and Lindsey, you guys supported me and believed in me. We would sit around for hours drinking wine and no matter how much I babbled about all my ideas or told the story of Alikye over and over again you always listened and offered your help any time I needed. You guys are the best and I couldn't ask for better friends.

Rebecca, my long time childhood friend, Thank you for the hours we spent together listening to my many ideas and even though you hate to read, you always said you would be the first to buy my book. If it weren't for you I probably would have never got through many of my writer's blocks because no matter the time of day, when I was stuck on a chapter you sat and let me talk it out until it was perfect in my head.

Thank you to Kaitlin Schultz and Ally Collette for being the best Beta's I could ever ask for, for loving every minute of it and bringing my characters to life by loving them as much as I do. Thank you for your support and feedback and catching the numerous mistakes I made because sometimes I didn't catch them.

Thank you to my editing team and design team, you guys are amazing and thank you for bringing my book to life.

And my biggest THANKS goes to my amazing and beautiful daughter Alix, I love you to the stars and back, more than cupcakes and candy and I love you more than pink. You were my inspiration to write, you were the reason I decided to put that pen to paper and create Alikye's life. I love you baby, ALWAYS.

And Thank you to my fans, you guys rock..............

24537176R10150

Made in the USA
Charleston, SC
26 November 2013